GW00863572

LOSING HOPE

A Novel by Nikki Dee

Losing Hope

Copyright © 2012 Nikki Dee

ISBN 13: 978-1508459439

ISBN 10: 1508459436

ALL RIGHTS RESERVED

All content herein remains the copyright of Nikki Dee, 2012.

The right of the author to be identified as the author of this work has been asserted by her in accordance with the relevant copyright legislation in her country of residence and generally under section 6bis of the Berne Convention for the Protection of Literary and Artistic Works.

This book may not, by way of trade or otherwise, be lent, re-sold, hired out, reproduced or otherwise circulated without prior consent of the publisher or author.

This work is a work of fiction. Name, places and incidents are either products of the author's imaginations or are used fictitiously. Any resemblance to any event, incident, location or person (living or dead) is entirely coincidental.

Published by WordPlay Writers Forum

www.wordplaywriters.com

Acknowledgements

My thanks go to:

Anthea and Heather, for listening

Charmian Brown, for typing

Simon and David, for reading

Mary and Maunce, for supporting

and

K.L.D., for never doubting

PROLOGUE
Portsmouth 2010

Chrissie Chambers sighed with pleasure as she drank her third, and then fourth, large coffee of the morning, whilst flicking through last week's papers. This was her ritual after a job and a way to get back the feeling of being at home and in touch. She never cancelled the delivery when she travelled away for work, regardless of how long she'd be away for, and would always try to read them in order and not stop drinking coffee until she'd finished.

She'd arrived home late last night, tired and drawn after a horrendous week, only to find her on-off partner, Sarah, waiting up and looking for a fight – a fight that Chrissie didn't have the energy or interest to join in with. The greatest benefit of not giving in to a row then, was that this morning she was being left alone to read and digest her papers, rather than kiss and make up.

Sarah busied herself by furiously banging things about in the kitchen. Her anger and hurt were reaching boiling point after being bottled up for so long. A row last night might have been a release for her, but, as ever, Chrissie had refused to be dragged into anything that wasn't on her own personal to-do-list. Last night's stand-off had frustrated her immensely.

"I know these people!" Chrissie exclaimed suddenly in surprise.

"What?"

"Look, here in the paper. It says the police urgently want to contact any of the people in this old photo that was found on the body of a man discovered in a warehouse fire. What have I missed? Where was the fire? What do you know about it?"

"Nothing much. I'm more interested in what goes on in my own home, unlike you."

"Sarah, don't play silly fucking games now. Tell me

1

what's happened."

"Well, okay, but you're too late to go rushing off to the rescue this time, so you can put your white horse back in its stable. That paper's days old."

"Sarah!"

"Okay, okay. There was a fire in one of the abandoned spice warehouses down in Old Portsmouth. It was two – no wait – three days ago. It was pretty bad by all accounts. The top floor was completely gutted. They pulled a couple of people out: a man who was dead and a woman who was as good as. They seem to think they were tramps, or squatters, or whatever the PC term is these days. You'd know that better than me. The building had been declared unsafe and was due to be pulled down. It's a mystery how anyone was able to get in. Anyway, they were asking if anyone knew who was squatting in there, cos they can't identify them. I haven't paid any more attention, so that's all I can tell you about it. The first paper report should be there somewhere.

"But listen to me – you've been away for a week and not phoned me once. If you call that number now, I'm off. I mean it this time, Chrissie. I'm sick to death of sitting here waiting for you to come home and then being ignored. I want you to spend today here with me or I'm packing. So, what's it to be?"

The phone rang then, shattering the silence, and the two women glared at each other one last time as Chrissie leaned to pick up. The moment she turned her back on Sarah with a shrug and gave her attention to the caller, Sarah walked away.

"Chrissie, it's me. Time to help an old friend?"

"Rich, I've only just …"

"I'm offering you a gift here, mate. Trust me, you won't want to be on the outside looking in when this breaks. Get a move on; you need to be here ASAP."

"The photo in the paper?"

"You've got it."

"You must know who they are by now, why do you need me?"

"You don't understand, I'm the person doing the favour for an old friend. I don't need you at all. I owe you one, and this is it. You in or not?"

"I'll be there in thirty minutes."

Sarah had heard the last few words, and she now spoke sadly.

"You won't need to worry about me, I'm off now. I was kind of expecting something like this. It's always the same with you. It's okay; I've come to terms with the fact that 'this', whatever 'this' is, is not what you want. I think I knew that all along, but I had hopes, you know." She waited for Chrissie to say something, but then realising that she really was wasting her time, she shrugged. "I'll fetch the rest of my stuff later."

Quietly but firmly, she closed the front door behind her.

Chrissie sighed again, this time with sense of guilty relief. In truth, Sarah going was no bad thing. Chrissie had done nothing but hurt the girl since they had got together, and, in doing so, had been left feeling like crap herself. Thank God it was over. Really over this time, she resolved. No more getting drunk and falling into her usual pathetic routine. Salt, shot, lime, pathetic phone call. Late night booty calls whenever she felt lonely or horny had to be a thing of the past. Or, at least, not to Sarah.

Twenty minutes later, Chrissie abandoned her car in front of a no-parking sign at the back of the hovel the local police were proud to call home. She scowled at the CCTV and marched to the intercom-controlled doorway.

Richard Dawkin was there to meet her and began speaking as he opened the door.

"Am I glad to see you! Don't ask me any questions yet, it'll only waste time, and we've none to spare. I'll take you through the events as we know them, and then we'll cover where to go from there." He took her arm and began leading her through the building, talking non-stop. "The

3

fire service got a call from a concerned dog walker. He'd seen flames shoot out from one of the top floor windows of the old spice warehouse. Our lads attended, naturally. When they got up to the top, they found a man – currently unidentified – lying against a locked door. He was dead, gunshot wound."

"Gunshot?"

He ignored her interruption. "Now, on the other side of the locked door, was a girl, young woman, whatever – again unidentified. She was in a state, not really making much sense at all. As I said, this is a mess, and we've no time to waste. We need to know who *she* is, who *he* is, and what the hell is going on. You've worked with all sorts of traumatised people – over to you."

"Wait a minute, I thought you were doing me a favour. Sounds like you *do* need me, you cheeky sod! As I'm here, and suddenly single again thanks to you, I'll stay, but I need a bit of background."

"No can do. You'll need to trust me here. I *am* doing you a huge favour. I've put my neck on the line to get you in on this, but I can't do more than that. We've got nothing out of her, but I think you could. Just sit with her and find out what you can, right?"

"No. Wait. Don't be in such a hurry. If I go barging in blind, I could do more harm than good. If she's in shock, which I'm sure she is, this could take quite some time. She's got to be made to feel safe and be given encouragement."

"Chrissie, we don't have any time. Upstairs. The men in suits think she shot a man and set a building on fire, and they want her arrested and charged. I think there's a lot more to it than that, but she won't help herself, and I'm worried that once she's arrested, we'll lose her forever. I'll buy you all the time I can, but right now, I need you in there working. There were a couple of interesting phone calls that came in after we printed that photo, and they've caused quite a bit of fuss and speculation. I'll be digging

4

into as much as I can out here, but I need you to be in there establishing some facts. Come on, love; we're both due a spot of luck. This is a career-changing case, but we're not going to be left alone for long. We have to make this ours. I need a break, and this could be it."

"Oh you bastard! For a moment there, you had me thinking you were feeling something for the victim."

"Hey, don't knock it, love. If it's good for me, it'll be good for you." He leered at her, and she mock shuddered before opening the door in front of her and walking through to the interview room.

***

The room was overly bright, with ugly industrial light bulbs humming and giving off far too much heat. A thin pale girl leant on the table biting her nails, she gave no sign that she had noticed Chrissie coming in.

"Hi there, my name's Chrissie. I've come to see if you've got everything you need. Can I do anything for you?"

The girl glanced up and then down again very quickly. A few seconds later she looked up again.

"Chrissie?"

"Yes, love, that's what they call me. What do they call you?"

"Auntie Chrissie," the girl whispered.

"What did you say? ... Oh my God."

The girl smiled faintly and whispered again, "I had an Auntie Chrissie once," she drifted back into a sleepy daze, focusing only on her raw fingertips.

Chrissie touched the girl gently on her shoulder and turned to leave the room, closing the door quietly.

Once the door was closed however she yelled out, "Richard, where are you hiding? Richard!"

"I'm up here. Don't make so much bloody noise, I'll come down."

"How could I have not put it together? Oh Christ, I should have worked it out. Why on earth didn't you warn me? What are we going to do?"

"You're going to interview her and we're going to find out who she is, where she's been, and why. We need answers before we release any information."

"You know what I'm thinking, don't you? And you know I'm connected to the family?"

"Yeah I do, and normally that would rule you out, but to be honest, I don't know where to turn on this. We're working blind here. Using you might be a mistake, but it could be the best possible thing to do. Either way, it's all on me, good or bad. Help me out, Chrissie."

"I don't know what to do for the best. They've all gone through so much since she went. What a bloody shock after all these years. I thought she was dead, I really did." She sucked her breath in and thought desperately. "Okay, give me a minute. It's important that I approach this the right way. What else can you tell me?"

"We've yet to identify the man who was on the other side of the locked door. She was almost catatonic and that hasn't changed. He had that photo in his hand, the one we put in the paper, and scrap of paper."

"Where is it?"

"Evidence."

"A slip of paper is evidence of what?"

"Christ almighty, Chrissie, we don't know for sure, okay? We didn't know what the fuck was going down. She wouldn't speak, and we did what we had to do."

"You need to let me see this slip of paper. She'll try to help us when she's ready, but I'll have to give her something first. You know how it works."

'she could be a murderer. Don't you get it? We've got a dead man here, and she's the only suspect. Letting you in to see her is the only chance she's getting. I'll let you see a photocopy, but there's no way you, or anyone else, is getting the original until we know exactly what is going on here. As it happens, I don't think she killed him, but she won't help me prove it. You're the last chance for both of us. I figure …"

"Just shut up and get me the photocopy. She may, or may not, be a murderer, but she definitely is a victim. Of something. When your bosses start calling her a murderer, remind them of that, will you?"

He nodded and walked away.

When he came back he handed her a photocopy of an old newspaper cutting. She glanced at it and looked at him again.

"Oh my God, Rich."

"I know. But it doesn't prove anything. Now, please, get in there and find out what you can."

***

"Okay love, it's only me, Chrissie. I want to talk to you if you feel like it."

The girl took her fingers out of her mouth but didn't look up. "What you mean is you want me to talk."

"We're trying to understand what happened to bring you here, but we can't work it out without your help. I can tell you everything we know but then I'd like you fill in the gaps for me. Will you do that?"

The girl looked down then simply shrugged her shoulders.

"I'll take that as a maybe, then shall I?" Chrissie was pleased to notice the hint of a smile drift across the girls face briefly.

"You were found in a locked room and you didn't have the key, so we assume someone locked you in. You were on the top floor of an old warehouse near the docks in Portsmouth. A fire had been lit that took hold very quickly, we have no idea yet whether that was an accident or not. We don't know whether you lit the fire or not.

"At some point, a man who was on the top floor but not

7

in the same room as you, was shot. We don't yet know who he is or who shot him. We don't know who you are or why you were there. We're hoping that you can help us. Do you feel you can talk to me now?"

The girl nodded and began to speak in slow monotone.

"You've just told me a whole load of what you don't know, so I suppose I'll have to." Again there was the ghost of a smile.

'she was so mad at me I expect she did it. Lit the fire I mean. Not him. He was very strict, but he wouldn't seriously hurt me. I know he wouldn't. She hated me, not at first, but she did hate me in the end. Didn't you find her?"

The girl began to shake and bite her nails again. She looked around the room wildly and tried to push the table way, then, realising it was fixed to the floor, stopped and slid off her chair to the ground and crawled into the corner where she curled over and wrapped her arms around herself.

"It's okay, you don't be scared." Chrissie spoke gently making no move to touch the girl. You're quite safe here and there's no need to panic. We don't know anything else and we've found no trace of a woman so far. I want to help you remember what did happen. Why don't you come back over here and tell me everything you know and we can piece it all together as we go?"

She waited then and it was a few minutes before the girl very slowly came back and sat at the table facing Chrissie.

"Good girl. Now, let's start with how you feel right now, I know you've seen a doctor, tell me about that."

"Yeah okay. It's weird. I don't remember much but I woke up confused. I had pains everywhere my head and my chest hurt the most. I could see pinpricks of red and green lights dotting on and off. I realised there were machines all around me, clicking and sighing. As soon as they realised I was awake it was tests, questions, poking, prodding, and mucking about. All sorts of people came to look and, I have to say, they all seemed happy enough with my body but very worried about my mind. Not as worried as I am though.

'the doctor told me I'm pregnant and that I'm 18 or 19-years-old, something around that. He said I've been very badly beaten recently, but also many times over previous years. Like I didn't already know that. I'm severely underweight and have a mouthful of sadly neglected teeth. I think the only reason he didn't call a vet and have me put down was because no one knows who I am, so who'd pay the bill? What else do you want to know?"

Chrissie realised the girl did remember being beaten and was determined to find out what else she knew. "Do you remember a time before you lived with the man that beat you?"

Chrissie cleared her throat before continuing. She knew it was vital to be on the same side of this girl if she was to find out anything useful. "Do you remember living with your mum?"

"No. But for as long as I can remember *he* told me that she didn't love me and couldn't cope with me because I was such a naughty girl."

"You just think back and tell me the things you do remember. You may well find that as you go back over the past other things will come to the surface. Just keep in your mind that I want to help you. We can stop for a break whenever you want."

"I suppose I need to know everything now. I've always known that normal people didn't live like we did. I had the television, you see. Well, if I was good I had the television. Once he realised how important it was to me, he would take it away sometimes, to punish me. Then, of course, I had to be extra good to earn it back."

The girl stopped talking and once more attacked her nails.

"Do you want to have a break now?" Chrissie asked her quietly.

"No. I have to remember. I know I do. Just stay with me if that man comes back."

"I'll stay with you as long as I can. That man, though is a policeman. You're quite safe with him."

"You don't know that. You can't know that. You have to promise to stay with me or I won't tell any of you anything."

"Okay, I'll stay, but please don't try to play games with these people. I know you've been through a terrible time, but, you see, they think you're the one who tried to burn that building down and they also think you may have shot the man you were with. They'll let me talk to you alone because I'm trained to interview people who've been through bad situations and the police know and trust me. They'll give us as much time as they can, but they really do need to hear your side of things. Now then, it's just us at the moment, so why don't you start telling me what you can, and then if I'm asked, I can show that we are making progress."

"I didn't shoot him for God's sake. If he were dead, no one would feed me. I don't know how they can think that I would do that."

"He had a newspaper cutting in his pocket. If you feel strong enough, I'd like to show it to you."

The girl held her hand out and took the slip of paper. She scanned the few words and then slumped back in the seat and closed her eyes.

PORTSMOUTH NEWS JUNE 16th 1995
A POLICE SPOKESPERSON ADMITTED TODAY THAT THERE HAVE SO FAR BEEN NO DEVELOPMENTS IN THE CASE OF 5-YEAR-OLD HOPE GIDSON WHO WENT MISSING FROM HER HOME TWO MONTHS AGO.
HOPE AND HER BROTHER WERE ALONE IN THE FAMILY GARDEN ON THE MORNING OF 16 APRIL AND AT SOME POINT BETWEEN THE HOURS OF

8AM AND 11AM HOPE WAS TAKEN. POLICE ARE ADAMANT THAT THE SEARCH CONTINUES.

Across the bottom scribbled in pencil was the word 'SORRY'.

**

Chrissie sat in silence and held the girl's hand. At last, she spoke in a whisper.

"What does it mean?"

"We've got to work together to find that out. I need you to tell me everything you remember about your past, and I promise to help you all I can."

"Oh god. I'm so scared."

"I know you are, but we have to tie up all loose ends in an event like this. You'll have to give a statement and appear in court once we've been through it all. It will be far, far better to be a helpful witness than a potential suspect. I'm sure you've seen enough television to know the wisdom of that."

"Yes I have. I'll tell you everything I can."

"Good girl. Now, relax and just tell me things, and like I said, you'll find more and more memories surface."

The girl nodded obediently and began speaking once again in that curious monotone.

"He told me that he would try to keep me safe, but it would only work if I did everything exactly as he said. So I did try. Sometimes, though, I must have forgotten, once I remember him saying it as he walked towards me holding a pair of scissors and I was so scared that I wet myself. He called me a dirty little beast and laughed at me. He was only going to cut my hair, he said, but now he'd have to get me cleaned up. He dragged me into the bathroom, just shouting over and over, 'do what I say and I won't hurt you."

"Sometimes there was a lady with him and we would

11

have some food together and watch television. Sometimes she did my hair and painted my nails and sometimes we played games, monopoly or scrabble. I liked it when she came.

"I want my mummy". I remember sobbing that. "When is Mummy coming for me?" I begged him. "Mummy won't be coming for you. She doesn't want you," he'd say. "You're a naughty, dirty girl and she wants me to look after you. And I will, but I won't let you be naughty. Now, come here and let me make you all nice and clean. Daddy's little angel."

"I screamed at him then, "You're not my daddy".

"I am now and you'd better get used to it." He always shouted so loudly and he would be so angry he shook. He would have white spit on his lips and then it sprayed on me when he shouted. I knew he was very angry with me.

"For the longest time I cried and screamed until I was sick. He'd discover my dirt, smack me, and then clean me. Over and over again. I eventually learnt what made him angry and what pleased him and things got better. Once I'd stopped wetting myself every time he came into the room, he'd let me wear clothes and then he stopped cutting my hair. Every day he told me that he was keeping me safe because he loved me and that my mummy threw me away because she didn't love me.

"Sometimes the lady was with us. She was kind and smelled nice most of the time. Sometimes she was cross and had a funny smell. Those times she would hit me if he wasn't there. She looked after me if I was poorly. I had to call them mummy and daddy and I hated it because I knew they weren't but it made them happy. I would lie in bed after they had gone and call for my mummy. I thought if I kept calling her she would hear me one day. I can't remember when I stopped believing that.

"I went to school sometimes when I was very little, but I changed school a lot and I don't remember ever having any friends. I was always dressed differently to the other kids and they said I was backward, or I smelled funny. I was at one place where the kids usually called me spastic or retard. When that started, he'd take me out and send me to another school somewhere else. I never made any friends – he wouldn't allow that.

"I don't know how old I was when he first got into bed with me. I do remember that's when I started screaming until I was sick again. He beat me and beat me. In fact, I think perhaps he always had. I don't think that he'd had full sex with me until I was about ten though. It was about then that I do remember I started to wet myself whenever he walked in. I would wet myself, scream and scream, be sick and he'd beat me. It seemed to last forever and ever. He would be so angry, screaming and spitting and lashing out with his fists and feet.

"Dirty, dirty little bitch! You're ten-years-old and you're no better than an animal. Don't you realise how lucky you are? Your mother threw you out when you were a baby and I took you in. What will you do if I throw you out? How will you live? Think about that my girl. I'm in charge and you do as I say. Now, go and get cleaned up and then come back to bed".

"I did, I accepted all of that as what had to happen for me to be safe. If I did what he wanted, things were fine. In fact, sometimes things were good. I spent a lot of time alone. When the bed thing started, he stopped letting me go to school at all, but he let me have books and a TV. I had food and clothes, though I never chose my own. Sometimes he'd talk to me about when he was a little boy. I liked it when he talked to me because he didn't mess with me then.

"I want your life to be better than mine," he'd say. "My dad was wicked and then my mum left me. There was no one to love me. I want better for you. You know how much I love you, don't you?" he'd ask me."

Chrissie hated to interrupt the flow but this was getting closer to where they needed to be and she wanted to steer things forward. She asked, almost casually, 'did he ever tell you anything else about himself?"

The girl didn't reply immediately but Chrissie could almost see her racking her brains trying to tease out a memory. At last she nodded. 'there was a photograph in the flat, it was always there but once he did talk about it. It was of him: tall and blond and so handsome with five others – two girls and three boys. They were all teenagers and looked so happy and healthy. The girls wore swimming costumes. "That was the last time I was really happy," he'd said.

"I asked him if one of the girls was my mum but he said no. This was taken before she came along and broke us all up. She caused some terrible things to happen. This boy here – she killed him. Just think; he's dead because of her. Slut."

"We never talked about it after that because I had thought that if my mum *had* killed someone then he really had saved me from her. If he hadn't rescued me she might have killed me. I was happier with him after that. Most times he quite kind, if things went his way. We would go out together if I'd been good, to the beach, or for a walk along the cliffs. As I grew up he would let me go shopping to a market or to a car boot sale with him. I've never been to the pictures or a pub though. I woke up one morning and I thought I was dying. The bed was all bloody and he hadn't been with me. I only ever saw blood when he visited. I was terrified and I didn't know what to do. It was two days before he came to see me and by then I was hysterical. I suppose I thought it was something terrible happening to me. He just called me a dirty little bitch, punched me really hard and walked out.

"When he came back, she was with him. She took me into the bathroom with a carrier bag of stuff and told me what was going on and why. I couldn't believe I'd be going through all this every single month, though her biggest concern was how to protect him from it.

14

"He's a good man," she said. "He just doesn't like all this business. You must keep it private. Don't worry him with it."

"Of course it worked in my favour. It meant that for one whole week every month he didn't come anywhere near the flat.

"I was always locked in, of course, and there was never a phone, but I had my friend, the TV, and I was happy. Trust me, my life was getting so much better. From then on, he came to see me less and less, for which I was truly thankful. Sometimes I would run out of food and that was a bit scary, but he always turned up with supplies eventually, and we'd have a night like we used to. That's how it was always, and it was okay. It was my life and I was mainly happy. Nothing ever changed. Well, until recently, of course, then it all changed. She'd turned up as normal with my monthly carrier bag, she went into the bathroom cupboard to put the stuff away and then came out looking really angry.

"You haven't used the things I brought last month. In fact, I don't think you used any the month before. What's happened?" She just stood there staring at me and she looked so unhappy. Like I'd let her down.

"It hasn't come this time," I told her.

'so when did it happen last?" she screamed at me then. She had her hands on her hips, and I thought for a minute she was going to cry.

"God, how am I supposed to know when it happened?" I said, now I was really scared. "I never know what day of the week it is."

'do you understand what this means?" She screamed at me and looked like a crazy woman.

"I was shocked. She was the nice one usually, but, this time, she was like a mad woman. I'd never seen her like this – she was beside herself.

"No, I don't know what it means," I cried. "Why, am I ill? What's wrong with me?"

15

"You're having a baby, you dirty bitch. You really are just like your sluttish mother, you stupid, dirty little bitch! After all I've done for you!" She ran out of the flat then and I was alone for a long time.

"I was so hungry that eventually it stopped hurting and I seemed to sleep all the time. I had plenty of water but I didn't want it. I needed food.

"I heard his key in the door at last and I tried to stand up, but I was just too tired.

"He hadn't brought me any food though. He told me it was my own fault. He'd tried to teach me right from wrong, but clearly I wouldn't learn. If I had not let myself get pregnant, we could have gone on forever, but I just had to spoil it, didn't I? So that was it. It was time to say goodbye.

"I cried. "Haven't you brought me any food? I'm so hungry."

"He went mad again. You only ever think about yourself, don't you? Christ, my whole life is ruined and you want something to eat. You're unbelievable."

"He was spitting as he screamed at me, then he lashed out, kicking and hitting me. I fell to the floor and just gave up.

"And then I was being poked about by that doctor and I don't know anything else.

"That's my side of the story and now I need to know the other side."

Chrissie thanked god for her training, it was all she had to fall back on now. She was certain this was Hope, her god-daughter. The adored child that she had mourned for fifteen years. Now she was the one to help this child and her family re-build their shattered lives. She guessed though that things would get worse before they could get better.

CHAPTER ONE
Spring 1983

Linda Edwards kept her head down and her eyes on the floor as she clumsily squeezed past the more sensible people who had allowed themselves enough time to get to their seats poolside and were now waiting patiently for the gala to begin.

The room was uncomfortably hot and the music was so loud that it felt like a wall of vibration that Linda was struggling to break through. Certainly no one could hear her mumbled "excuse me" as she squeezed past.

The Phil Collins song came to a very sudden but welcome halt, and, after a second of silence, the entire crowd joined in singing and swaying to "Electric Avenue" by Eddie Grant. Linda gritted her teeth and fought on.

She spotted Steve at last and sank gratefully into the empty seat next to him just as a whistle rang out and the crowd reluctantly fell silent.

"Ladies and Gentlemen, welcome to the grand opening of the Portsmouth Centre's Olympic standard swimming pool. I'd like to begin the day's celebrations with an important announcement."

A heckler in the back called out, 'don't tell us you've found Shergar hidden away in Paulsgrove?" causing the crowd to cheer and clap and the Mayor to frown and blow his whistle again.

"Ladies and Gentlemen, please. I would like to introduce to you the two people who will be the first ever to sample the delights of our marvellous new pool: Miss Deborah Edwards, our very own Hampshire champion, and Miss Julia Marchant, representing the hopes of Sussex, our worthy neighbours."

As the crowd broke out into semi-good-natured jeering, he once again had to demand silence. "Now, now, people. Let's give a generous round of applause please for these

17

two young ladies, who have agreed to have a friendly race to mark this occasion."

The whistle screeched again and the two swimmers slid into the pool causing barely a ripple. The local crowd watching screamed encouragement, primarily for Deborah, because everyone knew that between Hampshire and Sussex no race nor contest could ever be anything but deadly.

Linda finally stopped worrying about herself and her humiliating entrance and instead, gave herself over to supporting Deb, screaming her name and leaping to her feet in excitement. Her face was flushed and her voice hoarse from cheering on her sister.

Linda was, at best, a mumsy girl. She looked and dressed older than her age and could easily pass for someone in their mid-thirties, although she was, in fact, only in her mid-twenties. Today she was acting out of character and looked much better for it.

Her younger sister, Deb, was representing Hampshire, and Linda was as proud and excited as a mother would be. Today, all thoughts of being the sensible one were put on hold, and she threw herself into the moment. Turning to the boy next to her she gripped his arm as he grinned down at her. They were clearly very close friends but total opposites in looks. He was very tall and slim with fair skin and nearly white hair, whilst she was barely five foot five with tanned skin and wild brown curls.

"Just look at her go, Steve. Isn't she fast! I can't remember the last time I watched her swim. I'd forgotten how good she is. Go on Deb!" she screamed encouragement as the swimmers made their final turn.

As the pace in the pool quickened slightly, the cheering of the crowd became ever more frantic.

It was close, so close, but the first to touch the edge by a fraction was undoubtedly Julia Marchant for Sussex.

Linda slumped against Steve in disappointment, and, for just a second, it seemed as though the entire crowd slumped with her. Then, being the Portsmouth fans that they mostly were, they soon rallied and good-naturedly cheered Julia, and so, reluctantly, Linda joined in.

"Oh damn! She's trained so hard. I'd better go and start cheering her up, she'll be devastated," she muttered to Steve. "It's a shame; she deserved to win."

Steve shook his head. "She'll be fine. She's worked hard but only because she wanted to put on a good show. She's proud of the pool and loves the fact that she was going to be the first to use it. Winning or losing didn't really matter today, not to Deb. It was a great contest and great fun. You took this more seriously than she did."

Linda looked up at him with a slightly bemused expression. "When did you suddenly become so grown up and sensible?" she asked. "And, while we're on the subject, when did you grow so tall? You must be a foot taller than me. I didn't notice that happening."

"We're all growing up and sometimes you forget that, I think," he replied. Then, noticing her face had fallen; he felt a bit guilty so he looped his arm across her shoulders and after checking that none of his mates were watching, he kissed her cheek. "We'd both be lost without you though, Lin."

As they made their way poolside the Mayor of Portsmouth congratulated Julia on her win for Sussex and subsequently offer a slightly stilted "well done" to Deb for Hampshire, leaving no doubt that he personally was very disappointed in her performance.

That was exactly what she needed to clear her mind. She snorted with laughter at the pompous little man, linked her arm with Julia, and both girls beamed for the waiting journalists and family photographers. After the frenzy of photography, there was a small round of cheers and much patting of backs. Deb seemed happy to fool around for the cameras and was busy making friends with Julia, whilst enjoying all the attention from the press, who were out in full force today, mostly in anticipation of the free bar and buffet they'd been tempted with.

This whole day had been arranged to launch the opening of the new sports and leisure centre, mainly because the Mayor was wise enough to know that far too much money had been spent, and by challenging the county of Sussex to a contest, he would be guaranteed a crowd and could raise a fever of rivalry that just might help take the minds of the Portsmouth taxpayers away from how much this fabulous pool was actually going to cost each and every one of them in one way or another.

As the press pack remembered the promise of free booze they moved away from the girls and Linda seized her moment and began ushering Julia and Deb back together for a keepsake photograph. Steve walked over to the two girls, hoping for an introduction to Julia, and, just as the trio faced Linda, with their best camera faces on, they were suddenly jostled by three boys who were in the same class at school as Deb and were also hoping to get close to this lovely stranger.

Gary Daniels, black-haired with milky coffee-coloured skin, was in the centre at Julia's feet. At either side of him were Barry Evans and Clive Gidson, who were both tall, blonde, and athletic. All three boys had been determined to meet Julia by fair means or foul and were not going to be deterred by Linda or her camera.

Linda was severely put out that her keepsake photo had probably been ruined by three strangers but she knew she'd never get Deb to pose again so she put her camera away and tried to join in with the fun. She'd get the film developed later in the week and see whether she had anything worth keeping.

CHAPTER TWO
Spring 1989

Linda spent her day racing around as usual. What with the housework and keeping an eye on her dad, who preferred not to interrupt his very important reading by something as mundane as eating, she was kept pretty busy. The added responsibilities of working night shifts at the local hospital and a younger sister who was determined to live life to the full and not act her age, meant Linda felt she never had a moment to herself, and things occasionally got the better of her.

The family home was a typical Portsmouth town house, built many years before when Portsmouth was a bustling port that helped many men to make a fortune. In those days it was important to have a house that showed a man had wealth and, as the tiny island of Portsmouth had no more space to offer, houses had to be built tall, narrow and very close together. As there was no room for gardens individuality was demonstrated with ever more fanciful stone or ironwork bays, balconies and turrets.

Though perfect for those times, housing a large family with attendant servants, nowadays, these places were a nightmare of trudging up and down endless flights of stairs. The bills were enormous due to the fact that the wooden frames, beams and floorboards required extensive and expensive modernisation. The stone balconies were dangerous and scruffy and it was impossible to get warm in the winter. The damp didn't bear thinking about.

Most of the rows of houses had become shabby, with absentee landlords renting out rooms to anyone who had a little cash. Portsmouth, with her history of being a home to sailors from all around the globe, had now become a home to anyone and everyone who had nowhere else to go. People came and went, often leaving little or no trace of themselves behind.

Occasionally, a wealthy couple would buy one of the faded old houses in the hope of turning the wreck into a show home – ultra modern but with period details. This generally involved stripping out the entire interior and saving only the fireplaces – a practice that was not approved of by the locals.

The disapproval was, in part, because the local roads, which were already gridlocked several times every day, became even more chaotic with the addition of skips and builder's supply trucks. Mainly, however, the disapproval was caused by sheer envy.

Certainly Linda struggled to keep the place safe and tidy, but she knew it was a battle long since lost. She dreamed that one day one of the despised yuppies would knock on the door and offer to buy her dump before it fell down around their ears..

As she dressed for work in her sensible shoes and no-nonsense nurse's uniform, she daydreamed about the light, modern flat she would buy when that wonderful, life enhancing yuppie finally knocked on her door.

Of course, she'd need a car, because her dream flat would be just outside of town. She fancied a little blue Ford Escort, something reliable and economical. Deb would probably want a red sports car with a soft top. Linda smiled to herself as she acknowledged that the imaginary car choice perfectly demonstrated the differences between the two.

The voice on the radio announcing the eight o'clock news summary snapped her out of her daydreams. Switching the radio off, she dashed upstairs again to the study, which was on the top floor. This was the room her father had made into his own private space twenty years ago. It was totally impractical these days, as he now required constant monitoring, yet he would not consider giving up his private sanctum. Formerly a maid's bedroom, it now contained a chair and desk placed so that the sitter could work at the desk, or, by raising his head, simply gaze out to sea and dream. The walls were lined with overfull bookshelves, and apart from the piles of yet more books that were dotted about, the only other thing in the room was the old armchair that her dad refused to be parted from. He was sitting there with a book on his knee, wearing his glasses, but with his eyes closed.

"I've got to go to work now, Dad. I've made you a sandwich. Try to remember to have it with a cup of tea later. I've got to dash now though; I'm running late."

There was no reply, yet surely he was only pretending to sleep.

"Are you listening to me?" Heavens, perhaps he's dead. No, still warm, the nurse in her had checked. "DAD?"

"I heard you. There's no need to bloody shout. Go to work and stop nagging me. I'm busy, not retarded." He sat up and glared at her. "Sod off to the hospital and bully the poor patients there. They might need it, but I don't. Tell your mother to put the kettle on as you go."

She sighed deeply but didn't bother to correct him. It was just too tiresome and sad. Stopping briefly in the kitchen she wrote a note for her sister.

"D, can you make Dad a cup of tea and make him eat his sandwich when you get in. I know he'll forget. He's talking about Mum again. If it gets too much, phone me at the hospital. I'll come back if you need me to. I've asked Steve to come for lunch tomorrow. See you at breakfast. L"

She propped the note up against the photograph that she had taken that day years ago at the swimming gala. She glanced at it briefly and shook her head. That day in some odd way marked a change in the sisters relationship. Deb seemed to pull away and, try as she might, she'd never managed to pull her back. She knew the names of the boys in the photo but nothing more than that. She'd never seen any of them, except for Steve since that day. She, Deb and Dad shared a house but not a life. She shook herself out of her attack of the miseries.

"I'll see you at breakfast, Dad," she called up the stairs, and, not expecting nor needing a response, closed the front door and headed to the hospital.

She thought briefly about her dad's remarks and wondered if she was turning into a bully. No, surely not. Since her mother had died, they had all let her do everything for them: Dad, Deb, and even Steve had leaned on her, for food, clean clothes and occasional medical care and she simply had no time for indecision. She knew what should be done and when. And certainly, there was no point in having an opinion and then keeping quiet about it. Having an idea of how to achieve what must be achieved, was how Linda coped. And she would continue to do so. Deb couldn't be trusted and Dad would dream his life away if left alone. In fact, he had dreamed most of it away, every day saw him slip further away from reality. He'd done nothing but sit up there with his filthy, mildewed books since Mum died.

Deb had been just a little girl then, only three or four-years-old. She was, in effect, Linda's baby, and overnight Linda grew up. She made sure her baby sister didn't suffer through losing her mum, which, at the same time, kept Linda so busy she barely had time to miss her mum herself.

All these years later nothing had changed. Deb at twenty-one was barely more sensible than she was at four. She'd definitely inherited the laid back dreaminess from her dad.

Nowadays though, feeling the weight of her thirtieth birthday looming, Linda longed for someone else to be the sensible one for a while and give her a break. As soon as the thought entered her head, she chased it away with a whispered. "There's more chance of me winning the pools than that happening,"

She leapt off the bus just in time and was on duty in an instant. That was the great thing about nights on the casualty ward – there was no time for her to dwell on anything except the job in hand. The other great thing, of course, was that as a trusted employee in a poorly-managed NHS, it was relatively easy to get a small supply of a little something to help tide you over when things got tough. We all need a little help sometime after all, she thought, and it's not as though I can't manage without. I can stop whenever I want to.

CHAPTER THREE
Spring 1989

"I'm serious Gary, I need help."

Near the docks, in an old, run-down-looking yard, Gary Daniels listened with half an ear to the seagulls squealing and wheeling overhead, as Colin, his dad, built up a head of steam. The radio was on in the background, and Gary was absent-mindedly tapping his feet along to Wham, until he caught up with himself, that is. "Bloody crap music." He declared.

Colin paused, drew breath and relaunched. "Listen to me not the bloody radio, will you? I know you kids think you know what you're doing and life will take care of itself, but some things have to be thought about and planned a bit. I don't want you to work with me if you want to go on to university like Barry, or join the police like Clive, or do something I've never even thought of, but I need to know soon. I need help here, son, and if you're off, then I'll need to find a lad I can train up. I don't mind. Don't misunderstand me. I want what you want. I just don't know for sure what you do bloody want."

Gary finally took pity on him. "I don't want to be like Barry or Clive, thank you. I was thinking of following Steve's example, to tell you the truth."

"What are you talking about? Steve who?"

"Steve Dickson. He's moving into his family business, and I want to move into mine. We plan to see who can grow the biggest empire."

"He never is! I don't see how a lad of that age can want to get involved in old people's homes. That can't be right. Are you sure?"

Gary grinned at him. "Yes, I'm sure. There's big money in that kind of thing. He's not going to get involved with the old people at all. His dad and the board run everything with managers and staff doing the day-to-day work. Steve

26

will be taking on the properties they own and managing that side. He thinks the future of their company will be in property ownership… you know, renting out flats and shops."

"I didn't know it was that big an outfit," Colin said. "I was at school with his old man, you know. Miserable sod, he is. He's older than me so we weren't mates. To be honest I was the kind his sort never noticed. Working class you know. They considered themselves middle class, although we all said they were just stuck up. He always did have an eye for wheeling and dealing, even back then. It sounds as though it's paid off. They've got a lot going on around here then?"

"Yeah, they have." Gary nodded. "And not just around here. His dad's been buying up big old houses all along the coast for years. He's making a fortune renting stuff out to the authorities to be convalescent homes and hospices. The NHS rents one from him and it's used as a hostel for nurses. He's got a contract with the navy as well."

"How come you know so much about their business?"

"We're in the same boat you know, parents nagging us to grow up and take responsibility. We talk to each other."

"I guess he might put some work our way when he gets himself established," Colin said, perking up.

"He probably will. He's a bit like how you just described his dad. He definitely thinks of me as a worker, while he's a businessman, but that could work to my advantage. He thinks he's cleverer than me, whereas I know he's not. There'll be plenty of work coming our way over the next few years from him, and we'll be ready for it. After all, our workforce has just doubled."

"What? Oh right, I see what you mean. You're quite sure about that?"

Gary nodded enthusiastically. "You worry too much, old man. I'm here and I'm staying. Working with you is all I ever wanted to do. We're going to take 'Daniels and Son' into the nineties together. I've been waiting for this. It'll be great."

"Fair enough. Just one more thing though – call me old man once more, and I'll put you on your arse, you cheeky sod. I'm not forty yet."

"You think being thirty nine is still young then, do you?"

"You'll learn, now drop it. Let's be serious for a minute or two more. I'm bothered about your football and all that though. The most profitable side to our business is the emergency call outs, and they happen at nights and weekends."

Gary smiled and shrugged "Well, yes, because they wouldn't be emergencies at any other time would they?"

'Smart arse." Colin laughed and aimed a thump at him. "I meant that our most profitable business is done while you're out playing the fool with your mates. I'll do most of the calls while you're getting used to the idea, but you'll need to take on a fair share pretty soon. If you're in, you're in all the way, so I want you to think seriously about it. I can't have you starting and then buggering off somewhere. It's a big commitment, Gary. Make sure you know what you're doing."

"Honestly Dad. Football, swimming, and seeing my mates will fit around work from now on. We're having one last trip, August holiday-weekend, camping. We've all got things to be getting on with so we're planning on having one last blast and that'll be it. We'll all be sensible grown-ups then, okay?"

"That'll be something to see." Colin laughed "But fair enough, Daniels and Son it is, then."

Gary continued speaking, "I want Julia to see that our business is important to me. She's so full of her dad and his business, I don't think she takes me and mine seriously sometimes."

Colin tried to bite his tongue. He was worried about Julia, she was a bit grand for his tastes and he hoped that she wasn't just toying with his boy. She clicked her fingers and Gary jumped. He didn't want to seem to be against her though, that could push them together. "You're still fixed on her, are you?" He asked.

'she's the one, Dad. I knew the first time I met her and I've waited six years for her to realise that I was serious, and she's starting to get it now."

"I thought she was having a thing with Steve, though. Is that all over with now?"

"No, there never was anything going on there. Steve made a fool of himself over her, and she tried to let him down gently, but he just took a long time letting go. It wasn't her really, more the idea of her that he fancied – someone rich and from a smart background. He wants a nice smart person at his side, but I don't think he wants a *real* girlfriend."

"You mean he's ... you know?"

"No. I don't think he's anything. He's happy enough with us in a group but his main interest is his business, in fact his only interest is his business I think. He's like a machine when he talks about it. Dead keen, he is. I think he thought having Julia would be easier because they're already mates."

"It's different for you then?"

"Of course it's different for me. Bloody hell, Dad, I thought you knew me better than that."

"I mean, are you sure she's not trying to let you down lightly this time?"

"I hope not, but only time will tell for certain. I'm in no rush ... Back to business now, I'm on board full-time apart from the weekend of the August bank holiday. That will be my last one away. Okay?"

"Okay. I feel better now we've had a chat. Cup of tea?"

"Yeah, and it's your turn to make it. I'm a plumber's mate, not his maid!"

Gary knew his dad had been worried for no reason. Right from when he was a little lad, he'd wanted to grow up so he could work with him, and as he grew, his

29

ambitions for the business grew with him. He couldn't wait to get started, but he'd decided to take it slowly when it came to telling his dad about the changes he hoped to make in the business. The yard was something that had evolved over the years. It was a series of makeshift sheds and storage units with one telephone line that went unanswered when Colin was out on a job. He had fixed ideas about how things should be done and Gary knew he would have to work very hard to convince Colin that he knew what he was talking about. This business was all he'd ever dreamed of and he knew one day it would be his. If he had to wait a few years before he could make some changes, then that's what he'd do. As he'd just told his dad, he was in no rush.

CHAPTER FOUR
Spring 1989

Melanie Petersen rushed nervously into the surgery, and sat in the doctor's waiting room in a panic. She felt sure she knew what the result of the test would be but there was always a chance of it being something else. As she glanced around for something to take her mind of things, she put her hands in her pockets and crossed her fingers. The receptionist called her name and pointed to a door. Mel walked in to the consulting room, thankful that the waiting was almost over. The doctor confirmed her name and then offered congratulations.

"Are you sure you haven't mixed my sample up with someone else's?" she pleaded.

The doctor smiled at her and shook his head. "There's no mistake. You're definitely having a baby. You're a month or so along, which means you need to think very carefully and quite quickly about what you want to do."

'Do?"

"I mean if you plan to have the child, you must begin to care for yourself better than you have been. You're far too thin, and I suspect you're anaemic. You look very tired. Carrying a developing baby is hard work, and if you choose to do it, then you owe it to the baby to do it well. Our nurse here can help you with advice on nutrition and recommend some supplements for you, and we will want you to come along to the clinic for regular check-ups.

"On the other hand, if you don't want a child, there are options, provided we act quickly. A termination is a very safe and simple procedure these days."

She shook her head abruptly. "Oh no. There's no question of a termination. I can't think how I'll manage just yet, but I will. It's a surprise, but I'm thrilled, I think. Yes, this is wonderful. I'm having this baby. Thank you, Doctor, thank you so much." She began to cry.

31

Once again, he smiled at her. "I'm just the messenger, but I'm glad you're happy and you want to keep your baby. Make an appointment to see the nurse on the way out. You owe it to your baby to keep yourself in the best possible health from now on. I'd like you to promise to come along to our clinic in a month or so, just so that we can keep an eye on everything. I know you're not married and you're very young to be facing this kind of thing alone. Let us help you as much as we can."

"I will. But I'm almost eighteen, you know, and I've been alone all my life. I'll cope."

She almost skipped out of the surgery. There was a lot to think about and organise, but, for today, she was just going to enjoy herself. A husband, a house and a baby had been her master plan all her life. Never mind, she'd still get it all, just in a slightly different order.

As she walked around the edge of the Lido at Cosham, she smiled and held her hands over her still flat belly. Was it possible that she felt differently so soon? Yes, it was, because she did. Her baby was growing inside her at that moment, how could she not feel differently? She walked around for hours, thinking over her options and trying to consider all the implications. At last, she was clear in her mind that she could cope alone if she must, but, if she played her cards right she wouldn't have to. She was in a happier frame of mind as she caught the bus home to share the news with the one person who knew her and loved her.

Mel ran into the flat that she shared with her best friend, calling out, "Chrissie, are you in yet?"

"Bathroom. I'll be out in a sec," came the muffled reply.

"Hurry up, I've brought wine. We're celebrating!"

The bathroom door opened, and Chrissie stepped out wearing just her underwear and with a foul-smelling potion coating her hair. Mel gasped and stepped back. "Oh man, what a stink! When are you going to stop with the home perms? I've told you so often that I'll do your hair any time you want, but still, we have to have one of these disasters every few months."

Chrissie giggled and crossed her fingers. "I know, but I love playing with it myself, and it's only hair at the end of the day, whatever happens, it'll grow out. You professionals take it all too seriously. Now then, open the wine and tell me what we're celebrating."

Mel took a deep breath, smiled, and made her announcement, "I'm pregnant. Cheers." She drank the wine in one gulp and poured another one before her friend could react.

"Oh no!" Chrissie sat down on the bottom step of the stairs and looked up at Mel. "Not really? How? What are you going to do?"

"I'll answer those questions in order, shall I? Yes, really. In the normal way. I'm going to have it and love it, of course. Was it just the three questions you had? And when will I hear the congratulations?"

Chrissie stood up and looked directly in to her best friend's eyes, but, as she drew breath to speak, Mel spoke again. "Be happy for me, Chrissie. Please. This isn't the way I wanted things to happen, not yet. It'll work out right though."

"Work out, how? You've only been seeing this guy for a couple of weeks. It's far too soon."

"It'll be fine. I want a baby so much and that's the most important thing. I'm going to make this work, you'll see."

Chrissie sighed and threw her hands up in the air. "How, for fuck's sake?" she demanded. "You don't know each other at all. You can't get a guy like that. It's not right, and I don't think it ever works out. It can't. You're the one that dreamed of the little cottage, kids and dogs in the garden and a big man to look after you all."

Mel tried to speak but Chrissie just shook her head at her.

"You can't get it by cheating. And what if he doesn't want to know, what then? Look at this place. It's been a laugh for us two, but we couldn't keep a baby safe here.

33

The mad old bat downstairs will have us out on the streets. How on earth do you think you can make it work?"

At that moment, their landlady banged on the door, screeching at them for making too much noise. They both smiled sadly and continued their argument in a whisper.

"Oh, don't start on me tonight," Mel begged. "I haven't cheated, this was an accident. I didn't plan it, I swear. I don't know how things will go, but I'm having this baby and I need you to be happy for me.

"You were there in that home with me and you know what it's like to have no one of your own, no one who loves you. Well, now I'll have someone who will always love me. You know this is what I always wanted, so be happy for me. I will be the best wife and mum in the world, I swear." Mel was glowing, her eyes sparkled, and she looked as though all her dreams had come true.

"You certainly look as though it's the best thing that ever happened to you, and if you're happy, then okay, I'm happy for you and I'll do anything I can to help you, you know that. But just think about it and listen to yourself. You want to be the best wife in the world, but you're such a daft cow, he might not marry you. I can't believe you were so careless. That bloody home was evil for us, and all the others, and it was just because we didn't have a mum and a dad. Remember, unwanted little bastards, every one of us. You know what it's like for unwanted children, you're one, and so am I. And now here you are, broke, single and pregnant. And you know that bitch boss of yours will sack you the minute she hears that you're up the duff." Chrissie paused for breath.

Part of her anguish was for Mel, making a mistake that could misery to an innocent child but part was for herself. It had always been just her and Mel against the world. This could be the end of all that.

'my baby is wanted though, and it will be loved all its life. I'm hoping you'll be a friend to me through this." Mel began to cry. She'd never before felt that Chrissie wasn't on her side. She couldn't bear to lose her best friend. "I'll do whatever I have to, to keep my baby safe and cared for, alone, if I must. But I'd much rather do it with you. Don't let this come between us please, we need each other. "

"Okay, okay," Chrissie said, "I'm concerned for you, that's all. I'll be there for you whatever you do, always. Even if I do think you're mad. We'll have to talk about stuff though. Will you still live here? And when will tell that cow at work? Hell, I hope you know what you're doing, Mel. This is seriously big stuff. But, if you're going through with it, then I'll be there for you, just like the old days, me n you against the world. I'll do my best."

"I know you will. But if you don't want to be doing it with a bald head. I think you ought to go and wash that crap out of your hair pretty bloody quickly."

"Oh shit!" Chrissie screamed, as she ran back into the bathroom.

Mel poured herself another glass of the cheap wine and started thinking through the things her friend had said. They'd been through so much together since they first met and they both knew that they would be there for each other no matter what.

They had been two sad, scared and lonely little girls in the home and they'd become friends instantly. Nothing would, or could, come between them. Her friend would be there for her no matter what. The one lesson they had learned, faster and more thoroughly than any other while in the home, was look after each other and trust no one else. Once they'd met and recognised a friend in each other, everything improved. They turned to each other for comfort and reassurance. Their friendship had been the only thing either of them had ever had and it was very precious to them both. She would need Chrissie now to help her clear her mind. She knew she had plans to make and a few very difficult bridges to cross. It would be a tough time ahead; she was in no doubt of that. She had spent her first sixteen years in a run-down care home -

though care was more in name than nature - and the fact was by the time she was ten she was more knowledgeable and cynical than many adults. Childhood innocence was a luxury she and Chrissie, and most of the other kids in the home, couldn't afford to hang onto.

The bathroom door swung open and Chrissie wailed, "You've got to come and help me quickly. My hair's turned into a bloody ginger brillo pad, and I don't know what to do."

"Are we friends?" Mel tried to keep her face straight.

"Of course we are. And I'm going to love your baby like it's my own. I'll help you change nappies and read bedtime stories and I'll be chief babysitter and anything else you want, but, please, please, please, help me fix my hair," Chrissie pleaded.

As Mel ran her fingers through her friend's now tarnished and tangled crowning glory, she lectured her about messing with things she didn't understand and extracted a promise that from now on, she leave the hair care to Mel. As they agreed that a very short pixie crop was the only solution, Mel got busy with the scissors and carried on with her own confession.

The simple truth was that she wasn't entirely sure who the father-to-be was. There were two candidates, and she was in some confusion over which one to approach.

Chrissie was shocked all over again. "I thought we told each other everything. What else have you been hiding from me? You'd better tell me everything now. If you do want my advice, I'll need more information. I know you've been seeing this bloke Barry, but that's not serious yet, surely? And who is the mysterious other candidate?"

Mel began to speak. "It was that night of the Singles Ball in Southsea. Do you remember? You couldn't come because of that exam you needed to study for. I met this guy at the bar. We were both drunk, he, much more than me. It was just flirting to him at first, but I'd had a major crush on him at school, I led him on. He's older than me, by a couple of years. He's rich and handsome, and I was drunk and overconfident.

"Not one of the posh lot you were always mooning over when we were kids?"

"Yeah. I thought perhaps he'd just been too shy to approach me before and I was so excited that finally we were getting together. I was happy that the booze had given him the confidence he'd needed. We walked away together along the beach, just talking and having a kiss now and then. But it got heavy a bit too fast. I thought we'd just talk and fool around a bit, and get to know each other. You know, I thought it might be the start of something special, but it actually got a bit nasty. He'd got something different in mind and when he realised that I hadn't, he laughed at me, then he turned rough."

"How rough? Are you saying he raped you?"

"Not quite. He was bloody determined, though. I guess he thought I was more willing or playing hard to get. Or even more drunk than I actually was. Who knows what he thought?"

'so he raped you! Tell me his name?"

"No Chrissie. I led him on, that's what I'm saying. He wasn't to know I had something else on my mind, was he?"

"But when you said no, that should have stopped him. You should report him. Men can't be allowed to get away with that sort of thing, not these days. Report him to the police, Mel, you must."

"Listen to me, I was drunk and I led him on because he was there and I'd fancied him for so long. I'm not reporting anything, so drop it." Mel was adamant.

She continued her story. "I realised too late that he barely knew my name, much less secretly fancied me. I was drunk and I had made a complete fool of myself. I could have fought him off, I suppose, but he was a part of a dream I had, a lifestyle that I desperately want to be a part of. I kind of thought, well, this is better than nothing, and he might like me more when he sobers up a bit. When he'd finished he just shoved me away and said all of sorts of nasty things."

She stopped speaking and as she remembered the shame and humiliation she was overtaken by terror. She began to shake and then sobbed noisily. Chrissie stroked her back and waited in silence for the storm to pass.

"He called me pathetic, smelly Melly and said I was so desperate to be wanted that everyone knew, and they all laughed at me behind my back. He told me I wasn't anything to him and I wasn't to go near him or any of his friends again.

I ran away from him then, along the shore, until I'd sobered up a bit. I was angry and sick with myself for letting it happen, but I was even angrier with him for spoiling my silly dreams. Once I knew I had sobered up properly I started to head back. There was a man walking towards me and I thought for an awful minute it was him, so I just shouted out, "Leave me alone, you bastard", or words to that effect.

"But it wasn't him; it was Barry. He apologised for scaring me and asked if I was okay. I told him I'd had a problem earlier and was still jumpy, but that I was fine. He said he'd make sure I got safely back to the ball; which he did.

"When we got there, we both agreed we didn't want to go back in, so he drove me home and we had a couple of drinks in the Bear Hotel. That was my first night with Barry. I didn't sleep with him that night but I did a few nights later. I told you I'd met him that night when I got home, but I didn't tell you about the other thing because I was ashamed and I knew it was entirely my own fault. I just wanted to forget it."

"Okay, okay, I get it. Really though, if you won't report him for what he did, that's one thing, but you can't seriously be thinking that he might take care of you when he finds out about this. I mean, come on and get a grip,

Mel. That makes no fucking sense at all."

"It does make sense. I want a house of my own. I want my baby to have everything I never had, money and security. Barry's a lovely guy, he really is, but he's just about to go to university. He still lives at home with his parents. He wants to be a doctor. That means years of study and not much money. He can't afford a wife and a child. He'll be rich one day but I need it now.

'the other guy has everything I want. He only works in the family business now, but he'll own it one day. He lives in a great big house. He's good-looking and has brilliant prospects. He might not want to know, but I can't afford to not give it a try."

"Yeah, he's got it all and only the one downside, he rapes women to get what he wants."

"You have to stop saying that. I want a husband, but I need you and I need your understanding."

"How can I understand, you're saying that either one, could technically be the father, but you're probably going to approach the first candidate, who is not a nice person. Let's put it like that, shall we, because he is better off than the second one, who is the guy you've been seeing through choice."

Mel nodded slowly. "It all sounds so ugly when you say it like that but it isn't, really it isn't. I've made a terrible mistake and I know it. I'm talking things through with you before I do anything else because I don't want to make another one. I have to make the best of things and I don't need to be told again how daft I've been. I've worked that much out for myself. I'm trying to do the right thing for my baby, because it's not going to go away."

"I'm not judging you, I promise." Chrissie put her arm round Mel. "Well, I suppose I was, but only cos I'm worried about you. Do me one favour though, don't say anything to anyone yet. Just keep it to yourself and think about it. There is no need to rush; you can take a day or two. Sleep on it. Keeping the baby is one thing, but to risk everything with a man like that is something else altogether. A violent brute is always going to be a violent brute."

"I've thought and thought and now I'm ready. I'm going to try to see him, tell him to his face. Have a drink with me, for luck."

Chrissie just shrugged. "I'll have a cup of tea, and so will you. That's my niece or nephew in there, and too much booze is bad for babies. You've clearly made up your mind, so no more nagging from me. What happens next?"

"I'll have to tell the proud father and I'm going to phone him tonight, see if he'll meet me."

Later that night Mel dialled a number and clung on to the receiver in terror. He answered just as she was about to hang up.

"Hi, it's me. Mel."

"Huh. Who?"

"Mel Petersen. I need to talk to you. Can we meet for a quick chat?"

'thanks, but no thanks. I'm really not interested." He sounded irritated.

"I need to talk to you. It won't take long, but it's very important," she pleaded.

"It may be important to you, but not to me. I'm not interested in you or anything you've got to say. You're not my type," he said sharply.

"I was your type once, enough for you to get me pregnant."

"You're kidding yourself, love. I wouldn't touch you with a barge pole. Don't try peddling your trashy lies round here; it won't work. Phone me again, and I'll call the police. Whatever your little game is, I'm not playing. I have nothing more to say to you, except this: don't ever phone me again. Ever. You'll regret it if you do."

She hung up and breathed deeply, then, holding onto all that was left of her dignity, she walked back to the flat where Chrissie was waiting.

One look at her friend's face told her what she needed to know. "On to plan B then?" she asked. Met nodded sadly.

***

Mel sat in the bar of the Bear Hotel nervously waiting for Barry to arrive, at which time she would have to tell all. Or nearly all. Now that plan A had crashed, plan B had to work. Her baby would have both a father and a mother. She walked nervously around the ancient hotel and for the first time ever she didn't really appreciate any of it.

At last, Barry walked in and his face lit up when he saw her. "Not late am I?"

"No, I'm early." She waved away his concern. "I don't have far to travel, after all."

"Of course, your flat is just opposite here, isn't it?"

She nodded, and then smiled, as he bent to kiss her. "What would you like to drink?"

"I think I'd rather go for a walk now, and perhaps have a drink later. I'd really like to talk to you. Would you mind?"

"No. That's a great idea. Where shall we go?"

"I've always loved walking along the Hayling Billy trail when I have things on my mind," she said, looking up at him.

"Okay then. Let's go. You can give me directions and then you can tell me what's on your mind as we walk. If I can help you, I will."

Within a few minutes they were on Hayling Island and parking the car. They began walking in silence. Once they got alongside the oyster beds Mel stopped and looked behind her, past the old bridge supports and over the road to the old mill in the distance.

"I've actually been along here before but I'd almost forgotten about it. It's been years. Why is it called the

41

Billy trail?" he asked. "I'm sure I never known, or, if I did know, I've forgotten."

"This used to be the railway track used by the train called the Hayling Billy. Those are the old supports and this path is exactly where the train ran. For almost a hundred years from the 1860s to the 1960s the train brought holidaymakers here. Rich people from London and Brighton would flock here in the summer. Just think of it, a hundred years. All those different people coming along here, the track runs all the way alongside the sea to the far end of the island. I picture old folks that would come back time after time and young lovers seeing it for the first time. Husbands and wives with their children, then, when their children had grown up they would come here with their children. I love that and I hate that it doesn't happen anymore."

"Why did it stop?" He seemed interested in her story.

'the bridge from Havant to Hayling needed expensive restoration and the short-sighted idiots closed the line rather than pay to repair it, even though the service was very popular and hugely profitable," she told him.

"I don't know much about it. Hayling Island, I mean. It's a kind of old-fashioned place. There's so much more to do in other places, you know. Brighton or Southampton are the places I go to if I get fed up with Portsmouth. I've got a mate Clive, lives at Langstone. At least his parents have a place there but he spends most of his time at my house. My mum thinks she's got two sons, I reckon. She paints pictures – views and stuff – and some of her pictures are of this place. I recognise them, although I don't really remember it here."

"There's not much in the way of night life, but the surfing and kite buggy races are fantastic. The golf links are great and there are a couple of good sailing clubs. If things got a bit much at the home, I would get on the ferry and come across here to escape. I used to daydream about living here one day.

42

"That's partly why we got the rooms in Havant when we left the home. I didn't ever want to see Portsmouth again, but I can't imagine not being able to walk along here. I come here most weekends now. You should come along one weekend. We could go and watch the kite racing."

"Perhaps I will, and you can take me to see all your favourite things. I want to know everything about you, Mel. What makes you laugh and what makes you cry. I want to know what you dream of and what your plans are for the future. And I would like to show you my Portsmouth, I know you have some bad memories but I had a great childhood there and I want to tell you all about it. It's scary, in a way, how special you are to me. I know it's a bit soon, but you're important to me already. Did you realise?"

She couldn't wait any longer. She didn't want to spoil the moment, but she knew it was unfair not to tell him what was going on. "Stop talking and listen to me for a moment please, Barry. I have to tell you something, something very important. For a moment back then, I'd almost put it out of my mind, but I need to tell you this."

He looked at her, worried by the serious note in her voice.

"I'm sorry," he apologised, "I'll slow down. I know I'm going too fast and that there's no need to."

"Actually, there probably is a need to move things on a bit," she jumped in quickly. "I'm afraid we're having a baby."

"A baby …" He gaped at her. "How? Are you sure?"

"I'm sorry to blurt it out like that, but I've been so scared and I needed you to know."

"That's amazing …" He looked stunned.

"I'm so sorry," she said.

"But we only did it that first time without using … I should have had more sense. I don't know what to say. I can't get my head round this."

43

They walked together in silence, both thinking frantically and both horribly scared.

At last he spoke, quietly and slowly in a slightly wavering voice. "Okay. This is huge, Mel. I don't know how we'll work it all out, but we will." He stopped walking, looked at her, and said again, "We'll work things out together. Don't worry, I'm not going to leave you high and dry. I'm not like that. I'm bricking it, but I'm with you all the way."

He shrugged, "You know what? I think it's going to be okay. I was about to tell you I thought I loved you, but I was worried it was a bit to soon." He grabbed her around the waist and they walked faster along the track. Both talking now, their words tripping over each other's. They could manage, they would manage. He did love her, she would love him. Her baby would have a dad. It would all work out fine.

"Smile Mel, I'm going to be a dad. My mum will be so chuffed. You'll have to come and meet her. She's sure to love you. I know it. We'll be fine. We can look after each other."

"Are you sure? Barry, I'm terrified."

"So am I. Terrified, I mean. But I'm sure, sure about you. We'll work it out."

Then they were running along the track half laughing and half crying but holding hands all the way.

CHAPTER FIVE
Summer 1989

Several weeks later, Jean Evans was lying in bed looking at the damp stains in the corner of the ceiling and facing the fact that a new roof couldn't be put off for very much longer. Bugger it. These old houses were money drains. As soon as Barry was settled in a career and in his own place, she was determined that they would sell this huge, rambling, old wreck and move to a tidy little bungalow somewhere. It was far too big for the three of them, and she couldn't bear the thought of being here after Barry had moved out. It should bring in a nice little sum of money as well. Maybe enough to finally take that trip out to Australia they'd been talking about since before Barry was even born. She hated the thought of Barry moving out at all, but Ted had told her to be proud of him and his ambition. He'd said she should pride herself on having a son who wanted to do and achieve more than they had. And she did try but, in her heart of hearts, she was dreading it.

She knew that when he went away to university, he would be with different sorts of people, not his own kind, and she was worried that he would change, grow away from them. It was inevitable. She imagined a future where she'd have a monthly phone call, and perhaps a visit at Christmas. As far as she was concerned that was just plain wrong. It was nothing to do with holding him back, as Ted had once furiously accused her of. A career, a fat salary, and a smart car were all well and good, but she knew that a happy family brought more joy than anything else, and she wanted a lifetime of joy for herself and for her son.

The sound of the front door opening brought her back from her daydreams. She relaxed and clicked off the bedside light. She had never been able to sleep until Barry got home, but because he got cross with her, she hadn't sat up for years. Neither he, nor her husband, realised that she still never slept until he was safely home. That's what mums did.

She was only mildly surprised to hear a gentle knock on the bedroom door and a whispered, "Mum, I know you're awake. Come and have a chat with me." She grabbed her old pink bathrobe and opened the door.

She'd known for a couple of weeks that there was something on his mind and she knew that he'd come to her when he was ready. If this was the time, then she was more than happy to get up. She'd sit up all night if that's what he needed.

"Is everything okay, love?"

"Yes, Mum, I just want to talk to you, that's all. You make the tea, and I'll fix some toast. Then we'll talk."

She couldn't wait though. "Oh no you don't. Spit it out now while you work. Don't keep me in suspense any longer. Tell me what's going on or I'll only think the worst. I can't help it, I always do."

He took a deep breath. "I'm going to be a dad." There, he'd said it.

They sat looking at each other, drinking tea, and thinking what to say next. Their relationship had always been so secure they'd not had any of the teenage traumas that many families went through. Jean never allowed tantrums or sulks to cloud her home. She was a firm believer in talking through problems and being thoughtful when dealing with others. She'd worked hard to teach her son those things. She'd also always tried to think before passing comment or judgement. Eventually, she knew she'd have to say something and she struggled to hit the right note.

"Well, you're far too young, of course, and I suppose it was carelessness rather than design, but a baby is a gift and if it's what you want, then I'll do anything you need me to do."

He visibly relaxed, and she felt a pang as she saw the

46

tears of relief in his eyes.

"It's not so much what I wanted, Mum. I know it's far too soon and we hardly know each other, to tell you the truth." He began to explain. "But it's happened, and I do love her, I think. We were careless but only the once. We've known about the baby for a couple of weeks now, but I couldn't tell anyone until I'd got used to the idea. It was a shock for both of us. I wanted to get my head around it before I talked to you. We plan to get married as soon as we can and I don't know how we'll manage, but I know we will."

"Of course you will. It's not like you're the first person this has happened to, you know. As soon as a couple get into bed there's a chance of it happening. I know you're not far along in your medical training, but surely you knew that much. It's not a new discovery."

They both laughed and the atmosphere between them was at once more comfortable.

"It may not have been in your plans, but having a baby is not going to spoil anything truly important for either of you. I meant what I said earlier. A baby is a gift. We need to pull together and make some plans though. I think I ought to meet the mother of my first grandchild pretty soon and we'll have to talk to her parents as well."

The kitchen door swung quietly open.

"What on earth are you two doing sitting up talking at this time of night? What's going on? You've woken me up," Ted grumbled sleepily.

"Barry's just told me I'm about to be a grandma, which means that you are about to be a grandpa," Jean informed him.

"What nonsense! Jean, my love, you're far too young to be a grandma. The boy must be drunk," he said, reaching out and clasping Barry's arm.

"A bit of notice might have come in handy, son. I know it's old-fashioned to get married first, but I didn't even know you'd got a girlfriend. Last I heard you were heading off to uni. You'll have to wait for me to catch up a bit here."

"I made a mistake Dad, but only in being careless, she's the right girl for me. We do want to get married and it does mean the things I'd planned to do won't happen, but to tell the truth I'm over the moon. I can't wait for you to meet her."

"We'd better set something up soon then, we'll do as much as possible to help you both of course."

CHAPTER SIX
Summer 1989

Less than a week later Mel was smiling hesitantly as she was introduced to Barry's mum and dad. Jean immediately took pity on the skinny, frightened-looking girl who already had a tell-tale bump that looked way too big for her tiny frame. It was going to be up to her to make this timid child feel welcome.

"Why don't you take your dad to the pub for an hour or so, Barry? That'll give us two a bit of time to get to know one another and make some plans. Go on, you're making us both edgy. Come back later and we'll let you know what you'll have to pay for; we'll have done all the hard work by then." Jean laughed at them.

"Yes, go on. We'll be fine," Mel agreed.

Ted, with almost indecent haste, grabbed his old jacket and in less than five minutes they were gone, leaving Jean and Mel alone.

"Let's have a coffee and a chat now they've gone. I can see you're nervous so I'll start, and hopefully, I'll put your mind at ease. This situation you're in doesn't need to be difficult, and I want to do everything I can to make things easier for us all.

Mel nodded and smiled nervously. "You don't mind that we want to get married quickly?"

"You're having my son's baby and he seems very happy about that. We've never met you, and you've not been a couple very long at all, but my feeling is that if he loves you, then that makes you good enough for us.

"I do care for him and I won't let him down."

"I'm sure of that, Barry's happiness means everything to both of us. This isn't an interview or a test. We're a family now, I want to get to know you properly and I want you to know me. It will take time, but don't be afraid of me, please."

"You're being very kind, Mrs Evans. I half-expected you to be angry. Barry should be heading back to university soon, but instead of that he's going to be stuck with a wife and baby. I would understand if you blamed me."

"Call me Jean, please. It takes two to make a baby and I am not angry or disappointed. You're carrying my first grandchild and I'm absolutely thrilled about that.

Hearing this Mel at last began to relax. She was relieved that this family had been opened up to her with no hesitation at all. It had all been so much easier than she'd expected but she was beginning to believe that she had cracked it.

"I longed for a baby of my own right though school, you know." Jean had decided to share as much of herself as she could. She'd always longed for a daughter and was determined this girl would be the next best thing. "I knew I was born to be a mum. I knew Ted even then. We went through secondary school together and neither of us ever even looked at anyone else. He was the only one for me. That's how it was for us two. We didn't have the choices and chances that there are today, but you know, when I look back, everything that happened was right. It was meant to be. I wanted to live here and have a family. If I had to choose again, I wouldn't change anything. Family is everything to me.

"Oh me too, all I ever wanted was my own family. It's just a shame that Barry may not go to university now. I feel very guilty about that."

Jean smiled and shook her head.

"Barry and Ted both know I didn't want him to go to away to study. They both thought I was being daft and old-fashioned, but I know people whose kids go to university, or they get jobs in other cities, and such like. They come back clever and well rounded, of course, all set up for a career, true. But they're sometimes ashamed of their parents and family. They're ashamed of a dad working in a factory, or a mum who cleans offices at night. I can't help thinking that something that makes a child feel too good for parents who work hard for a living is a very bad thing.

"If Barry decides to get a job and stay here because you're pregnant, then you'll have a friend for life in me. I believe a happy family is the most important thing a person can have.

"Ted's only brother, Peter, lived in Australia. He married, started a business, had a son and then died. All that, without the two of them seeing each other for over twenty years. I think it's tragic that his son doesn't know his Uncle Ted. Ted's mum died without ever having met Peter's wife.

I've had nightmares that something like that could happen to us. Now, I know it won't. I'm pleased that he'll be staying nearer to home."

As Jean told her stories about the family, Mel relaxed and could see how kind and welcoming this woman was being.

"I thought you would think I'd ruined his life. I'm so … well, I don't know what I am really."

Jean stood up. "Come on, no silly tears now. This is a time for celebration. There'll be enough tears in a few months when all your hormones go haywire. Let's go and sort out some lunch for those two daft beggars. See how handy you are in a kitchen at the same time."

"No problems there; I'm a brilliant cook. Provided you like omelette or toast," laughed Mel.

"Well, we'll do sandwiches and a bit of salad. There's no telling what time they'll come rolling back, and, of course, it'll be my fault because I told them to go."

As they worked together preparing the lunch, they talked about what lay ahead.

"So, exactly how far along are you? Do you have a date?"

"The baby's due mid-December."

"And what plans have you made so far?"

"None really. We've both been getting our head around things. We wanted to be clear in our minds that we could cope with a baby. I feel we should be married, and Barry agrees. He wants you and his dad involved in that. So, apart from agreeing with each other, that's as far as we've got."

"Well, that gives us a few months. I'm sure we'll work things out in time. I suppose finding somewhere to live is going to be pretty high on your list as well."

"Yes. But first, Barry needs to find a job, so we thought we'd wait until then and get a flat as near to his work as possible."

"Makes sense, I suppose. I'm sure we can get him in with his Dad until he sorts something out for himself. Now then, Barry told me that you've no family of your own. Is that so?"

"Yes, I live with my best friend, Chrissie. She's as good as a sister to me. We were at St. Agnes's Home together and when we had to leave, as you have to when you reach sixteen, they helped us to find a flat. Well, it's just two rooms with a kitchen on the landing really, but it's home for us. She's all the family I've ever had."

"You've no family at all?"

"No. I was left at the hospital as a newborn baby. I was sent to the convent first, and then when I was about five-years-old I moved into St. Agnes's. I've never known any more than that and I don't really want to. It's mad, I know, but I have a picture in my mind that my mum was just too young to have a baby. I couldn't bear to learn that I simply wasn't wanted."

Jean needed to know more. Family and a history had always been important to her. She couldn't imagine what it would be like to have none.

"It was okay. I mean it was all I knew, so, of course, it was okay. As I grew up and made school friends and saw things on TV, I realised that there was something missing, you know, that I was different. Not the mum and dad thing really. I'd never had those and I knew kids who had mums and dads that no one would want. No, it was something much bigger than that. I knew it was something very important, but, for a long time, I didn't know what it was.

"When Chrissie came along, I realised all of a sudden what it was that I was missing. I needed someone to love me that I could love back. I was five years old and she was six, and neither of us had ever had anything to call our own. I can't tell you how wonderful it was to have her. People might think it's odd, but it was like all at once I knew what it was like to have a sister and I know she feels the same about me.

"The home wasn't a cruel place at all, but some of the people who took care of us, really, you wouldn't leave them in charge of a dog. Others, well, they were just doing a job, and when it was home time they went home and another lot took over. Until Chrissie came along, there was no one for me to tell my little secrets to. There was no one to give cuddles or stuff like that. She changed everything for me. We weren't allowed to get too friendly with each other officially. They said it would make us soft and clingy, so we made a game of it. They would change our dormitories every so often. They thought having close friends could be a bad thing. In a way, I understood, cos we never knew who was staying or going. Some kids would be there for a few weeks and then they'd get fostered or go back to their parents. We were never allowed to say goodbye either. You'd just get up one day and someone else was missing. We all had job schedules, you know, housework and stuff that we had to do as well as homework. They made sure you weren't on the same rota as your friends."

"So how did you and Chrissie manage to continue your friendship?" Jean asked, fascinated. She wanted to understand and love this girl that had suddenly become so important to her family.

"Oh, that was mainly down to her. We made it a game,

you know, like James Bond. We pretended we were undercover agents. We could act the way they told us to in the home, because we had as much time as we needed at school to be together.

"She was a year in front of me at school, so no one there thought we would be friends anyway, so they didn't watch us very closely. On the bus into school and then back to St Agnes's at night, we would tell each other everything. At night, we worked out a code of nods, or taps, or even the colour of our T-shirts to get a message to each other. When we were in the home, we acted like we didn't like each other. We never spoke or smiled at each other."

"That's the saddest thing I've ever heard." Jean was genuinely upset.

"No, not really." Mel smiled. "When we started it was quite exciting. Two little girls sharing a secret, having a game that no one else understood. As we got older, we knew the rules were stupid and we enjoyed getting one over on the wardens. We kept the secret agent thing going long after we needed to because it was fun. We got a kick out of it."

"Were they called wardens? It sounds a bit like a prison."

"It felt like a prison sometimes. When we spoke to them, we had to call them "Auntie" or "Uncle". We did think of them as jailers though.

"I swore that when I grew up I'd get married and have a few babies, and they would be the happiest babies in the world. I knew I would be able to do that because I know what causes unhappiness. I know what scared me, I know what hurt me and I know that I can make sure none of that happens to my baby. That's always been my dream, to have a happy home with a husband and a few kids."

"What about Chrissie? Did she dream of having those things as well?"

Mel laughed. "No way. She reads a lot and her favourite author is Barbara Taylor Bradford. She wrote a book called *A Woman of Substance*, and Chrissie always says that's what she'll be. She says she'll never have children because no one can keep them safe. That's up to God. And he can't be trusted."

"Oh. Now, that is sad." Jean's soft heart was melting.

Just then, the door opened to admit Barry and Ted, who had been celebrating the forthcoming addition to the family, and who were both considerably relaxed and had decided that a new baby was such a great idea they had almost planned it.

During the meal they established that Barry and his friends would go, as already agreed, away for the holiday weekend. This could serve as his stag night and would save disappointing anyone. Meanwhile a quiet registry office ceremony would be arranged for the following Saturday.

"Will you be going along on the camping trip with the gang, love?" Ted asked Mel, as he picked up the photograph that had been taken six years ago.

"No," she said with a smile, "I'm not a part of that group. In fact, I don't know them, I used to see them at school of course, but none of them ever noticed me. And I wouldn't be going out on his stag night in any case. I want Barry to enjoy his last weekend of freedom without worrying about me."

"Have you seen this photo? It's the only one we have of them all together, the whole gang. You know Clive, of course, and that's Gary, kneeling between him and Barry. The back row is Deb and Julia either side of Steve. It was taken at the swimming pool opening years ago."

Mel nodded uncertainly. "As I said, I used to see most of them at school but they were a year or two ahead of me and I've never seen Julia at all."

"She used to go to a school in Sussex," Barry explained. "That swimming gala was the day we all met her for the first time. She and Deb became good friends so she just joined in with us. Clive has been my best mate since we were at junior school. Gary played football on the same team as us then, and Steve has always been around cos he's a mate of Deb's. He's okay, a bit of an oddball, but okay. Anyway, like I said, I'll stick to the August plan, but then I don't expect to see much of any of them, except for Clive, of course."

"Because of me and the baby?"

"Yes and no. Deb is planning to go away to teacher-training college in September. Gary is going to work with his dad, and I know he puts in long hours. Julia and Steve are Deb's mates anyway."

Jean cleared her throat. "And you're going to have all your spare time spoken for, for the foreseeable future. And so are you, Ted. I've been thinking about a few things today as Mel and I talked." She grinned as they both groaned.

Ted turned to Mel. "Word to the wise my love, whenever she says "I've been thinking", look out! It means trouble, you mark my words."

Jean laughed and shook her head at him. "Now we have a wedding almost planned and a baby on the way, I think you two had better resign yourselves to doing a little bit of DIY in your free time."

Staring at her Ted asked, "What are you talking about, woman? What have I missed? DIY?"

"Well, I don't think my grandchild is going to be entirely happy in a rented flat somewhere," she explained. "And I think the novelty would wear off for Mel pretty quickly as well. We've got more than enough space to make two big flats here, one for us and one for them. We needed to get some work done anyway, so it seems to me that *now* is the ideal time to turn this place into two large flats. This is Barry's home and it will be until he's on his feet. The first couple of years here will help them save some money, ready for when they want their own place."

She looked at Mel a little uncertainly. "It will also give you babysitters on tap. If you'd like to, that is?"

Mel grinned as Barry said, "Grab your hammer, Dad, you've work to do, by the sound of it."

CHAPTER SEVEN
Summer 1989

Linda opened a second bottle of wine and continued debating which was more pressing, the need to repair the plumbing that was making some very interesting noises, or having a look at the cost of double glazing. Deb really didn't care either way. They both looked up in relief, as they heard a tap on the door, welcoming anything that would delay the talks about money.

"Whoever you are, the entry price is food or drink," Linda called out.

"What do you mean "whoever you are"? Who else would it be? And would I ever turn up empty-handed?" Steve called from the kitchen. "I've got sweet n sour pork, chips with curry sauce, and two bottles of cider. Come on girls, dive in."

"That's a perfect choice. I couldn't have picked a better menu. It's just what I need – comfort food." Linda loaded a plate and smiled happily.

"I know how to keep my women happy. But why do you need comfort food? Have you been getting upset about your dad again?"

"Oh no. We've moved on from that. No, we're talking about house repairs and what we can and can't afford."

"You know, if you need a bit of help, you've only to say."

"Good God, no. We're fine, Steve. I mean, thank you, but no, we are fine, really."

"Lin, I'm practically family. I've got cash; borrow some."

"No. Thank you."

And, as she saw Deb nod in agreement, she continued. "The reason I said I needed comfort food was because I'm thinking of leaving the hospital and I've got myself in a bit of a state trying to decide what's the right thing to do. You can both help by giving me your advice. I don't need comfort as much as reassurance, I suppose."

"But you've been at the hospital forever. What's made you think of changing now?" Steve sounded shocked.

"That's part of the reason, actually. It's the only place I've ever worked and I feel it's time to spread my wings. I want something a bit different and it's now or never. I want something that pays better than the NHS as well," she responded.

"How long have you been thinking like this?" Deb asked her.

"Just since I realised that you two were getting on with your lives, really. I feel as though I've been standing still almost. When you both go away to college, I'll need something else to focus on. I haven't made my mind up, but I'm seriously thinking about it."

"What would you do if you did leave?" Deb asked.

"Agency work pays really well and I've thought about that. Then again, I could perhaps move to one of the private hospitals. It's got to be nursing of one kind or another, because that's really all I can do."

"You must have been there more than ten years. I can't remember you ever going anywhere else."

"It's nearly twelve years actually, so I'm almost institutionalised. Anyway, to be honest, I've probably had a bit too much to drink to talk about it anymore tonight. Fill my glass up, there's a love, then tell me what's been going on with you two."

"Has Deb told you the news about Barry's latest disaster?"

"No. She never tells me anything. The last thing I heard was that he was heading off to university and preparing to be a doctor. I thought he was really going places, what's changed?"

"He's gonna be a daddy. Didn't learn enough in school to stop a slapper getting in the club. Daft bugger's planning a wedding and converting his dad's attic for a

59

flat. Twat. He could go anywhere and do anything and he's been trapped by some little slut into giving it all up. She's got a name for being a bit of a bike," Steve said.

"He might not even be the father, you know. In fact, come to think of it, she might not be pregnant at all. He's soft in the head, I think," Deb declared firmly.

Linda shook her head. "Oh, well, that sounds like you two have kept your usual open minds. Why are you both so bothered? You're not that close to him now, are you?"

"No, I suppose not. I just don't want to see a mate being taken advantage of. I don't know her, but I know of her. I asked around when Barry told us his news," Steve replied.

"Well, if he's happy, it's nothing to do with anyone else. I can't believe you two sit gossiping like a pair of old biddies. I'd watch that if I was you."

"I didn't come round here to gossip. You asked for the latest news and I was just making sure you were up-to-date. I came round to talk to Deb about the August bank holiday weekend."

"Oh, go on," Deb sighed, "What else has changed?"

"Clive can only stay for the Friday night, Saturday morning he's got to be back at the police factory, sober."

"Oh, that's just great. Julia rang me earlier this afternoon to tell me she wants to leave Saturday night. She's got a family christening to go to on the Sunday. I wish we could just not bother with it at all. As it is, it's turned into a stag do for Barry instead of a lark for all of us ..." She stopped and thought. "You don't think they're up to something do you?"

Steve struggled to keep up with her. "What, Julia, with Clive? You pissed? Get a grip on yourself. He's far too uptight to be fooling around with the princess. And she's never going to settle for a lowly copper, is she? If she was up to anything naughty, you'd be the first to know anyway."

"Yeah, I suppose I would. It bugs me that people can't stick to the plans we made though."

"It's nothing to get bothered about. It's just a boozy weekend with some mates. Those who want to can join in, and those who have better things to do can do the other thing. Chill out."

Linda stretched and muttered, "Open another bottle, Steve, and pour me a drink. You said this August weekend thing is going to be reinvented as a stag do for Barry, so they've actually set a date?"

"Yes. It's all set for the weekend after and that's the last we'll see of him I reckon. We're all going our separate ways soon. Gary's had to promise his dad he'll knuckle down at work for a bit and Clive's police training means he can never be sure what time he can have off. This will be our goodbye weekend."

"That's what I meant earlier," Deb sulked. "Everything's changing so quickly, and yet no one seems to care about keeping our last weekend special."

"Oh grow up Deb's for fuck sake." Steve opened another bottle and filled her glass quickly. She was his best mate but she was a moody cow sometimes.

CHAPTER EIGHT
Summer 1989

Jean and Mel had agreed that while Barry was away having his last weekend as a single man they would go through the attic and try to scavenge enough bits to furnish the flat. They had started with good intentions but they kept finding things to talk about. It was hot, dusty work and they were both getting tired and fed up.

Jean uncovered a box of almost forgotten photographs, and so now they were perched side-by-side on an old trunk, as Jean gave Mel a brief, illustrated history of the family. They were both still enjoying the feeling of the contentment that being together had gave them. It was as though they had both been able to resolve a need in the other. At the moment they were giggling at the photographs of Barry as a small boy. Or more honestly, at the ridiculous clothes he was wearing.

Jean smiled and patted Mel's rounded tummy. "We'll soon have another little one to photograph. I can't tell you how excited I am."

'me too, but we won't be dressing her up like that. Oh Jean I can't wait to meet her and start to see things for the first time with her. I'm so excited."

"What makes you so sure you're having a little girl?"

"I don't know. I can't even remember thinking about it. I just know I'm having a girl. There has never been a minute when I wasn't certain," Mel replied.

They heard the doorbell echoing up the stairs.

"Oh damn," Jean said, 'Ted's still out. I'll have to go down and get that."

"I'll come with you, It might be Chrissie, she's as excited as I am about the baby. She keeps going shopping and buying the daftest things. We'll sit and have a cup of tea and a gossip. I'll bring this box down and we'll go through it later," Mel said. As Jean headed downstairs, she followed on.

At the bottom of the stairs, Mel could see the outline of two people, one of whom had raised their hand and was ringing the bell again. Not Chrissie then.

"It's okay, I'm here," Jean called out, as she opened the door. She was startled to see two police officers standing there.

"Mrs Adams, Mrs Jean Adams?"

"Yes, that's me/" Jean smiled at them in her normal trusting manner.

"Can we come in please?" the female officer asked, in a brisk voice. "We need to talk to you."

"Why? What's happened?" Jean realised suddenly that she was about to hear some very bad news. She reached out blindly toward Mel. They could see from the expression on their faces that they were bringing her the worst possible news.

Mel held Jean's hand tightly and turned to the police woman. "I'm her daughter-in-law. Come in, please and tell us what's happened. Has Ted had an accident?"

"No Miss. It's about Barry. Barry Evans."

"My son?" Jean screamed. "Why, what's happened? Is he hurt? My God tell me what's going on, where is he?"

"Mrs Adams, I'm very sorry, it's very bad news. Barry died in a car accident earlier today." The officer stepped forward quickly as Jean slumped to the floor pulling Mel down with her. Eventually they got Jean onto a chair and Mel was able to sit beside her and hold her as she howled out her grief.

"Is the kitchen through here?" she asked. "I'll make us some tea."

"I can't believe you people are stupid enough to think making tea helps anybody. My son, my beautiful son, tell me he's not dead or get out of my house now."

She and Mel clung to each other in shocked sadness and exhaustion and waited for the nightmare to end.

63

CHAPTER NINE
Summer 1989

Linda checked the clock on the wall and sighed with relief. She was about to finish her shift at the hospital and was looking forward to a day off. The bank-holiday weekend had, as usual, been chaotically busy. Sometimes it seemed that the more important a holiday was to people, the more likely it was destined to end in tragedy.

A holiday weekend always brought with it a huge increase in the number of accident and emergency incidents for the hospital to deal with. There were so many people on the roads causing chaos and those that stayed at home seemed honour-bound to try their hand at DIY, using power tools that they were not familiar with, and, frankly, had insufficient respect for.

She heard the emergency alarm ring and automatically picked up the phone in one hand and began filling in an admissions form with the other, as she listened to the dispatcher read out the details of who was on board the next ambulance coming in.

"We've got three more on their way in for you. They'll be there in fifteen minutes. Four more kids in a car crash. One female, early twenties, has several broken bones and possible internal bleeding, a severe head wound and is not conscious. Two males, early twenties, both suffering from shock and bruising mostly. The driver's on his way to the morgue."

"Okay. Give me the details. Do you have any identification for any of them?"

"We do. The female is a Deborah Edwards, the males are a Steve Dickson and a Gary Daniels."

***

A week later Linda sat in the semi-dark hospital room

holding her sister's hand and listening to the beep of the machines that had kept her stable since the accident a week ago. She'd almost lost all sense of time. Steve had needed to remind her that today she'd be on her own as he had to attend Barry's funeral. He didn't want to go but she'd told him he must. She hardly noticed, focused as she was on her sister, willing her to wake up. Nothing else mattered. The shock of the accident had barely registered with Dad which meant that having a team of her own workmates calling in to feed and monitor him as and when they could was fine.

Linda knew every inch of this hospital and had always felt completely confident striding around and reassuring visitors that their loved ones were in the very best place and that she was in control. Where was all that confidence now when she needed it?

She wiped away a tear as Steve walked in, still dressed in the suit he wore to Barry's funeral.

"How's she doing?" he asked.

"No major change so far, but the specialist was here a few minutes ago and he's quite pleased with her and he was very encouraging. I keep thinking that I can see her move out of the corner of my eye, but I know she's hasn't yet. It seems to be more likely that she'll be okay. The longer she goes with nothing going wrong, the better the prognosis. It's going to take time, but, of course, we don't know how much. She's not in pain though and she's in the best place. I wish I could do something more, but it's just a waiting game.

"I know, but I'm with you Lin. We'll get through it together."

"For the first time I understand how helpless and frustrated people feel when someone they love is in the hands of someone else. They've told me to go home or to go for a walk, but I can't. I need to be here when she wakes up. She'll be so scared. I'd feel guilty if I went home. I want to be here with her. When she's better and

I'm back at work, I shall be a bit more understanding of other people though, I can tell you that."

"I know Lin, I know."

"Anyway, what about you, how was it?"

"It was absolutely bloody awful." He began pacing the room. "I've never been to a funeral before. I mean, people are always dying in the homes, but they're not people I know and they're old. I mean, he's my age, was my age, and he's dead. Fuck it, Lin, we haven't done anything with our lives yet. We've only just started talking about our plans and hopes for the future. I keep thinking about all our conversations. All six of us. Who'd be the first millionaire and what we'd be doing this time next year, what car we'd buy. And now he's gone, and Deb's so messed up she doesn't even know he's dead. I can't get my head around it. Just a couple of minutes and everything has changed. I feel like shit now for talking about him the way we have been."

He dropped into a chair and held his head in his hands.

"How are his parents coping?"

'they're both wiped out but trying to be strong. They didn't say much, just clung onto each other's hand. They seem to be the stiff upper lip generation, you know. Mel is making herself one of the family by the looks of things. She's moving in this week as planned, so she's well set up.

"Ted's family were there, over from Australia. They're going to stay for a few weeks so they'll be able to keep an eye on things. They seem like nice enough people. They've never been here before, apparently, or met Ted. They'd been saving to come here on holiday, but when this happened they moved their plans forward. It's going to be a great help; they're family, after all. Meeting each other for the first time is giving them all something to talk about."

"And the others?" she asked, trying to care. "How are your other friends?"

"Julia seemed pretty upset, but that would probably be

66

attention-seeking, I expect. She's such a bloody princess sometimes. Gary had to take her home early, but, fair play to him, he's never been one to miss a chance, so I don't blame him. Clive was being his usual Mr Charming, organising everyone and acting special."

Linda smiled at him and raised her eyebrows.

"You were all so close when you were kids, but it seems that that growing up has done an awful lot to change that. Or were you pretending all the time?"

"Not pretending, no. We do like each other, but it was like wheels within wheels, you know. I mean, me and Deb, obviously are like brother and sister, and none of the others come close to that. Barry and Clive are also that close to each other. Oh God, I suppose I must learn to say were, not are."

He sighed, rubbed his face with hands, jumped up and began pacing restlessly around the tiny room again. He picked up his chair and moved it closer to the bed then continued. "Gary was in the same class as Clive, and they play football together. Deb kind of brought Julia in after they met at the swimming county-championships that time.

Linda smiled faintly. Thinking back to that happy day as Steve talked on..

"Deb invited her out with us to celebrate and she just kept turning up after that. And, of course, the football and the swimming at the centre meant we all saw each other every weekend and it was fun, sports mates we were. As time went on, it began to become get more competitive. You know the sort of thing. A bit of a race to be the first to go to university or to pass the driving test. Within the group there are close friendships but we aren't individually all that close. We all have our own lives and friends.

"To tell the truth, I don't care if I never see any of them again. Deb is my best mate; the others can get on without us. This bank holiday was always going to be our last big get together. It was time for us all to move on.

"As it was, Julia and Clive only spent the day with us. She was off with the family that night for some posh do or other, and Clive was going back to the police school. We were all making an effort to get on well, but in truth, we were all happy to head home early. Now though, Christ, Deb is lying there all messed up and Barry …"

He choked up, and Linda saw again the sad little boy that she cared for alongside her little sister.

"Come on now, I know it's all been a lot to take on board and it's really sad about Barry, but Deb is going to be okay, I'm sure. We've got to be strong for each other now. I need you and you need me."

As she put her arms around him, she felt a small pang of guilt to find that she was taking comfort from the fact that both Steve and Deb needed her again. She'd missed that so much.

The last few years they'd been growing away from her. Perhaps this tragedy had brought them back.

As she held his hand and watched Deb, she thought back to her mum and how this had all begun.

Her mum had become friendly with his mum in the maternity ward. Steve and Deb were born on the same day twenty-one years ago. Steve's mum suffered horribly from depression, at a time when the only help available, was a brisk, pull-yourself-together from a well-meaning friend or relative. She was menopausal when she fell pregnant and never got back to normal after the birth.

At ten yeas of age, Linda was often left in charge of the two babies while her mum did what she could to help her friend.

When Steve was three-years-old, his mum fell down the stairs and broke her neck, at which point, Linda began to take care of him, as well as her sister, as her own mum had returned to work.

Steve and Deb were like her playthings until they began school and started to have their own opinions and certainly didn't want to be hers to rule any longer. That was when she had evolved into a kind of mother figure to them both.

She still loved them both, but, as they became teenagers, they were determined to show they didn't need her looking after them any longer. The trouble was, that looking after them, had been her main source of happiness, and she was unwilling, or unable to stop.

Now, here he was, a grown man, true, but still sobbing in her arms. She allowed herself a small smile. At last her patience would be rewarded, she would be invaluable in their moment of need.

CHAPTER TEN
Winter 1989

Mel found herself waiting for the quiet tap on the back door that heralded her daily visit from Clive. He appeared to have appointed himself Mel's protector and she was surprised to find she was grateful for it. He'd been wonderful: from the dreadful accident, through the horrendous funeral to now, the imminent arrival of her child.

"Hi there. How are you doing? Good morning, baby." He nodded to her bump "You seem to get bigger every day now. Are you feeling okay?"

"I'm fine, but I'll be very glad to have this load in a pram soon. I can't believe how big and heavy I am. Thank God I've only got a week or so to go."

"Ah well, that's what I wanted to go over with you. Just to be sure we all know what will happen when the time is here. You've got my phone number and Gary's, right?"

"You know I have. Don't worry, I know the drill. When something happens, I call you first, and in the event that you're not available, I'll call Gary. My bag is packed and is sitting in the hall by the front door. Once I've phoned you, I will sit in the hall with my bag at my feet and wait. Either you or Gary will come and pick me up and take me to the hospital. Sir." At that she jumped to her feet and shot him a salute.

He grinned at her. "Sloppy posture, that's the wrong hand and your uniform is in a shocking state. Still, you got the drill right so that's something. We're both on standby and we'll keep in close touch with you and each other."

"I know. And I really appreciate the way you're both taking care of me. It must be difficult for you both sometimes."

"Believe it or not, looking out for you and the baby is helping me. I feel that I'm doing what Barry wants me to do. Although it sounds a bit soft when I say it like that. Anyway, how do you think Ted and Jean are getting on?"

"Not too badly under the circumstances. Ted has more Scotch at night than he should and Jean cries herself to sleep most nights. I think they just have to do what they can to get through it one day at a time."

Clive filled the kettle and raised his eyes in question. She grinned and nodded then finished the update. "They're both eating, though not very much, and one or other of them comes for a walk with me once or twice a day. Just around the block. I've told them I need to do it for my circulation and I need one of them with me in case I go into labour. I don't want them to be afraid to go out, you see, and this way, they see people that they know and can exchange a word or two. I think it's important that life for them carries on as normally as possible."

"It's great that you get on so well with them."

"I love them both. They opened their home and their hearts to me from the very beginning, and I will never let them down. As far as I'm concerned, they're my parents and I will put them first, always."

"I know you will. What about Aunt Chrissie? How's she getting on with that Social Services course?"

"She loves it so far. It's exactly what she hoped it would be. Though when the place first came up, she thought about putting it off to stay and look after me. Bless her.

"She's hearing about some terrible things, of course, but she's itching to get out and start helping. She's working on what they call 'scenarios". They work on files of cases that are mainly now resolved but in a classroom situation. You know the sort of thing. Given X, Y, and Z, what would you do in this scenario? The students then can work together to develop a plan of action and set a time frame, and when they've finished, they can see what the actual social worker did do and how it worked out. She's talked to me about some of things they've worked on, and I'm realising now how lucky we were in St Agnes" house. I didn't think so at the time, but now, my God, we were lucky. But, I guess, that's no surprise to you, is it?"

"No. I had a pretty sharp reality check about that kind of thing within a few days of joining up. I'd had a bit of preparation though when my dad realised that I was determined to follow him into the force. He made sure I knew what might be thrown my way. He didn't want me to risk spoiling the macho image he likes to think he has, by fainting or throwing up at my first grisly scene.

"I'm grateful to him for that. It's helped me no end. I'm still staggered at the levels people can sink to, but I can put a bit of a poker face on if I need to. Some folks are good all the way through though. I do see a lot of both."

"Yes, you're right, of course. Just look at Ted and Jean, a perfect example of the good."

"Exactly. Anyway I'd better be off. I just wanted to look in on you and make sure we're ready for the big day. I'm off to see how Deb is getting on now."

"Is she still in hospital?"

"Yes. It didn't look very good for her for a while, but things seem to be getting better now quite quickly. Her bones have healed up well, but she's not quite regained her sense of balance and gets confused and panicky."

"It must be very hard for her sister. Will she make a complete recovery in time?"

"All the signs are that she will. Linda's a nurse, so she's more aware than most of how fragile Deb's health is at the moment, but, on the plus side, she's able to help in the day to care, and that been good for her. She's very strong and Steve is on hand night and day for them both."

"Well, I wish them well."

"I'll tell them. Now sit down and rest. Not long to go now. Bye."

Lying in bed that night Mel felt unusually restless. Normally her days were so busy that she slipped into sleep quickly and gratefully. Tonight though, it was different, for some reason she couldn't settle. Eventually

72

she got up, made a cup of tea, and began to daydream about her baby. A tiny little person that would love her and whom she could love wholeheartedly. She was filled with a deep joy and also felt so excited. She was almost certain that given time she'd have learned to love Barry, but when he died, she knew she didn't feel the desperate pain that his parents felt. She'd told Chrissie how guilty that had made her feel, and her friend had tried to put it into perspective for her.

"He was a new boyfriend for you. What you had may have been real love, but you hadn't spent enough time together to know. You may have in time. But there can be no doubt that from the day he was born, he was the most important thing in the world to his parents. Your baby will be to you. There probably isn't another kind of love that deep. And there probably isn't a deeper pain than when that love isn't there."

She shivered and realised that she'd nodded off in the chair, but as she began to stand, she felt a sharp pain in her side. "Not yet little one", she whispered. "You stay in the warm for a little while longer."

She flicked through a magazine and tried to ignore the discomfort she was feeling. Another sharp pain doubled her over then a warm wet gush told her that her baby was not prepared to wait any longer. She walked slowly to the bathroom to clean up and get changed. Then she tried to calmly make her way down the stairs to the telephone, but she had to stop halfway, as another much more severe pain tore through her body. Then she panicked.

"Jean, Jean! I need help. Wake up, Jean, please!"

Lights clicked on, and Jean, swollen-eyed and grey-faced came down the stairs. "It's okay now, I'm here. Just relax if you can love. Won't be long now."

"My waters broke. Oh God I'm so scared Jean."

"Of course you are. But I promise I'll be with you every step of the way and before you know it you'll be a mum." Then, turning away, she called out, 'Ted, come on. We need you to drive us to the hospital."

"I heard you both. I'm ready," he said, coming down the stairs fully dressed but with sleep-ruffled hair.

Mel remembered the agreement she'd reached with Clive. "I'm supposed to phone Clive or Gary. I promised them I would."

"You sit here quietly and wait," Jean was taking over completely. "Ted, you go and get the car ready. I'll phone Clive to let him know."

"Ask him to phone Chrissie for me," Mel asked, then she gave herself over to Jean.

"Chrissie won't be left out, don't you worry."

At the hospital Mel was wheeled away and Ted and Jean sat down in the grim waiting room. It was painted a pale green and cream and furnished with unmatched chairs, the only light came in through windows set so high up the wall it was impossible to see anything but grey skies above. Someone had set up a threadbare little plastic tree in the corner, and the few little bits of tinsel did all they could to brighten up the dismal little room. Jean stared at it with a jolt. She'd entirely missed Christmas this year.

Ted nudged Jean and nodding his head at the windows said, 'do you think they get many folks trying to break out of here?" She bravely raised a smile and gripped his hand for dear life. For the first time since August she realised that they both had something to look forward to.

Within thirty minutes, Gary was there as he'd promised Clive he would be. He began offering to fetch tea, simply because he didn't know what else he could do. Once Clive got here he'd be able to relax, maybe. Though what use Clive thought he would be was a mystery to Gary.

"No news yet?" he said as he came back in carrying in some cups of grey tepid cup liquid that by no means fitted the description of tea.

"No, but it's not going to be very long now. They're just settling her down and then we can go in. They said we'd

74

come too early when we first arrived but they've changed their tune a bit now. So we're staying put. In fact, I'll just pop in and see what's what," Jean said.

"Clive's on his way. He'll stop off in Southampton to pick Chrissie up on the way. Do you want me to go and get you anything Ted?"

'sit down and relax, they're not going to ask you help if that's what you're twitching about. We'll be quite safe in here. Let's be honest if anything needs to be done Jean would be beating off all comers anyhow."

Seconds later Chrissie and Clive ran down the corridor towards Ted and Gary, who were sitting in silence in the waiting room. And at that moment, Jean burst back into the waiting room, beaming from ear to ear and in floods of tears.

"It's a girl," she cried. "We've got a little girl, Ted."

He wrapped his arms around her and for a moment they stood together quietly giving thanks. Then "Can we go in and see them?" He said, coughing to clear the catch in his voice.

"Yes, but only for a minute. Come on."

"What, all of us?" Chrissie asked.

"Yes, of course, all of us. We're her nearest and dearest, after all. A girl needs all her family at a time like this. Just let them try and stop us."

They all pushed into the room and surrounded the bed in awed silence. Mel looked up at them and smiled as she proudly brushed the covering aside so that they could all meet her daughter. "Everyone, say hello to Hope."

CHAPTER ELEVEN
Winter 1989

Jean's constant tweaking and pacing had started to grate on everyone, but they were all trying to ignore it and get on with their given tasks. They'd planned a party to welcome Mel and the baby home. It seemed important to Jean and Ted, that Mel was helped to realise that she could lean on them both for a while, they were strong enough now. Jean wanted to make sure everything was as perfect as it could be.

Ted watched her move a cushion a fraction to the left and finally snapped, "For Christ's sake, Jean, sit down and have a stiff drink. You're making me bloody edgy, love. There's nothing to panic about. Do you think anyone is going to care if the cushions are not lined up properly?"

"No, they won't, but I will." She smiled at him. "I'm just putting them over the worn patches on this settee. And, let me tell you now, there will be no more swearing from you in this house. Not once my granddaughter has moved in." She smiled again. "My granddaughter. I can still barely believe it. It feels so good just to say it. My granddaughter, It's a miracle."

"I know, love." He gave his wife a quick squeeze.

"Now, now; there's no time for any of that mucking about, you two. Where do you want these sausage rolls putting?" Chrissie called out.

Jean pointed. "On the table there please. Thanks for helping us with this. I know it's probably daft, but Mel has been an angel over the last few months and we thought a little welcome home party would be fun for her."

'she'll love it, I'm sure. Now then, Gary's been doing a bit of work in the garden and I think you should both come and make sure you like what he's done. He needs your approval."

Ted groaned. "Come on, Jean, this sounds ominous.

Let's go and see what he's been up to."

Gary was balanced with one leg on a ladder and the other on an ancient apple tree, tying one end of a bright pink banner to a branch. The wind was whipping around his ears and rain was dripping off his nose as he struggled to keep steady and stretch at the same time. "Good timing, Ted," he shouted. "Stay there a minute and make sure I get this level." He leapt down and carried the ladder over to the corner of the house and began to attach the other end. In clear white writing the banner read, "HOPE LIVES IN THIS HOUSE".

"Oh Gary, that's lovely. Thank you so much. It's perfect. You are clever," Jean was moved to tears once again.

"It was Julia's idea. She suggested it," Gary said.

As they all looked up at the little pink banner, the dark miserable day seemed suddenly brighter.

'tell her I think it's a lovely sentiment and we're very grateful. It's a shame she couldn't come today and join in the fun." Jean wiped her eyes again, and Gary grinned at her.

"Don't worry about Julia. She'll be having fun enough. Her mum's taken her shopping. Now, I need some help. We've got a stack of balloons to blow up before your guests arrive in about half an hour, so come on. They won't blow themselves up. Everyone, chop chop."

CHAPTER TWELVE
Winter 1989

"How did the homecoming party go down then?" Julia asked Gary later that night.

"Great. I know you thought it was a bit naff, but this baby is going to be a lifesaver for the whole family and I wanted to do all I could to help. I'm glad I did. I just wish you'd come with me."

"Not my thing at all. Sorry."

"God, you can be so snotty at times. Barry was your mate too, and I think it's about time you put yourself out for his mum and dad. And what about that little baby? Don't you want to help out? What exactly is your sort of thing? You don't want friends. You won't put yourself out for people. You don't want a job. You're not sure whether you're my girlfriend or not. I mean, what do you bloody want?"

It was the end of a very long, difficult day for Gary and his patience was exhausted. He'd struggled to be the fun, doting "nearly uncle" as he'd billed himself. He didn't want anyone to discover how bitterly upset he was that Julia had refused to attend. He was facing up to the idea that their relationship was about to change. It had to.

"I don't know why it all means that much to you. Chill out. You're twenty-one not forty-one. You're so serious these days, I feel like I'm going out with an old man."

His heart sank, she just didn't get him at all and he couldn't let it go on. Perhaps it was time to clear the air.

"Yes, I know I'm serious about this because I think this is quite serious, actually. You know I care about you, very much. But I'm happy with the way I am and I'm happy with my friends. I don't want to spend time with someone who wants me to change. You wish I earned more money and you'd like me to change jobs. You've decided that the people we've both been friends with for years are not good enough any more, and I'm fed up with the feeling that I don't quite come up to the mark. I always wanted you to be happy, but I want a girl who wants the same for me."

He stood up, almost as though he'd made a decision. "I'll take you home now. I know it's early but I think we both need some time to think. You need to know that Mel, and her baby, are now a part of my life. I do care about you, but I'm not about to change my life, or my friends, for you. I want you as you are, but you want me to be someone else, someone I don't want to be. Can't you imagine how that makes me feel? "

Julia listened to him in horrified silence as she followed him to the car. She was used to having her own way and had never, ever, been spoken to like that. She had never felt the need to explain or apologise and wasn't going to start now.

The journey continued in silence and after Gary dropped her off at home, he decided to go into Chichester for a drink before heading home. There was a pretty decent pub opposite the cathedral where a couple of his mates went. He could use a bit of time with people who hadn't known Barry. He'd just struggled through the worst four months of his life and was in desperate need of a break.

CHAPTER THIRTEEN
Spring 1990

The atmosphere in the car was tense. Linda and Steve were bringing Deb home at long last and they were both unsure how to deal with the fact that Deb had really wanted to stay where she was. The doctors were confident that she was well on the road to recovery now and would continue to improve at home. It was also important for her mental well-being that she started to live back in the real world again. Linda had initially tried to persuade the doctors to let her bring Deb home a few weeks earlier after Deb had said that she felt so safe in the hospital that she wouldn't mind if she never left. As a nurse, Linda had seen people become almost institutionalised. It was very easy to switch off and accept that life in hospital, whilst undoubtedly dull, was wonderfully stress-free. She knew that Deb had to be eased back into real life sooner rather than later. Things needed to be decided about Dad's future soon, and although the hospital had been very understanding, she knew she'd got a lot of favours to repay. Added to that was the fact that she had been finding the free supply of a variety of medications a little bit too useful at times. Things had to change. Sleeping pills were one thing, but now she found she needed things to pep her up during the day, and then, of course, she needed extra pills to send her to sleep. Those pills made life so much easier.

Only yesterday, Steve had almost caught her out. "Steady on, Lin. We don't need you developing a habit like that. A little bit of help is one thing but you seem to be a bit heavy-handed to me."

Her protests that she just had a headache seemed to set his mind at ease but she took it as a warning anyway.

"We'll soon be home now," Linda said, trying to break the silence. Deb had been terrified at leaving the hospital and Steve was very quiet. "What do you fancy for tea?

Your first meal that's not from the hospital kitchens should be special. Shall I cook or would you like a takeaway?"

She found she'd automatically fallen into her briskly cheerful nurse persona when speaking to her sister, forgetting how irritating that was to just about everyone. A lesson she'd only recently been on the receiving end of.

"I'm not hungry. I think I'll just go to bed." Deb sounded thoroughly fed up.

"Deb …" Linda began to remonstrate but she noticed Steve shake his head gently in her direction and he spoke. "Let's just take it one step at a time. We'll get you home now, and then if you want to go to bed, fair enough."

Linda shrugged. "I guess so. But it's important for her to build her strength up, you know. She's not going to get better if she won't eat."

'she'll eat," he said. "She's not hungry now; when she is, she'll eat."

"Hello. I'm still here and fully functioning, almost," Deb snapped. "Stop talking about me as if I'm still in a fucking coma. I can hear and respond. I'm just not hungry, okay?"

The journey continued in an uneasy silence.

CHAPTER FOURTEEN
Summer 1990

Gary parked his shabby little van on the immaculate gravel driveway and walked slowly towards the wide stone steps that led up to the huge wooden double doors. The stone pillars at either side that were holding up a vast terrace were blindingly white in the hot sunlight. On each step was a brilliant white pot containing a fantastic red flowering display. Very lovely, but Gary couldn't help thinking that his mum's dustbin was not quite as big as these plant pots. The house itself was redbrick, but the windows and doorways were white stone, the same as those huge pillars. The lawn looked as though it had been manicured and, sure enough, in the distance was an old chap snipping and trimming away at some bushes.

Gary had long since learned that there was no point in trying to feel at home in a place like this. He had to keep reminding himself to close his mouth. It made him angry that he'd been seeing Julia, though not officially as her boyfriend for almost a year, and yet, coming here, he felt he was little more than a tourist visiting a stately home, or perhaps a taxi driver picking up and dropping off the rich folk.

As he reached the intimidating doorway, he pressed the bell quickly, not giving himself time to change his mind. He began to feel like a bit like a character in one of those terrible costume dramas his mum loved to watch. The door swung open and he let out a nervous laugh. Thank God it was Julia on the other side. If a butler had been there, he'd have lost it for sure.

"Come on in and say hi to Mum and Dad," she said. "We've loads of time, haven't we?"

This was a change. He'd never actually been invited inside the house before. Were things looking up at last he wondered. Perhaps the falling out they'd had, had made her think a bit. It had certainly cleared his mind. They'd stopped seeing quite so much of each other and had both enjoyed the change. It had been a time to take stock.

"Well, only quick hello, but we've not got a lot of time to spare. We've to be there for three o"clock. I know you don't want to go but I do, so don't try and make me leave it too late."

Of course a quick hello wasn't on in this house. Silver tray, coffee pots and china cups were produced just as Julia's mum made her entrance. Thinking her back up had arrived Julia wasted no time going on the offensive.

"Oh Gary, please. Wouldn't it be fun to play twosome truant? We could go to Brighton for the day, almost like our first date."

"Jules, stop winding me up. I have to go to this christening; I've promised. I'd love to spend any other day with you, and you know it. We can't do it today."

"I know that. It's just … oh, I don't know. Mum, have a say, what do you think?"

"Darling, If Gary gave his word then he must go of course. If you hate the idea then stay here with me. We could go shopping, or a manicure. Oh darling, yes, lets have the day together."

This was not quite what Julia had in mind.

"I just think that Barry's been gone for a year now and we should all move on, well most of us have. It's hard for me to understand why you are so interested in the family. You didn't really know them before he died and I think perhaps they should have moved on as well. Things like today event feels a bit like we're bringing it all back. Don't you know what I mean? Can't we all just let it go? We're not a gang of kids any more. We hardly know each other nowadays, let's be honest."

"I'm sorry you feel like that, but I don't. I'm going because I want to, now, do you want to come with me or not?"

She realised she'd pushed him as far as he was going to

83

be pushed, for today at least. She pinned on a brilliant smile. "Silly, of course I'm coming with you. Come on, let's go. Sorry about the manicure Mum."

As soon as they had driven out of the gates, Gary felt himself back in control a little bit. He hated that it was the fact that her family were so rich that intimidated him.

He began to speak. "Today is for us all, you know. It's for the baby and Barry's family, of course, but they want to share it with their friends, and we are their friends. They've booked this particular day in honour of Barry. It's a sign that they are ready to move on. As his friends, we must support them. Can't you imagine how hard it's been for them? It's been so much worse for them than for us, but they're much happier now. They want to celebrate and they want to let all his friends know that it's okay to move on. We've got to put them first one more time.

"I said it's okay Gary. Let's leave it now. I understand that I'd got it wrong and I'm really sorry. I'm trying to be more understanding; it's taking a bit of time, that's all."

"Just let me explain though, everything was changing for all of us anyway. But nothing has been spoiled for us. Think about Barry's mum and dad and that gorgeous little girl. We'll be her honorary aunt and uncle. You don't really begrudge spending time with them, do you?"

"It sounds like I'm such a selfish little cow when you say it like that. Of course I don't begrudge the time. I'm so stupid sometimes," she said with a smile, "and you're very wise, for a plumber."

"I'm a kitchen designer, thank you very much. And another thing, don't forget this will be Deb's first social event since the accident. It'll be great to see her dressed up and out. I was beginning to wonder if that would ever happen."

"Yes, I know she's had a tough time, but she's getting better every day now. She's no fan of Mel either you know. It's not just me, but a day out is a day out. I'll behave and we'll have fun, but only for you, Gary.

84

CHAPTER FIFTEEN
Summer 1990

Mel sighed with pleasure as she walked into the room that was supposed to be her own private space. Although the plan had originally been to completely divide the house into two flats, Barry's death had changed things. Hope and Mel now shared the house with Jean and Ted, except for this one room that was totally hers. It was very dated, having last been decorated in the seventies when Jean and Ted were newly married. Thankfully, the violent orange and brown swirls of the wallpaper had become tolerably muted, but, unfortunately, the same could not be said for the foul orange shag carpet. Although the change in circumstances meant that decoration was not a priority, the carpet had to go. Once it had gone, Mel found her therapy in scrubbing, sanding, varnishing, and then loving the old floorboards that she brought to life as she helped Jean and Ted heal.

Walking into the room now gave her a feeling of immense satisfaction. She sat down on the floor and holding Hope in her arms talked to her quietly, breathing in the sweet baby smell and stroking her plump baby limbs.

She'd fallen in love with her baby before she'd been born, but the sheer depth of emotion that she had felt when this tiny bundle first nuzzled in her arms had taken her breath away. This precious little person totally satisfied Mel. All day, every day, they talked and cuddled and laughed.

Today though, they had duties to perform.

"It's going to be a long day, precious. Lots and lots of people are coming just to see you and I know you're going to make them all fall in love with you. This is your special day and you're going to be wearing a very special outfit, an outfit that used to belong to your daddy. What do you

85

think of that?"

Hope blessed her with a glorious smile that had just a hint of teeth and rather a lot of gum.

"I think we'd better put our party frocks on and go downstairs, princess," she said, as she fussed about with the rather fancy and quite heavy christening gown.

This whole event was not what she'd have chosen but she knew that both Ted and Jean were viewing it as a turning point for themselves and she was prepared to do anything within her power for them.

"Car's ready, love," Jean's voice rang out. "Do you need a hand?"

"Yes please, Jean. Come in and help me with this child. She's into everything. She needs a firm granny's hand, I think."

Jean came in smiling and placed a kiss on Mel's cheek saying, "You're a darling and I thank God every day for sending you to us. Now, where's my little angel?" And picking up her granddaughter she left Mel alone.

With a final check in the mirror Mel was ready to go and face the day. She'd spent a lot of time worrying about what outfit to wear. It was so important that she showed everyone that she was as good as them. She knew that Barry's old friends were not her friends but she was determined to show them that she was a good, decent person, worthy of Barry's love and that she would be a good mother to his child. She would never fit in with them, she knew, but she would never let them think they were better than her.

As she walked downstairs she could hear her friends, Chrissie and Clive, teasing each other as they waited with Peter and Sally for her to appear.

"I think you'll find that a godfather has seniority over a godmother," said Clive.

"Only if your name's Marlon Brando, pal," Chrissie said. "The "ladies first" rule applies in this, as in most other situations."

86

"Yes, but we've come all the way from Australia to participate, so surely we have seniority," Sally laughed.

"Now, now children, don't spoil the day by falling out with each other," Mel said, as she joined them in the hallway.

"You look lovely, Mel. What a fabulous dress." Chrissie grinned at her friend. "Suit of armour, is it?"

"Just a little bit of power dressing … just in case," Mel replied.

"Do you feel in need of protection, Mel?" Peter asked.

"I do, every now and then. I think I was a shock for some of Barry's friends, and one or two of them are still not entirely comfortable in my company. It'll pass, in time."

"Well, just remember we all love you and we're family. Hold your head high, girl. Now, we'd better get going, I think."

The church was full and the christening of Hope Abigail Petersen went according to plan. Clive and Chrissie clearly took great pride in their roles as God-parents, as did Peter and Sally. Hope behaved like the angel that she was spending the entire afternoon smiling and raising her arms for a cuddle to everyone. Just as Mel predicted, she made everyone who met her fall just a little bit in love with her. It was an incredibly emotional and moving ceremony.

Ted's idea had been to throw a party afterwards. He hoped that this would give him a chance to talk to the group that he had expected to address at his son's wedding. He had things he needed to say to every one of the people that he had invited. He waited for an hour or so, wanting everyone to have a drink and relax after the formality of the church service. When he judged the time was right he stood and tapped his glass for attention. He began to speak, quietly but clearly.

"Let me start by thanking you all for being here today with my family, helping us have a happy day. As you all know, it's been a year since Barry, our wonderful son, died. Just one year ago I didn't think I would have the strength to go on living. Jean, Barry's mum, felt the same."

Here he paused to take Jean's hand. "Just two things gave us a glimmer of light in those dark, desperate months. One of those things was the friendship and caring we had from all of you sitting here today. We'd lost our most precious thing, but you all helped us to get through it. Your phone calls, your visits and the cards we received, all made a difference. At the time, we weren't able to let you know how important you are to us. Today we can, and we do thank you all from the bottom of our hearts. Each and every one of you helped us move forward, one day at a time."

His eyes moved over everyone. He needed to make sure they all knew they were included. Only when he was satisfied, did he continue to speak.

"The other thing that helped us was Mel. We didn't know her very well then, but we did know that Barry loved her and that was good enough for us. She carried us both in those first few dreadful months. She shopped, she cleaned, she cooked, she organised and she kept us on track. She paid the bills and kept us safe. The knowledge that she was carrying Barry's child and was therefore family gave us the strength to keep going.

"Hope's arrival at Christmas was what took us from barely functioning to actually looking forward to getting up each day. Mel has allowed us to enjoy bath time, bottle time and even nappy changing time."

Here he stopped speaking, raised his eyebrows and grimaced. A gentle laugh swept the room.

"There could only ever have been one name for her. Hope. Our Hope. To christen her in the same month that her Daddy died is our way of celebrating the link between them. Not all of you know Mel very well, but I want you all to know she is, to all intents, our daughter and I hope you will all take the time to get to know her better. Thank you for being there for us in the bad times. I look forward to seeing much more of you all through our good times. Now then, let's all have a drink and get this party started, shall we?"

A little later, once everyone had taken the time to catch up with everyone, Gary found Julia and said, "We can head off any time now, if you still want to."

She shrugged. "No. I don't think so, not just yet. I want to spend a little bit of time with Deb first and then perhaps I'll have a chat with Hope and Mel. We'll never be friends if I don't get off my high horse, so I'm going to make an effort."

He nodded his approval. "Brilliant. I'll be over there in the bar with the lads. Give me a shout if you want anything."

CHAPTER SIXTEEN
Summer 1990

After picking Deb up from the christening party Linda parked the car on the road as near as possible to their house. The roads in Portsmouth seemed to get more and more clogged up every day. It was often quicker to walk than bother driving. She leaned back into the car to help her sister get out, and they made their way slowly into the side door that opened into the kitchen. Once in, Deb kicked of her high-heeled shoes with a sigh of relief.

Linda opened the kitchen door and shouted up the stairs. "We're home now, Dad. Tea's on its way."

A gruff voice floated down to them. "It's about time too. I'm dying of thirst up here."

"I should make you come down here and fetch it yourself for that remark, you cheeky old sod." She looked at her sister for support and noticed she'd turned deathly pale. "Sit down quickly. What's wrong? Have you got any pain? Do you feel dizzy?"

"I'm okay, no pain. I'm just a bit light-headed, you know, shattered."

"Well, it's been quite a long, tiring day. Just sit still for a moment, I'll go and make us some tea, and then perhaps you ought to think about having an early night."

"Maybe. Though a glass of wine of would be a far better idea. It was an interesting day and I'm so glad I went. I've got such a lot to tell you. It was great to be out and about like a normal person. I'm okay, don't worry. I just got a bit tired all of a sudden."

"It's to be expected, I suppose. You've been in bed for most of the past year. I guess it'll take a while for you to get all of your strength back. Never mind, we're home now, and you can rest all day tomorrow," Linda said

"I won't though. I've got far too used to doing nothing and then resting, and it's time I got on with my life now. I need to get going again."

"Oh?"

"Let's have that drink and I'll tell you what I'm thinking of."

As Linda made herself busy getting drinks, Deb told her what her plans were.

"You know I was all set to go to teacher-training college before the accident? Well, I'm almost fully recovered now and I want to apply again. There's no reason why I shouldn't get in. I had a perfectly valid reason for not taking my place last year, so I don't envisage any problems in starting this year. Same course, just a year later."

"But are you sure you're ready this quickly? Why not wait a little longer?" Linda said. "I mean, look at you, after just one day out, you're wasted. I don't think you're ready yet. There's no point in pushing yourself."

"I think there is. I'm okay. I've just got lazy and I need to get myself in shape. You've made it too easy for me to do nothing. Being out today with my friends has made me realise that I'm missing out on so much now."

"Missing out?"

"I read the paper and watch the soaps every single day. That's as close as I get to real life. The Sunday supplements are the most exciting thing that's happened to me since the accident. I'm nearly twenty-three and it's time I got on with things. All my friends have moved on. Gary and Julia look like they've settled down with each other. Shame for Steve, but that's life, I guess.

"Policeman Clive's got his future all worked out. He'll be chief constable one day. Or whatever title it is that a top-dog cop has. Even Mel's talking about going to go back to work in the hairdresser's. Admittedly, Steve doesn't do much apart from go to meetings but he wears very nice suits and he looks quite important."

They sat in silence looking at each other for a moment and then Linda started to laugh.

91

"I know. He does look important when he dresses up nowadays. What did you mean though when you said it's a shame for Steve? What's wrong with him?"

"Well, he's only really got me. He's so odd about girls but he won't talk to me about it. He's had one-night stands but he's never really had what you'd call a girlfriend. I think he …"

"He what? What are you saying?"

"Oh, I dunno. I think that's why he's a misery sometimes. He's lonely and he hasn't got anyone except me to turn to. And I'm moving on. I have to. Gary and Julia don't mean to exclude him but they're a couple, and he's the odd one out now. It was okay before they kind of got together, but it's different now."

Linda didn't know what to say. To think of him being lonely and not feeling he could turn to her broke her heart. She thought she had shown him she was always there for him. Obviously not clearly enough.

Deb continued speaking. "I'm so grateful for the way you've put your own life on hold and looked after me. But, you know, I can't go on acting like an invalid forever. I've got to start my life and you need to get a life too."

"I've always looked after you and my life is fine thank you very much," Linda retorted.

"It's not really though, at least, I don't think it is. I mean you could have come to the party today, no one would have minded."

"I didn't want to come, they're your friends not mine, anyway I was busy."

"That's what I'm saying, just think of the numbers and you'll see what I mean."

"What numbers? What on earth are you talking about now?"

"If I'm nearly twenty-three and thinking I've left it as long as I could, then you, at nearly thirty-three have almost missed the boat," Deb explained. "You should be getting married and having babies. In fact, you should have had your babies by now and I should be getting married and having them. We seem to be locked in this little bubble here watching life go past just outside our window. I want to join in now though. Don't you?" Deb asked.

"I don't really understand what you mean. This is my life here with you and Dad. I've got a job and a family and I don't feel that I'm missing out on anything." Linda felt very defensive and a little bit scared. She'd spent her life looking after Deb and now she had to keep an eye on Dad too. She didn't expect thanks, but to be told she was letting life pass her by was a bit rich.

"I think you are missing out though, and I'm not being unkind, honestly. I know how much we let you do for us and we're all in the wrong. None of us are disabled, but we've become far too reliant on you. You're not a servant and I feel awful for letting it go on this long. I did need a lot of help when I came out of hospital, but I probably didn't need as much as I took, and I certainly should have been up and about at least a month ago. There's nothing I can do about that now except apologise and stop it now."

"It's never been a problem. I love looking after you and I don't want it to change. Please don't go off to college, not yet anyway. I'd miss you horribly and I'd worry all the time. You had some terrible injuries and I don't want you to risk being hurt again."

"I've made up my mind Lin, sorry. It would be so easy to stay as we are but it's not right for either of us. You're my sister and I want you to be a sister, not a substitute mum. You should be a real mum to your own kids, before it's too late. You know you'd be brilliant. Try to understand me, please. I want you to have a life, a social life, I mean. You know, friends, parties and concerts. When was the last time you went to the pictures or a museum?"

"What's brought all this on, changing my life, as well as your own?" Linda asked.

"It was today seeing Mel, who's younger than both of

us, with that lovely little girl. And Jean and Ted, who've been through so much, and are now so excited and looking forward to a full life with her. Even Chrissie, who I always thought was a bit thick, she's a social worker, well almost. She's still on probation, but she's on the way.

"I was watching Julia and Gary carrying on a ridiculous grand passion. You know niggling and picking and taking it in turns to break up, then make up, and both clearly loving every minute of the drama it causes. And then there were Peter and Sally, over here from Australia, just to get to know Hope and keep involved in the family. They are both teachers and they were so full of life and energy. It all kind of made me look at us, look at me, mostly. I could do any of the things all those people do, and more. I want to start now, trying things and going places. I want to meet loads more people and then I want to fall in love and get married and have a family. I feel excited, almost energised at the thought of all of it. I can't wait to get started."

"And to think you thought about pleading a headache and not going today! And all of a sudden it was good enough to make you want change your life, and mine."

Linda scrabbled in her handbag for her pill bottle.

"I know. It was the most fun I've had for such a long time. It was quite a wake-up call. I think that's why I'm so shattered now. I wish you didn't need to take so many of those pills though, Lin. Is it your headaches again?" She yawned and stretched. "You should talk to one of your pet doctors. Get it sorted out."

They were disturbed by the phone ringing, and as Linda went answer it, Deb drained her glass and started to pour another.

Linda came back in looking worried. "That was Steve. He's at the hospital. His dad had a massive heart attack this afternoon. He was lying on the floor when Steve got home and he's not doing very well. He's at the hospital and I think I should go and sit with him."

"I'll come with you," said Deb.

"No, you stay here. I know you're all fired up about joining in with life, but you look really tired now. You stay here and rest. I'll phone you if anything happens. I promise."

"Okay. Bring Steve back here if ... you know."

"I know. Go to bed. We'll talk more tomorrow."

Linda dashed to the hospital and used the staff car park. As she raced along the corridor, she gave thanks for her intimate knowledge of this place. She knew where Steve's father would be and got there in record time. As she reached the corridor, she saw Steve standing looking out of one of the windows.

"Steve?"

'thanks for coming, Lin. The panic's over though. He's gone."

"Oh, I'm so sorry, Steve." She put her hand on his shoulder and he turned to her. "It must have been awful for you, finding him on your own. You should have phoned me sooner. I'd have been with you."

"I'm not. Sorry, I mean ..." His voice was slightly muffled against her shoulder.

"Steve, don't say that." She'd slipped into nurse mode automatically.

"Don't give me all that 'mustn't-speak-ill-of-the-dead' bollocks. You know what an evil bastard he was." He pushed her away and turned back to the window, staring out at nothing.

"You don't need to drag all that up now though. It's over and he'll never hurt you again. Don't say things you might regret later," she said.

"It's a relief that he's dead and you know it. I'll never regret saying that. I just couldn't get away from him no matter how hard I tried. He only had to look at me and I lost all my confidence. He didn't want me but he wanted to control me. He never showed me any kindness, ever. But that wasn't the worst of it. You can't imagine what I had to go through at his hands." He put his head in his

95

hands and groaned.

"Don't do this now Steve. Let's go home and rest. If you want to talk tomorrow, I'll listen, I promise," she said.

"I'm going through it now because this is it. It's over and I'm laying the ghost here and now. After tonight I'll never mention him again and I won't listen to anyone who does. This is the last night he'll ruin for me. You can listen to me or not. That's up to you. I'm pretty sure you knew what was going on anyway, didn't you?" he asked.

"I don't know what you're asking me. Don't upset yourself. Let's just go home."

"Did you know he was abusing me?" he persisted. "He raped me for the first time the night we buried Mum. I was a scared little boy whose Mum had died but he just said if she couldn't stay to take care of him, then I would have to. He killed her, you know."

Linda shook her head and tried to hold him but he pushed her away and kept on talking.

"He always said she fell down the stairs drunk, but it's a lie. She jumped down the stairs drunk. He beat her and abused her all her life. Didn't she realise that if she wasn't there to look after me, he'd turn on me? Or didn't she care? When she died, he just carried on exactly as he had before.

You've never said anything, but I know you know. When did you guess? For fucks sake, Lin, talk to me! Why do you always try to pretend shit doesn't happen? You always want to make out everything is clean and nice, and everybody is good inside and the world's a happy place. It's a crock, Lin. Be real, if only for tonight." He was shouting now and pacing back and forth.

A passing nurse tapped on the door as she opened it and asked them to keep the noise down, then apologised as she recognised Linda. Nevertheless Linda knew she needed to calm him down.

"Okay, okay, I just don't see how this can help, but if you want to talk about it, we will. But please stop shouting, I can't afford to get kicked out of my own hospital.

"Sorry, but I need to get this off my chest. Now. You know about it don't you?

"I knew you were being treated very badly. My mum told me some of what your mum had gone through and we knew that things couldn't be any better for you. I was very young at the time and I didn't know how he abused you – violently, sexually or mentally, but I didn't doubt you were abused. Your dad was a cruel, hard man. My mum made me swear I'd never go into your house alone, or let Deb go."

"Does Deb know?" he asked.

"No one knows except me, as far as I know. It's not something I would ever repeat. My mum only told me so that I could know to be gentle with you when you needed me to and to keep Deb close. I can't imagine what it must have been like for you."

"I thought it was normal, it happened so often. He came to my room every night. I was so young when it began that I didn't even think too much about it. Once I started going to school, I realised that most boys didn't have to do what I did every night. I knew it was wrong and I was so … I don't know. I hated him but I loved him and I felt sorry for him as well. I put up with stuff even after I was big enough to stop him. That makes me as sick as him, huh?"

"No, Steve, no, it doesn't. Not sick, or weak or any of the things you might accuse yourself of. He was wicked to take advantage of you. You were a child and you loved and trusted him and he abused and manipulated you. None of it was your fault. I think you just did what you had been conditioned to do."

"Do, you don't despise me?"

"Me, despise you! Never. I love you. I'll never judge you. I loved you as a baby and I love you now. I always will," she reassured him. "Don't ever think otherwise. I'm in your corner come what may."

97

"I thought I'd be happy when he finally died. But I feel angry, no, furious and let down. He went without telling me why he never could love me the way a father should. Now I'll never know."

"And I can't help you with that but I can tell you that I love you with all my heart. When you were a little boy I just adored you. When you were a stroppy teenager you pissed me off so often, but still I loved you. And now, you're a good man Steve, and here I am still loving you. If ever you want to talk I'll be there. Now come on, let's go home."

He couldn't speak and he looked quite overwhelmed. She simply linked her arm through his and they walked out into the night side by side, both feeling that something fundamental had shifted in their relationship.

CHAPTER SEVENTEEN
Autumn 1990

Once again, Gary and his dad were standing in their yard nose-to-nose. They were so alike both in looks and temperament. Their bodies were tense, their hands were at their sides, but their jutting chins were almost touching. A casual observer might think they were close to exchanging blows, but that had never happened and never would. Passion ran through their veins, they thrived on it.

Colin looked furious, but, in reality, he wanted to see how serious Gary was about his latest crazy scheme. There seemed to be no end to the ideas he was coming up with and so far they had all proved to be good ones. Colin was reluctant to admit he'd underestimated his son. He would give this latest idea a chance, provided he could see Gary was absolutely committed to it, whatever it was. Gary had been dropping hints for months now, so this was clearly going to be the big one.

"What are you talking about, we need a facelift? Where the hell did that idea come from? This is a storage yard for a plumber. What would we want to spend money tarting it up for? I've made my living doing this since I left school and this yard has been good enough for me. It's brought in enough money to feed and clothe you and your mother and it's paid for a roof over our heads, but now, here you are with your poxy little A-levels and no bloody experience, thinking you can tell me where I've been going wrong all this time. You're a cheeky sod. I swear, I don't know where you get your bloody thinking from sometimes. Unless it's Lady Julia giving you grand ideas."

Gary took a deep breath. "Just listen to me for a minute, will you? I'll explain what I mean if you stop jumping down my throat before I can even finish a sentence. I'm not saying anything is wrong here, okay? This business is doing great and I'm proud of it. This isn't personal; it's financial. You read the papers and you know there's a recession on. People are struggling to get by and there's a lot of 'make do and mend", right?"

"Yes, but I don't see your point. We're doing okay, more than okay, in fact. I don't want you to think that we're about to go out of business or anything," Colin said, instantly defensive again.

"I'm not worried at all. Just the opposite, in fact. If we're doing well now, think how strong we'll be when this recession ends. People know us and trust us. If we were to take on a couple of lads now … no Dad, listen, hear me out. If we took on a couple of lads to do some work here, then we, that's me and you, could carry on with all our normal business. There are good men around without work right now – builders, carpenters, and the like. We could get a couple now and put them on this place to build a showroom here." He paused for breath and realised that for once his Dad was actually listening. Gary decided to plough on. "I've done some drawings and worked out some numbers. Come and have a look."

For the next hour Colin listened as Gary outlined his plans to turn the emergency plumber's into a kitchen and bathroom installation business.

At last Colin spoke. "So, where do I fit in to these plans? I can't see me in a poncy showroom walking around in a collar and tie, can you?"

Gary laughed. "I don't see any change for either of us for a long time. We'll carry on working our business in our usual way. We mustn't change that. It's what our reputation is built on. That's paid for everything always and I know how important it is. I know you've worked all your life to build it. I want to add to what we do, not change it or take anything away from it. But, just think, how often do we go and work on things that have broken because they were put in the wrong place to start with? We work on kitchens and bathrooms that were laid out badly. We repair boilers that should never have been put where they are, and at least once a week a customer asks me what I would do to make their kitchen easier to work in. They must ask you those sorts of things too?"

"True enough, they do, and I give them my best advice. So, what are you saying now? Are we to tell them they've to pay for our advice?" Colin demanded.

"No, we tell them the opposite, in fact. We give the best advice as always. Then we tell them that if they decide to make some of the changes we've suggested, we'll do the work at cost price. When it's done, we'll want photographs of the job and their permission to use those photographs in our catalogues and as references. Word will spread that we're doing top-quality work at rock-bottom prices and we'll get more work in. We'll get photographs to use as advertising and displays in the showroom."

"Okay, I see where we're going with this, but sometimes the sensible thing means knocking down a wall or ripping up a floor. We're not big enough for that kind of work," Colin said.

"We're not, not yet, but we would be if we hired a couple of good, skilled blokes now to start working on the showroom. When they've finished that, we'll have outside work lined up for them," Gary said.

"Yes okay. I'll admit you've worked it all out very well. It sounds as though you've put a lot of thought into this and you might, only might, mind you, have hit on something."

"That'll be down to my poxy A-levels, I expect." Gary grinned, relieved now that he'd given it his best shot.

"Don't push it," Colin laughed. "You'd better start getting some kind of a schedule worked out then, hadn't you?"

"You mean you're going to go for it? Just like that?" asked Gary.

"Well, this is half your business now and one day it'll all be yours. If you think we need to do this, then I trust you. I'm going to have to start to one day. Today's the day. Put your money where your mouth is. Get a schedule of works, sort out the building regs, oh, and you'll be doing the interviews as well. If it's your baby, it's your job to change the nappies."

"I thought I'd need at least a month to bring you round," Gary said.

"Your ideas make sense, and I think you've got the enthusiasm to see the project through. You've done a good year's work with me and you've gone a long way towards proving yourself. I'll risk it. Just remember, if you cock it up, it's on your head."

***

Later that night, Gary sat in his local, pen and paper to hand, immersed in plans and dreams. At last he'd be able to build something with his name on. Something his dad would look at with pride and that could carry on until he had sons of his own to bring on. Julia crept up on him and tapped him on the shoulder. "What we doing tonight?" she asked.

"I want to work on a few ideas I've had for setting out a schedule for when we start building the showroom. You can come and help."

'so, the showroom is not top secret any more then? You've talked to your dad about it today?"

"He loves the idea. God, I can't believe it. He thinks my plans are really good." Gary still sounded amazed.

"Of course he does. I told you, you've worked it all out so well, and your dad's a smart bloke. He can see you know what you're talking about. I'll bet he's dead proud of you. How do you feel about it now it's out in the open?"

"Elated in one way, but terrified as well. He's run that business since he left school and it's absolutely solid. What if I mess it up? He's given me the go ahead, but I've got to do all the work. I think I've got cold feet."

"I understand that, but don't be soft. You've thought of

102

nothing else for so long. You know it's the right thing to do. Nothing can stand still for ever. It can't stay solid without changing. Business has to move forward and keep up-to-date. That's what my dad says anyway," Julia said.

She was much happier these days and seemed to accept that he had to work so many hours, but she still seemed to need far more cosseting and spoiling than Gary had time for. He knew he'd got to develop this business if it was to provide for his mum and dad and his own family in the years to come. It was a hands-on, personal business, and he simply had to work seven days a week when there was work to be done. The work could dry up at any time. Those were the days he could spend making plans for the future. She didn't always allow for that because she had never had to ask twice for anything before in her life. When Gary said no, her assumption was that he didn't care for her as much as she cared for him. He knew that now he'd got the go ahead for his project, he'd have no time for messing around at all.

"I really can't take time out to go out and about much right now. I want to draw up this time schedule and then start talking to a few likely blokes. Developing this new showroom is the most exciting thing I've ever been involved in, but it's got to be done properly. I'm working every job that comes in and I'll be overseeing that project as well."

"I know, don't worry," she said. "I've made a decision that will help us, I think. I've decided to get a job, and you're the first to know."

"But you're a princess" he said.

"Fuck off."

"Sorry, but you, working?"

"Look, I know you're busy and I actually feel a bit useless sitting around waiting for you to spend time with me when you've got so much on, I thought having a job made sense."

"It does, make sense, I mean. I think it's a brilliant idea.

What sort of a job will you look for?"

"I'm going to open a shop."

"You're opening a shop? Christ, what sort of shop are you thinking of?" he laughed.

She took a deep breath and began to speak. "Arts and crafts with gifts and cards. I want to have it set up as if it were a gallery. I'm going to have open evenings where I can serve wine and let people browse around. I'd like to think I might even get some commissions. Several of the people I knew at college are struggling to find an outlet for their work, so I imagine I'll have some kind of a sale or return arrangement."

It was her turn to laugh as he sat with his mouth open in amazement. "Did you think you were the only one with plans and ambitions, Mr Daniels?" She smirked at him.

"Well no, of course not, but I'm surprised. You've never mentioned any of this before. Have you just come up with the idea?"

"Yes and no. It's an idea I had a while ago, but the time wasn't quite right, or maybe I just couldn't be bothered. It may not be the right time now to do it, but I certainly want to start talking to people about the idea and get some advice. I know you're going to be really busy for a long time to come and I want to have something I can focus on. Do you think I'm mad?"

"I think you're brilliant. And you've got guts Have you started looking for a shop yet?"

"No. I wanted to tell you before I actually did anything. I'll start things off now though. I was going to mention it to Jean, Barry's mum. She's a quite a talented water colour painter, you know. She's done a few local scenes that I've seen and I think they'd go down a storm."

Gary struggled to keep his poker face on. He'd never heard Julia show any signs of ambition and he didn't want to hurt her or knock her back. As long as she was kept busy making her plans it would give him free time to work on his own business. Things were looking up.

CHAPTER EIGHTEEN
Winter 1990

The issue of one party or two was the topic under consideration.

"I think we should have two. If you're worried about money I'll chip in, I know you don't want Hope to be spoiled, but having her own special day is very important. It is for everyone, and I don't think she should miss out just because her birthday is five days after Christmas." Jean was determined.

"I know, but it's her first one. She won't know or care whether it's one or the other. When she's older, yes, absolutely two parties, but this year I think one's enough."

Hope beamed at them both. She was a child that smiled all the time. If anyone smiled back, she raised her arms for a cuddle, and, consequently, she learned fast that the world was full of kind people that loved her and would pick her up for a cuddle given the slightest hint of a toothless grin. Mel and Jean kept trying to encourage her to walk, but Hope seemed quite happy working on her sideways crab crawl for the time being. She could travel from one side of the room to the other faster than Mel could. She could occasionally be persuaded to stand up straight and look around but she always made a conscious decision to drop back down onto her bottom rather than step out.

"And that's not a money-saving idea," Mel continued. "I'm not too worried about money, to be honest with you. We're doing okay financially, and work would like me to do another day and a half. I've said no, but it's nice to know it's there if I need it," Mel said.

"Don't think about need, think about want. If you want to go back to full-time work, you know you don't ever have to worry about babysitters. I'd always volunteer for that job, but I don't want you to do more work simply for the money. We've plenty put away, and it's all for her anyway so if you need anything, you've only to say. Work to have fun and meet people; we've got money enough for all of us."

"If I needed anything for her, I would ask you. I promise you, she'll never go without. As for me, I have enough. I love being back at work two days a week, and for the moment, that's enough."

"Okay, you're the boss. Now then, let's see if we can get her walking in time for her first birthday party."

As Hope crawled around the floor, refusing to walk but managing to delight them both at the same time Jean told Mel about Julia's reaction the sketches Jean had shown her. "Obviously she can't know what will or won't be popular in her shop yet, but she's very keen to have half a dozen of my paintings in her stock."

"I'm so pleased, I knew she'd love your work once she had the opportunity to see some. Why were you so reluctant to show her some examples?"

"Because she started gushing about how much she'd love to see some of my paintings when we were at Hope's christening and at that time no one had seen anything I'd done for years. I thought she was bit too keen before knowing whether I could actually do anything."

"So how does she know that you used to paint?"

Jean snorted and laughed. "Well, that's the other thing that put me off a bit. She overheard Peter ask me something about my paintings because he'd got a small one that we gave to his dad years ago and he was kind enough to say he'd always admired it. Julia must have been listening. I thought she was just a bit pushy and to be honest she is, but I actually quite like her. She's just very ambitious and wants to do something for herself, or at least that's the impression I have now. I've only spent a couple of hours with her so I guess time will tell."

CHAPTER NINETEEN
Winter 1990

The entire downstairs floor of the Portsmouth house had been given over to the party for Hope as this gave enough space for a bar area with a buffet that Jean had prepared and there was a small room that opened onto the tiny back garden that had been designated for the smokers. This became the room Julia had privately earmarked for herself to hold court. This being her first opportunity to practise a little bit of net-working, she wasn't going to miss a chance.

She and Gary were enjoying catching up with old friends, they'd been so busy in recent months that had dropped out of their normal social scene entirely.

Both of them were today glowing with a sense of achievement and loved showing off to anyone who'd listen. They were telling Deb what they had been busy with for the last few months.

"I've finally found the perfect spot for my shop. It'll be in Chichester, I've decided." Julia was buzzing. "The local people are pretty well-to-do. There's a good range of shops that already draws people in from miles away, and I've found a lovely little shop right in the centre. I'm going to call it The Gallery. It's all about sourcing the right stock now. In fact, I want to talk to Jean about some ideas I've had for some local landscapes. I can't wait to get my doors open."

"When do you think that will be?" Deb asked.

"I'm aiming for the first weekend in March. I could probably do it a bit sooner, but I want to make sure I get it right first time, so I've allowed loads of time to find exactly the right things to stock. I also want to offer some custom-made gifts, and I've got to make sure that the people doing the work won't let me down."

"I'm impressed," Deb said. "I'd never have thought of

you doing anything like that, but you seem so excited by the whole idea. It suits you. Will you have to start wearing suits with big shoulder pads and bright red lippy?"

"I might, and if I do, I won't be taking any nonsense from students like you, so I advise you to start showing some respect! Seriously though, I'm so excited. I don't know why it took me so long to figure out that I was bored. I was so spoilt and lazy that I hadn't bothered to worry about finding a career and making something of myself. I'd got used to using Dad's name and money, but, to be honest, when I saw how hard Gary and his dad worked and how much pride they got from that work, I realised that I was missing out. I wanted people to admire me for something I had done rather than for my dad's money. Mad, huh?"

Deb laughed at her. "I don't think it's mad at all. I'll bet your parents are proud of you."

"They are. Anyway, enough about me. What about you, are you fully recovered now?"

"Yes, completely. I've got right back into studying and I've caught up, so just recently I've been chasing up training courses and brushing up on things. I've let my brain get a bit rusty but I'm back on track now. I'll be starting a course at Easter. There's a training college in Worcester that has offered me a place, and I've accepted."

"You're definitely going away then?" Gary asked.

"Yes. Linda worries about me whatever I do, and I'm feeling a bit stifled, to be honest. I worry about her in a different way. I don't think she lets herself have a life because she scared to let me out of her sight. By living apart we can both move on with life and remain friends."

"Are you starting to fall out then?" Julia asked.

"Are we ever," Deb smiled sadly. "She tidies my room if I'm out, which is extremely annoying and a bit intrusive, then last week she opened a letter that came for me. She thought it looked official and as she didn't want me to be worried by anything, she decided to read it to see if there was something she could fix for me. That caused a huge row. She thinks she's protecting me, and I suppose she is, but it feels as though she prying or stifling me. I don't want to be protected. And I will not put up with someone opening my letters or sorting through my room when I am out."

"I'd have killed her, the nosy cow." Julia sounded shocked.

"It's partly my fault. It was so relaxing after the accident for me to not have to do anything, and I admit, I did sit back and let her do everything for me. It was like having a maid, so it's not all her fault that I'm trying to get back something that I let her take. I think my going away is the best thing for both of us."

Gary leaned forward suddenly. "Sorry to butt in, but have you two seen Steve? I'd never have imagined he'd be good with kids, but just look over there. He's lying on the sofa with Hope crawling all over him."

"I know," Deb said, "He's totally besotted with her. He talks about her to Linda all the time. She was always asking him about Hope and I think that's why he started to visit them at first, but I think he comes to see them every week now. I never thought men would get broody, but I think he is," Deb told them. "He seems to have gone baby mad."

"Is it Hope he comes to see, or could it be Mel?" Julia wondered.

"No way," Deb said. "He still can't stand her. They're both civil to each other on the surface but no more than that. It's really odd because he does seem to adore Hope. I guess he was closer to Barry than I realised."

"Don't you two start acting like nosy old women and making up stories! I think it's great that he's started to lighten up a bit and let his hair down. I wanted you to see it but I don't want you starting a line of gossip," Gary instructed.

"It's fact, not gossip," Deb defended herself. "He and

109

Mel dislike each other so much that it fascinates me. Let's be honest, I've no time for her either. But I do know, he is genuinely fond of Hope. Let's face it, she's adorable. But having said that, I don't think juicy gossip is a bad thing. There just isn't any here. Okay, Gary?" Deb teased.

"I know there isn't any here and I also know you two are more than capable of making something up. Don't do it. Okay?

"Yes, sir," the two girls replied in chorus, laughing at him.

He shrugged and walked away saying, "I think we ought to mingle a bit, don't you?"

Julia quickly agreed. Everyone who had attended the christening was here, and many others beside. Few, if any of them would leave without knowing about her forthcoming shop opening.

CHAPTER TWENTY
Spring 1991

Mel tried to apply a slick of make up and run a brush through her hair, whilst at the same time make sure that Hope was kept out of trouble. She was staggered to think about how her life had changed so radically in such a short time. She smiled when she thought about how hard she had worked to paint the walls of this room in time for the day she brought her daughter home for the first time. The white walls had looked so lovely against the bare floor boards Ted had helped her uncover and then polish.

There was no doubt that having a toddler was a joy but it had its drawbacks. Certainly the scuffs on the floorboards and the scribbles on the walls, drawn in lipstick, were not what she'd planned to have in her little haven. She seemed to permanently have a pile of clothes on the arm of the sofa waiting to be folded. The laundry basket always had stuff in and she knew for a fact it had been a year since she'd painted her nails. But she wouldn't change a thing.

She was disturbed from her daydreaming as Jean called up the stairs to tell her that Clive was on the phone. She bundled a wriggling, giggling Hope under her arm and made her way downstairs to deposit Hope with her Gramma Jean.

She wedged the handset under her ear as she tried to untangle Hope's arms from around her neck. "I hope you're not calling to cancel," she said to him. "I'm battling to get free here and I hate being stood up. It's taken me hours to get ready and here I am waiting for you.

"I'm not standing you up exactly, more postpone. I can't get away. Not yet, anyway," he said. "And you were not just waiting for me so don't lie. It's dead on time and you're always late. I'll bet you haven't got your make-up on yet, have you?"

111

"Well, as you're standing me up, I guess you'll never know."

"Mel, I'm really sorry."

'don't worry, I'm teasing you. We'll do it another time. It's not a problem at all. We'll just turn tonight into a girl's night out. A nice romantic film followed by a few glasses of bubbly and a large dose of gossip will suit me fine. Don't worry. Go and do your job. Honestly, it's no problem. Go. I'll talk to you tomorrow, I expect. Bye."

As she hung up the phone she saw Jean hovering nearby.

"Change of plans?"

"Yes, but only slightly so don't fret, I still need a babysitter. We were going to meet up with Chrissie and catch a film, but he has to work, so that means we get to choose the film. It was going to be *Silence of the Lambs*, but now it looks more like we'll get to see *Thelma and Louise*."

"You do know he's very fond of you, don't you?"

"Yes, he's been absolutely great. He's like a brother almost."

"I think he'd like to be more than that though." Jean spoke seriously. But Mel shook her head in denial. "Oh no. You're imagining things, Jean."

Knowingly, Jean said, "I'm right. I know I am. I've known him since he was at primary school with Barry. He couldn't keep a secret from me if his life depended on it. You pay attention and you'll see. That boy spent more nights here with us than he did at home. I know him very well."

"Well, I hope you've got it wrong this time because that's a complication I really don't need. I'd hate to hurt him but I'm not thinking along those lines at all. The last thing I want is a relationship. It hadn't even crossed my mind," Mel said.

"So, don't think about it. I only told you because I was certain you hadn't noticed and I thought I should make

112

you aware. If you're happy with the way things are, then carry on."

"How long have you been thinking like this?"

"It was at Hope's christening that I first realised."

"But that was last year. Why have you waited until now to mention it?"

"It was awkward. I didn't know how *I* felt about the situation then. You know you're Barry's girl to me. But I do know you're so much more than that and I think Clive feels the same way. I just didn't want to see what was in his eyes and not try to help. I'm very fond of him, you know, and the fact is you're an attractive, young, single woman. You should have boyfriends and choices and fun. All the things girls your age take for granted. I don't want you to miss out on life and I don't want Hope to not have a dad." Jean was red faced and clearly struggling not to cry.

Mel threw her arms around her and they stood in silence for a few moments.

"Don't go getting upset. Hope has so much more than a lot of kids. As well as me, she's got the best gramma and granda in the world living with her and half a dozen surrogate aunts and uncles, all dancing to her tune. Hope and I are fine as we are. Now, stop crying. You're chief babysitter tonight and I want you to enjoy it. I don't know what to say to you about Clive. I've not thought about anyone that way since Barry and I'm not thinking that way now. Don't cry, please."

"I'm okay," Jean said, giving a shaky smile. "It's still hard for me to talk about Barry sometimes, but I needed to clear the air. I'm sorry I let my emotions take over but I meant what I said. Ted and I have talked about you and your situation endlessly. We love you dearly and we both know you *will* find someone else in time. Maybe not yet, maybe not Clive, but when the right man is here at the right time, you will have our full support. I've wanted to say that to you for ages, but it's just, well it's been difficult. We want to see you enjoying your life a bit more.

113

And neither of us would want you to think for one minute that anything you do will hurt us."

"I understand what you're saying and I thank you. You two have such big hearts and I feel so lucky to have found you. You're always going to be a big part of our lives. You know that, don't you?"

Jean sniffed and nodded. "Go on then, go on out and let me be a gramma in peace. You have fun, I know for sure we will. We'll see you later. Give my love to Chrissie."

CHAPTER TWENTY-ONE
Spring 1991

Gary had spent an hour or so walking around Julia's shop, just prior to the grand opening and now he stood at the back of the new gallery watching Julia as she paced back and forth checking every single detail. She looked happy, confidant, and totally in control.

"She's in her element." Tommy, her proud father, said to Gary.

"I know. She chose every piece in here. She knows who made it and she knows what else they can do. I think this place is going to be a huge success," Gary replied.

"Are you surprised? Tell me the truth," said Tommy.

Gary grinned at the older man. "When she first said she was opening a shop, I was so surprised I actually laughed. I thought she'd been winding me up, but, since then, she's not stopped. When she was about to sign the lease she managed somehow to get the chap who owns the building to pay for a few extras to be added in and her let her choose the new fittings. She's so serious about it. It's very important to her. Yes, I'm surprised, but I'm very proud at the same time."

Tommy snorted. "Us too. But she's worked like a Trojan, even to the point of working through the night on one or two occasions. I had to do that a few times when I was building my business, but I never thought I'd see my princess doing it for herself. I'm bloody amazed. She's been spoiled by me and her mum all her life. I think you've been good for her. We'll go for a pint later if you like?"

"Great." Gary was shocked into silence. His relationship with her parents had been polite but distant. He'd been into their home many times but never felt as though he actually fitted in. He'd never been invited for a drink with Tommy and was delighted but also apprehensive. Was he fitting in

115

better or was he about to be warned off. His dad had once told him he thought he was punching above his weight a bit with her. Oh god.

CHAPTER TWENTY-TWO
Spring 1991

"Are you sure you've got everything you need? Painkillers, a drink? You've checked that they're expecting you at the B&B?" Linda was fussing and getting away with it as they both knew it would be the last time.

"I've got everything sorted out for now. When I get fixed up with more permanent accommodation, I'll let you know what I need, if anything. Don't nag, I promise if I get in any bother, I'll call you and you can come dashing to the rescue."

"Tease me all you like. Just remember, if you need me, I'll be there," Linda said.

"I know. But you remember to get out and enjoy life, test ride a few men, and try and sort out a good one for yourself. You're far too young to be a dried up old virgin. And please think about sheltered flats for Dad. I know you hate the thought, but he wouldn't mind. As long as he has his books he's not bothered where he is. He rarely knows who we are anymore. And it wouldn't be a bad idea to talk to one of your doctors about yourself, I reckon. You're taking too many of those bloody pills. If you get headaches that often, get something done, Lin."

"I'll think about it. I am thinking about it. I'm also thinking about looking for a different job. I was going to a couple of years ago, if you remember, but I lost my nerve. I think the time is right for a change."

"Do it. A challenge and a new circle of people, what could be better? We can write to each other every week with our news, and you should have as much, if not more news than me."

"Take care. I love you."

"Love you too. Bye"

***

117

It was just few short weeks later when the ringing of the doorbell recalled Linda from her daydreams.

She had initially been furious that her sister had been completely out of touch since she'd gone back to training. Now however Linda had passed from being frantic with worry to acceptance that she was no longer vital to Deb. As a result of this awakening, she'd been making a few changes to her own life. She made her way towards the front door, but was amazed to see her sister. She draped her coat and handbag off the stair rail and had dropped a large rucksack on the bottom step.

"Deb, I wasn't expecting you! How lovely, there's nothing wrong is there?"

"Everything's fine, don't start," Deb said. "I've got a lot of bookwork to do this weekend and I figured I could do that here as well as there and it would be a chance for us to catch up."

"Well, yes, it would have been lovely, um... but, ah, well, I'm not actually going to be here." Linda was torn between being apologetic and rather pleased that she had plans of her own.

What do you mean? Where will you be?"

"I'm going to Eastbourne for a couple of days. I've planned to spend a couple nights there, in fact, just relaxing." Lin was thrilled to be saying it aloud.

"What? On your own?"

"Well, no, since you ask, I'm going with a friend," Lin said.

"Who? Anyone I know?" Deb didn't really care about that. She was, however, hugely put out that having lugged that bloody bag all the way here, it was looking like she'd be doing her own laundry anyway. What on earth had happened to her boring old sister in such a short space of time. Deb had fondly imagined her sister would be quietly waiting at home for her return. Wrong.

"I'm going with Steve," Lin said.

"Do you mean *my* Steve?" Deb was horrified.

"No. I mean our Steve. Is that a problem?"

"You're going away for the weekend with Steve, who you practically brought up. Not in the best of taste I'd have thought. I know I wanted you to see some men, but I was thinking of men your own age. I think you're being a bit random to be honest. How soon are you going and who'll take care of Dad?"

"Steve's picking me up in a couple of hours. I've got a nurse coming to stay here while I'm gone. But, as you're here, I'll call and cancel her if you like. It'll be nice for you to have some time with Dad on your own," Lin said.

"Er, no thanks. I've got tons of work to do. I'll have something to eat and a bath and head back to college then, I think. There's no point in my staying here if you're off gadding about. I must admit, I expected a bit more of a welcome than this," Deb sulked.

"I don't think there's very much food in actually. I didn't know you were coming or I'd have shopped. I've let the fridge run down because of going away. Sally will be bringing in her own stuff, of course."

"Linda! I know I said I wanted you to get a life but I didn't think you'd forget all about me. This is my home too, you know."

"Of course it is, and you must come here whenever you want. But, if you want me to cater for you, you're going to have to let me know when you're coming. You quite clearly told me you were sick of me acting as though I were your mother. You wanted me to be your sister. Well, I am. If you want to eat, then go shopping. If you want a bath, switch the water on. Stop whining and grow up."

Deb was so shocked she stepped back and had the grace to look embarrassed.

"Bloody hell, have you had a personality transplant or something? I know I should have let you know I was coming, but I just fancied a catch up, that's all. It didn't cross my mind that you'd have got a life so soon. I'm a bit

119

surprised, that's all. And I would like to talk to you."

"Yes, okay, but talking has to go hand in hand with listening because I'm not interested in being lectured by you, " Linda warned her sister. She brushed past her and walked back out in to the garden lighting a cigarette on the way. She knew she had to hold firm, it would be so easy to give in and let life carry on as it always had but she knew things had to change. Now was as good a time as any. She sat down on their old swing and tried not to notice how bad the windows frames were looking from outside. And as for the guttering, oh god. She watched as Deb opened the door and steeped out.

"Sorry." She mumbled. "I've become so used to you always being there for me and taking care of stuff for me that it's a bit of a shock really, you going on a date. I'm happy you are, don't misunderstand me. When I told you I hoped you'd start dating and that I could imagine you as a mum, I meant it. I'm very happy being in college and getting on with my life and I'm glad you are."

Then, seeing that Linda was about to interrupt she said quickly, "No, no, please let me finish. It's your business, not mine, I know. I'm happy for you. I was just surprised. I mean, come on, Steve? Your life seems to be changing much faster than I thought it would, and I haven't kept up, but I will, keep up, I mean. Just don't shut me out, please."

Linda reached out and touched the back of her sister's hand as she replied.

"Lots of things have changed very quickly for me. It's been two years now since the accident. Barry died, and for a while, I thought you would too. When we realised you were going to get better, I knew things would never be the same as they were before, not for any of us. As you got stronger, you talked of nothing but how soon you would be well enough to go to college. You were going to live, but I had still lost you."

"No, not lost. I've grown up and changed a little, that's all."

Linda smiled, again touching her sister's hand. "Yes, I know, and that's what's happened to me now. Dad needs a level of care that I can no longer give so he's going to need help facing up to the changes that have to happen, and that's partly what this job I'm going for could help to achieve. I've not gone anywhere yet but I've changed too. I'm different. Before you went away to college do you remember what you said to me?"

"I do and I'm sorry for that too."

"Don't be. You said I was a 'dried up old virgin living life through you.' You were right. I was a step removed from all feelings and emotions. It was safe. When you went away, I immediately began to build a life for me. You were being cruel, but accurate. I am your sister, not your mum. And we can talk about anything you want. We can agree or disagree, but I'm not your housekeeper any more."

"Wow," said Deb.

"Yes, wow indeed. So what do you want to talk about?"

"Have you got any wine in the fridge, sis?"

"I've always got wine in."

"Good. Let's have a drink and you can tell me about your new life. I don't want details about you and Steve though. I still think that's creepy. What does Dad think about the new you?"

"Dad is Dad. He's not aware of much these days. In fact, if I don't insist, I don't think he'd even bother to eat. That's something I want to talk to you about. I had hoped to come and visit you after this weekend. But, just to set your mind at rest, I'm not having a thing with Steve. We are going to Eastbourne for the weekend for me to have an interview at a care home. They're looking for a nurse/manager. I think I'd be good at it, and the great thing is there's a place available for Dad if it seems suitable. He's said he's not bothered either way. So my thoughts are, if I accept the job and he's okay with it, we'd both move in there."

121

"Thank God. Not about Dad, that's a bit sad. I mean about Steve. I felt a bit sick thinking of you two together."

"Oh, grow up. It could still happen, you know. You wanted me to get a love life, and I will, but don't think for one minute that I'm about to let you choose my partners. Anyway Dad's happy enough. He simply wants to be left alone. He reads his books over and over again and is content. It was you who put the idea in my head, after all."

"I didn't think you'd actually do it though. Or at least not quite so quickly. Were you just waiting for permission."

"Maybe I was. I certainly wanted to be around if ever you needed me and I know now that you don't need me in that way anymore. Perhaps that was what I was waiting for. I can focus on Dad's welfare and then, when that's sorted I shall be officially making myself number one!

TWENTY-THREE
Summer 1991

The biggest department store in Portsmouth had heavily promoted that an end of summer sale had begun and the bargain hunters were about in great number.

Mel had forced herself to come in to town, despite knowing it would be hell, simply because Jean and Ted had a wedding anniversary coming up and she wanted to find a gift for them. They had just got through the second anniversary of Barry's death and they'd not mentioned their own special date to her. This was their silver one though and although she was certain a party wouldn't be welcome for them, she knew a gift from her would be very special. They were everything to her. Mother and father and so much more. She truly loved them both and in loving them, had become a far better person herself. There was nothing she wouldn't do for them.

"I'm so grateful to you for offering to come with me." She shook her head and grimaced at a ghastly vase Clive held up for her approval. "I love them both dearly but I'm hopeless with presents and I was hoping you'd be useful but, judging by that vase I guess I was wrong." Mel smiled up at him.

"I can promise that whatever you choose, I'll carry it home for you, but you're on your own when it comes to choosing. I've made several suggestions and they've all fallen on stony ground. It's over to you now." he said folding his arms.

"I was hoping for a bit more input than that. How about a few appropriate suggestions?"

"I would love to help, but since you were so quick to reject that vase I realise I obviously wouldn't know where to start, but I'll buy you a coffee while we have a think about it though."

"I should have left you at home to keep them both busy

and brought Hope along instead. She'd probably be more help than it appears that you're going to be."

"I'm sure she would, but it's too late to change your plans now though. Hope is taking care of the oldies and you're stuck with me. Now, come on. I've only got the day off, not the week." He was clearly getting bored.

Mel laughed at him. "Oh, no you don't, this isn't going to be done in a hurry. You volunteered, so get used to it. And let me tell you, if they ever heard you referring to them as 'the oldies", you'd be in the doghouse. You know how worried Ted is about his age and his thinning hair. They'd never forgive you. Come on, let's have a glass of wine. That sounds a lot more interesting than a coffee. I'll buy something for them within the next two hours if you buy me a glass of wine now."

"Two more hours! I don't think I'll live that long," he said.

"Okay then, buy me two glasses of wine and I'll choose a present in an hour."

'that's my girl. Deal." He grabbed her hand and led her towards the nearest bar.

"I don't know why you volunteered to come with me though if you're not interested in the present I'm buying," she said, once they were seated with drinks in front of them. "Cheers."

"Cheers. I volunteered to come along in order to spend some time with you."

She looked at him in feigned surprise. "We see each other most days. What do you mean?"

"I don't mean when I'm being Uncle Clive, or when I'm talking cars with Ted or doing some decorating for Jean. I mean time alone with you."

"Oh." Her instinct told her that he'd decided to make a move at last and she hoped she'd be able to deal with it, without hurting him, or the friendship that she'd come to depend on.

He laughed and nudged her elbow. "Oh. Is that all you

can say? Didn't you guess?"

"No, I didn't. Well, maybe I did, but I think of you as Barry's mate and Hope's uncle and my friend. I don't want to think of you any other way. I would hate to spoil a really good friendship."

"Well, that's okay as far as it goes, but I'd like to be much more to you, and so I'm hoping you'll start to think of me differently in future. I've no intention of spoiling anything. I rather thought I'd try to improve it.

"I'll get us another drink, and we'll think about this present. That's the job for today. I'd like to take you out at the weekend though, maybe Friday night. Just you and I. So, think about it, will you?" He sounded uncertain.

"I'm not sure that that's a good idea. We're all happy right now and I would hate to see any of that change. Hope's my number one priority and I don't want anything to disrupt her little world just yet. She loves her Uncle Clive and I don't want her to lose that. I depend on your friendship. So, let's not rock the boat, please," she said.

"I'll be there for you both whenever you want me and that won't change but I want to be more to you, not less. I know you're happy with things as they are but you're too young to give up on life yet."

"I haven't given up on anything. I love what I have at the moment. I'm a single mum and I'm putting my little girl first. I don't want to have a relationship with anyone until she's older. She doesn't need to see people come and go in and out of her life. She needs you as an uncle and she needs Ted as a grandpa. Boyfriends, we don't need. She's never known a dad and she won't until I'm one hundred per cent certain that the man I take home to her is the one that will stay forever. Her real dad died before she met him and I'm determined to fill her life with people that will stay forever, no matter what."

"I'll stay. That won't change, I swear."

"If we began a relationship, then we'd change because that's what happens. Then, if the relationship ends, we

125

could never come back to this, and this is so important to me. If you're serious, then prove it by staying as you are."

"I will, I promise. Now, will you come out with me on Friday?"

"No, definitely not. You're not listening to me. If you ask me again this time next year, I might say yes. If you ask me before then, I'll say no."

"Mel."

"No, don't say any more, please." She smiled at him. "I'm very fond of you but I won't do anything to change things until Hope is ready to go to school and her world expands naturally. That gives you a lot of time to really learn about me and it leaves me a lot of time to focus on Hope. She's the most wonderful thing in the world to me and I would need to know that she means as much to you before anything could ever happen between us.

Now then, that's enough talk, we have a shopping mission to complete."

"Aw come on Mel."

"You stay here and wait for me if you like I know exactly what I'll get. You've given me inspiration. I won't be long." She dashed back to the ground floor and there it was. A canteen of cutlery, very simple and understated. The pattern was called Love Story and she felt thrilled to have spotted it. Perhaps it was an omen. She had paid much more attention to Clive since Jean's warning, in fact she'd paid more attention to herself as well. Nothing could be easier than to allow things to continue the way Clive would like but Mel had learned a lot in the last few years. This time around she had a different set of priorities, she also had as much time as she needed to do the right thing. Once she knew what the right thing was.

126

CHAPTER TWENTY-FOUR
Autumn 1991

Gary pulled up in the driveway outside Julia's parents" house and looked at the imposing building. He wasn't quite as intimidated by her family's wealth now as he had been, but he still couldn't imagine ever actually living like this, and every now and then he was struck anew by the difference in their lives. As their relationship began to settle down though, he now felt quite happy that this lovely girl from a wealthy background had decided that he was the one for her.

He had achieved a level of confidence in himself and her, and now he could be the first to joke that at last he'd found a girl to love him for himself and not just for his money.

They were going away for a weekend, the first that Gary had taken since he'd joined his dad's business, and he was looking forward to having two whole nights alone with Julia. They'd been together for a long time now as friends, but Gary had never looked at another girl since first meeting her.

Julia, on the other hand, had a much wider social circle, and her parents ensured that she spent as much time with other people as she did with Gary. They both liked him very much but were determined that Julia would not rush into a steady relationship too soon. A fact which had suited Julia just fine, as she'd never been quite as certain as Gary that they were meant to be together. She loved spending time with him but also loved being free to go out with the girls she'd been at school with, and their older brothers. They had more money than Gary and there was something very seductive about the champagne lifestyle. Lately though she found she wanted something else entirely.

The imposing wooden doors swung open and Julia skipped down the stone steps and launched herself into the car. "Hi, sweetheart. God, I am so looking forward to this break," she said. "I love my shop but it's been non-stop. To have a couple of days to do nothing but relax seems like bliss right now."

"I know what you mean. Sometimes I think we must both be crazy, working the way we do."

"Yes, but it'll all pay off. One day we'll be rich and important and have people working for us, and then we'll be able to live the way we want to."

"And how is that? How do you want to live? What would be the dream for you?" he asked her.

"I'd like to open a few more shops all along the coast, like the one in Chichester, but featuring local artists so that each one is slightly different."

"You're serious?"

"Why do you sound so surprised? You know how much I love my shop."

"Yeah, but I thought you were just keeping yourself busy. I imagined you were looking forward to the day you'd become a lady of leisure once more. I didn't know you saw it as a long term career."

"Well, I do. It's so much more than just keeping busy. I'm absolutely certain that I'm good at running a business and I can't actually see me stopping now. I thought you might have realised that. I'll never be a lady of leisure again. I like the feeling I get when I think about my shop and the people who work for me."

"I see you've got a taste for power. You like being the boss. I'm just so busy at the moment I don't see anything except my business. I've not really stopped to think about where you might be heading. I just assumed we were going in the same direction. You've turned into a tycoon and I didn't notice."

"We are heading in the same direction. Stop sulking. Your mistake was thinking I was following you, when, in fact, I'm alongside you. You'd better get used to it because I'll never be the sort to follow on quietly behind anyone.

128

In fact, I might overtake you one day!"

She smiled in satisfaction at the stunned look on his face.

CHAPTER TWENTY-FIVE
Autumn 1991

It had been a long time since Mel had allowed herself the time to enjoy her much loved walk along the old track and it was all the better today for being able to share it with Jean who was looking for ideas for her paintings. Ted had stepped in to be babysitter in chief so they were both enjoying their freedom.

"I just love it here, everywhere you look there's one kind of beauty or another. Mel sighed in contentment as she lay down in the still warm grass."

"I know what you mean, I've been so inspired since I picked up my paint brushes again. I'm sure it's this place." Jean was amazed both at the thought that complete strangers had paid good money for her paintings, and also the fact that Julia felt that she could sell even more. She was determined not to miss this opportunity.

"I've decided to put aside the money that Julia is giving to me for these paintings of mine and when I've got enough, I'm going to take us all on holiday."

"Mmm nice idea, but there's nowhere I'd rather be than here. I mean, just look around. It's paradise. Where did you have in mind?"

"Australia."

"How much are you earning?" Mel laughed out loud. "I thought you were thinking of something like a week at Butlins in Bognor."

"I'm earning quite a lot, in fact. I obviously don't have enough yet, but if I can keep this going for another year or so, then Australia's definitely on the cards.

"Julia is a fantastic saleswoman, you know. She constantly amazes me with her ideas and energy. I think coming from such a wealthy background helps. She has no shame in asking extortionate prices for things. I'd never have the confidence to charge what she does.

"Money talks," Mel said, and was surprised to find that she no longer envied the wealth of others.

Jean nodded in agreement. "Anyway, it would be great for Ted to see where Peter and Sally live. And I want Hope to see her cousins in their own home. Wouldn't you love it?"

"Yes, of course I would. It would be such an adventure. I know they'd love you to go and live there. Are you actually considering that?"

"It's an appealing thought, to be near all the family, but we could neither of us bear to go anywhere without you and Hope. If you'd think about coming with us, then, yes. Australia is such a place of opportunity at the moment, I think you'd be able to make a future out there just as well as you could here. And we'd all have the support of Peter and Sally. What would you think about it?"

"I was terrified that you might be about to tell me you were going ad leaving us here. But I had never given a thought to us going too. How could we though? I mean, work? Money? I don't think we could."

"Well, we all could. The thing is to plan ahead. If you think about it, we could decide to go in a few years time. That would give us all time to sort out work and a place to live. Ted could easily get a job with the business. His brother left it to Peter and him jointly. Peter was never interested in it, so it's been sadly neglected, but it stumbles along.

"You're a qualified hairdresser so you'd find work. I could do anything – help Ted out, or a bit of cleaning, or be a school dinner lady, anything."

"You could even continue selling paintings. I think it's absolutely great that your paintings are selling so well. You could do that anywhere. The fact that you were a painter was the first thing I knew about you."

"Oh?"

"Yes. When I first knew I was pregnant I brought Barry along here to tell him. I've always loved this old track and

I used to come here when I was worried about anything. I felt uncertain of his reaction so I brought him here. Anyway, I was talking to him about the old railway and how I love to think of all the people who travelled on the train in their finery. He told me that when he was small he used to come here with you, and you used to paint the things you saw."

"Yes, that's right. I once thought I'd make my living through my art, but then we began our family, and I knew that being a mum was more important than anything else to me, so I just painted for pleasure. I think that's when my work improved to be honest. I was never top-class but I'm producing work now that I'm proud of.

"I'm so glad Barry remembered those walks though. He was very young. As soon as he could walk though he was looking for trouble and I was struggling to keep him under control here." She laughed, a little sadly. "He was a devil, he could slip away and be out of sight in seconds. I had to stop it. I couldn't keep him safe and concentrate on the painting, and he always came first."

"I didn't mean to make you sad," Mel said.

"You haven't. I miss him terribly, of course. I always will but I can think of him now and remember the good times we shared. And I have you and Hope, so I do know how lucky I am. It's just that sometimes …" She shook herself. "Sometimes I get daft.

"Now then, be an angel and sort out the picnic and I'll do a little bit of work. Keep Australia in mind though. You know, sometime in the future, maybe?"

Once the seed was planted Mel found it difficult to think of anything else. Jean and Ted were a huge part of Hope's life. They must not lose that, Mel knew that her daughter must have the family support, that vital link with a past that she herself had never known. How she let them go so far away? She'd have to go with them.

But then there was Chrissie, Hope worshipped her and Mel had loved her for so long, the thought of not seeing her whenever she wanted to was actually painful. Chrissie was Mel's family That decided her, she couldn't go away from Chrissie.

CHAPTER TWENTY-SIX
Winter 1991

Clive raced about in the rain picking up Hope's discarded toys and getting totally drenched in the process. Mel, and Chrissie were watching happily from the window. The storm had come from nowhere and had already turned most of the garden into a mud bath.

"He's being a hero for you Mel."

"Shut up."

"Ah, be nice, You know you want to."

"Do not."

"Yeah, you do."

They both giggled then stopped suddenly as Clive ran in. They threw him a up towel and settled down over a pot of tea, dunking biscuits and enjoying one of those comfortable silences that only really good friends can share, when Clive straightened up, took a breath and began to speak.

"I've waited as long as I can and I think the time is right now. Will you come out with me tonight, on a proper date? We can see a film, or have a meal or go bowling. A walk, anything?"

"Don't start that again, please," Mel said.

Chrissie smiled as Clive put his hands on Mel's shoulder.

"I waited until the three of us were together because I wanted Chrissie to be here to back me up. It's the right thing for all of us. Come on, Mel; take a risk. What do you say?"

"What I said before. It's too soon for me and I'm not prepared to disrupt Hope by starting a relationship. And Chrissie will simply have to keep her opinion to herself. I can't believe you're ganging up on me."

Chrissie threw her hands up in a gesture of innocence. "It's nothing to do with me. I'm an innocent bystander. I didn't know he was going to do this. But, if you want my opinion …"

"I don't, thanks. This I can decide for myself."

This time though, Clive wouldn't give up as easily. "Look, Mel. We're good friends now, so we're in a relationship. I'm in Hope's life and yours. I'm not going to disappear whether you say yes or no. I'm asking you to come and have a meal with me. No more and no less. Chrissie is welcome to join us and I'll bring a mate from work. We can just have a fun night out. So, come on, say yes?"

She smiled as she shook her head.

Chrissie spoke again. "I'll keep my opinions to myself regarding you two if I have to. But, I'm not interested in being fixed up with a desperate bobby who can't sort himself out. I'll keep out of your business but you can keep out of mine. Now, for heaven's sake, make up your mind and go for it. I've got to go now. One of you phone me and let me know if you're on or if you're off. I'll sit with Hope if you need me to. I love you both. Bye." She left them to it.

Neither of them spoke. They just sat and looked at each other. Eventually Mel shrugged and said. "Okay then."

He punched the air in relief. "I was expecting to have to ask for a few more months before you said yes. I thought the sooner I began, the sooner I'd get there. I was also expecting to have to go through a load of reasons why it was a good idea."

"You still can if you want," she said.

"No way. An okay is almost a yes. Where would you like to go?"

"Let's take it slowly. All the reasons I gave you for not wanting to do this are still valid. I don't want Hope to think of anyone as my boyfriend, get used to them and then perhaps have to get used to not seeing them. We can go for a drink together, but I don't want things to appear any different to the way they do now to her. Can you agree

135

to that?"

"Of course I can. I love her as much as you do," he said.

"I know you do. My only worry is that you may find that I'm not the person for you and that might cause a strain in our relationship, that would affect her," she explained.

"I understand that totally, but the thing is I've known you now, very well, for two years. We're good friends and we know a lot about one another. I can't imagine that we're going to learn anything that we don't like about each other. Since Barry died I've seen you nearly every day. I saw how you looked after Hope through all sorts. I saw you care for Ted and Jean as though they were your parents. That tells me all I need to know. And I would never do anything that would cause a problem for you or a disruption for Hope."

She shook her head sadly.

'there are things that you don't know about me though. For one thing I wasn't in love with Barry and I can't let you go on thinking I was."

"I know that and so did he. Barry was my best mate, Mel. I knew that your relationship had hardly begun. You were going to get married because Hope was on the way and you would have made it work because you were going into it honestly, and you both would have put her first every single day. He loved you and he was sure that in time you'd have loved him. I know you'd never let him down and he would never have let you down."

Mel sat silently, knowing this was the best chance she'd ever get to clear the slate completely.

The truth, the whole truth. He loved her and he loved Hope. Surely the fact that Barry might not be her dad couldn't change that. Or could it? If he walked away now, how much would that hurt her and what would it do to Hope?

Why rock the boat? Ted and Jean had to be considered and, after all there was only a slim chance that Barry wasn't Hope's dad. Having her had saved their lives, she was in no doubt about that. Surely telling all could only hurt people needlessly now. Less said, soonest mended, wasn't that the saying.

"Fair enough. Let's go for a drink, then. One day at time, no rush."

CHAPTER TWENTY-SEVEN
Winter 1991

Since the weather had turned cold and wet Jean felt that she could no longer use the "I'm too busy gardening" ploy to avoid decorating the house. The building work that Ted had started in order to make a home for Barry and his new family had changed as the circumstances changed. They had got as far as adding a new bathroom but they'd never got around to installing a new kitchen. Mel had her own couple of rooms and a bathroom but they all pretty much lived as a family, sharing the kitchen.

Jean and Mel sat together sipping coffee and gossiping, which turned out to be much more fun than sandpapering. When Ted popped in to see what they were up to they explained that they were discussing paint colours and wall paper samples and would he like to give his opinion. He beat a hasty retreat.

Jean began relating a newly learned snippet about the latest bust up between Linda and Deb. The fact that Linda had moved herself and her Dad to a nursing home somewhere along the coast had been well known. Although no-one could be sure whether it was Bournemouth or Eastbourne.

Every now and then Mel responded with a nod or a smile, she never been a friend of Deb's and had never quite forgotten that Linda had refused to come into the party to celebrate Hope's christening. As far as she was concerned they were a pair of anti social cows. But Jean seemed to be fascinated with them so she feigned interest.

"So when Deb came home and saw the For Sale sign outside she was livid."

"For Sale?"

"I've got a friend in an estate agents and I just mentioned to her that we might think of selling. I wondered what properties like this were fetching. She knows them and told me about it. Linda put their house with them, she needs to release the cash to pay for care for their dad. Deb had come back to visit friends and driven past their house, seen the signs and gone mad."

"Spoilt madam. But Jean, are you serious about selling this?"

"Yes and no. At some point we'll need to and I wanted to start thinking that way. I should love for us all to go to Australia and selling this would give us a chunk of financial security. On the other hand if we decide to stay then I think a smaller place with a bigger garden might be better for Hope. The bottom line is we have to decide how we're going to finish off the work we started. As it is it's virtually unsaleable."

"Surely not."

"Well, according to my friend the estate agent we'd only expect a very low price if we advertised it like this. We've done more harm than good and I think we should do all we can to finish the work and make look like it works as a large family home and not two almost separate flats. Truth is we've messed it up a bit."

"Why don't you talk to Gary before you spend any more. He's got a great eye, and he'd never try to profit out of us."

"That's a thought. Anyway, we'd better get this mess cleaned up before madam gets home from her day out with Aunty Chrissie."

"Jean, please wait a minute. I want to talk to you."

"I thought you had something on your mind. You sound serious."

"I think it is. I've been out a few times with Clive, you know. Just as friends, of course. It's just that … well … um."

"You think it's more than just friends?"

"I know it could be more than that but I wanted to talk to you about it. It's all so strange. I don't know what to think or do. I wouldn't want to do anything to hurt you and

Ted ever."

"We know that and we've seen this coming for a long time. We were wondering how long it would take you to catch up with the rest of us." Jean smiled at her. "Clive was smitten from the start, and I was the one who told you about it. Remember? We wondered how he would feel about being a father to Hope, but it's clear that he loves her. I could see how comfortable you were with him, and, to be quite honest, I'd half expected something to happen before now."

"Well, nothing has happened yet, but I wanted to talk to you before anything did. I haven't mentioned Australia or anything long-term. I needed to know how you'd really feel about me seeing him. You're not hurt then?"

"Mel, I wish that things could be different. I wish my son were here taking care of you and bringing up his daughter himself. I'd give up almost anything to have that. However, he's gone, and I accept that things can't happen that way. That said, I couldn't ask for a better mother to my grandchild than you, and I've loved Clive always, so the fact that you two might just get together is the best possible thing that could happen. I would welcome it if it's the right thing for you.

Just take your time, for Hope's sake. Just let things happen naturally. Get to know each other properly and don't dwell on us going to Australia. If you stay here, we stay here. We will never want to be anywhere without Hope, so it doesn't need to be an issue," Jean said.

"You're so understanding and brave. I can't imagine how I coped before I met you."

"Stop now with that silly talk and let's just get rid of these paint charts. And before you ask, I admit how right you and Ted were about this colour – it's absolutely dreadful!"

CHAPTER TWENTY-EIGHT
Winter 1991

"Hi Deb. It's only me. How have things been up there this week?" The only sign that there was anyone on the other end of the phone was the familiar sigh of boredom. She was about to speak again when at last her sister spoke.

"Oh hi Lin, Look I'm too busy to talk to you right now. Can I ring you later?

Linda now took her turn and sighed in exasperation, "Of course you can but don't leave it too long please. We've things to sort out, you know."

"What things? You've moved Dad into an old people's home which I agreed with. But now you want to sell our house, which I don't agree with. But as per normal you know best. What on earth is there to sort out? You've got it all under control."

"For God's sake, don't start that again. You didn't agree with me moving Dad into a home, you bloody suggested it. I've managed to get him a place here, but it's not free, you know. In fact, it costs a sodding fortune. That house is his and the money is needed to pay for his comfort.

"I can't believe that you've turned even this around to be about you. It's not about you, or me. It's about him. Stop being a sulky, spoiled child and think about someone else for a change.

"I'll go now. Call me when you've thought about things, and perhaps we can talk like adults about where we go from here. It was you that wanted to be treated like an equal because you were fed up with me protecting you, so grow up, and get used to it. Goodbye." She replaced the handset and heard a voice behind her.

"Blimey, that sounded like tough love."

Linda turned and saw one of the nurses smiling at her. "Hi Susie. You still on duty?"

"Just finishing up for today and then I've got a day off

tomorrow as well. Bliss. Sorry, I couldn't help overhearing your call."

"No privacy in a place like this. Don't worry about it. A whole day off? You lucky thing. Do you have anything planned?"

"Well, I think a few large drinks in the bar tonight, and then tomorrow it's housework, laundry and shopping. You know what it's like to be a working girl. But you're in charge of the shifts so you should be able to make things easier on yourself."

"Oh no, I couldn't do that. We all have to do the rota. I'd have no friends at all if I cheated." Linda was appalled at the idea.

"RHIP Lin. RHIP."

"What?"

"RHIP. Rank Has Its Privileges. There's no point in being in charge if you don't make life easier for yourself."

" I couldn't do it."

"No, I know. Too good for your own good, that's you. But you're off tonight though?"

"Yes, I am."

"Well, come and have a drink with me. We've not had time to get to know one another, and if we're going to be working together, it might be a good idea. You'd be doing me a favour as well, because I'm determined to have a few, and people here talk about women who drink in bars on their own. What do you say?"

"Sounds great. I could use a drink myself."

"Okay good. We can go to The Crown just down the road. Get your coat."

One hour and two drinks later Linda and Susie felt as though they'd been friends forever. Linda had talked non stop about Deb, Steve and Dad and was feeling like a burden was lifting slowly but surely.

"So, let me recap. You've spent your whole life, since you were ten-years-old, looking after your sister and a little lad whose mum died. Now they've grown up and left

142

you, you're doing a job that allows you to keep looking after your dad. Have you ever done anything selfish in your life? When are you planning to put yourself first, I wonder?"

"Oh, you know what it's like. Events just take over sometimes and you have to make the most of it. Tell me about you."

"Not much to tell. My mum and dad live in Hastings and I see them most weekends. They say they wish I still lived with them, but they'd hate it if I did. I've got a little bed-sit down the road.

I was engaged for ten years before I woke up and realised that we didn't really want to marry each other, but we were both too bloody idle to do anything about it. We broke up last year, and I'm now saving hard to have a year off to go backpacking all around the world. This time next year I'll be away.

"I'm not going to wait for anyone or anything. I've wasted too much time already. I'm thirty-three and about to become a teenager."

"I'll be thirty-three next month but I don't feel anything like a teenager. In fact, I don't think I ever was a teenager. The thought terrifies me." Lin said.

"Ah, that's because it's a new idea. Give yourself time. You'd make a cracking nineteen-year-old. Trust me, I'm a nurse. You should think about coming with me. It might be just what you need."

"Oh no. I'm not the backpacking type. I couldn't possibly." Linda didn't find the idea appealing at all.

"Only because it's a new idea. You said no far too quickly. You should try saying yes once in a while. After all, what's the worst that could happen?"

"Well, I don't really know. But, I mean, I couldn't leave my dad."

"He's in good hands. And yes, you could leave him. You're not solely responsible for him. I'm not planning to leave the planet. India, Thailand, America and Australia are all part of the civilised world, you know. I'm serious. We're both very lucky and I think the trip would be more fun if there were two of us."

"Go on, I'll bite. Why do you say we're both lucky?"

"Most women our age have a husband, mortgage and kids. We've still got our freedom. If we don't do something wild now, maybe we never will. Just think, we can go see the world, get laid in half a dozen different languages and still be back by the time we hit thirty-five. Just in time to find a man and have a baby and all that stuff. But think about the memories we'd have to fall back on for when it all gets a bit blah."

"It's just the most ridiculous idea. India, America ... I couldn't though, could I?"

"Yeah, I know. Ridiculous, but you'll think about it. Right?"

"I will think about. Now, let's have another drink and you can tell me more."

CHAPTER TWENTY-NINE
Spring 1992

"Will you marry me, Mel?"

"Oh Clive, no. Please don't start that again."

"I have to, so don't say no. I didn't want to say this wrong, but I probably will. I love you and I love Hope. I swear I'll spend my life making you both happy and safe. You love me and I know we'd be happy. Please marry me?"

"I do love you, you know I do, but it's far too soon. It's such a huge step and I can't do it. Not yet."

"It's not too soon at all. Hope will be three at the end of this year. She's never known a time without us both in her life, so nothing will change for her. I was there when she was born and I'm a huge part of her life. She's a daughter to me and I want you to stop pushing me out of your lives.

"I'm not pushing you out." She protested.

'ted and Jean would be delighted and so would my mum and dad. And I think Hope needs a brother or a sister before she gets much older."

"Whoa, slow down. You've just leapt from me refusing to marry you into having more children. You've missed a couple of crucial steps out here. What makes you think I want to have more children? And where are you proposing we'll live? We've never talked about any of these things."

"No, because I've never asked you to marry me before. I think we should talk about all of it now though," he said. "I've given it a lot of thought and I have a few suggestions. But understand this – I love you both with all my heart and I want to take care of you. If you turn me down, I won't go away and I won't stop asking. We are meant to be together and we are going to be together. Let me tell you how it could work."

She opened her mouth to speak so he leaned forward and kissed her into silence.

"I'd like us to move into my parents" place at Langstone. They want to move to their flat in Eastbourne when Dad retires later this year, and I'll be living there then anyway. But if you say yes, then I don't care where we live. Even Australia.

"I love you and I want a baby, or even two, with you. Hope can be a big sister – she's bossy enough now, so I feel sure she'd excel in the role."

"Permission to speak, Sir?"

"Granted."

"It's obvious you've thought a lot about this. Would you really move, just like that?"

"Absolutely. You and Hope, that's all I want."

"I've always said it's all about Hope, but I do have a few opinions myself, you know. I'm certainly not ready to even consider having another baby. Hope's got used to having her own way a little bit too much and she's becoming quite a handful. I couldn't cope with two like that."

"Okay, so let me get this straight. You're saying no to a baby, but yes to a marriage. Good, one step at a time, I think you once said. I don't think we need to have a big splashy wedding, unless of course, you especially want to. You must think about that. I thought we could have a simple, quiet ceremony, then perhaps a party at my house."

"I haven't said yes yet."

"No, but you haven't said no either, and I'm afraid you've run out of time. I've started making plans now. You couldn't be cruel enough to want to cheat me out of my special day after leading me on, surely," he said laughing.

"Oh, stop it, you fool." She laughed along with him. "What are you like?"

"Say yes. Come on, Mel, you feel the same as me, I know you do."

"Yes, I do, but I can't do it. It's all mad."

146

"Okay then. No problem," Clive said.

"What do you mean "okay then, no problem"? You're giving up on me just like that?"

"I'm giving up nothing, but if you just won't do it because you think it's too mad, I'll soon bring you round. You admit you love me and that's the important thing. I've been worried sick that you were only going out with me because you like having sex with men in uniforms!"

Her laughter silenced him. "Shut up and kiss me. That's what you're supposed to do now. Then let's explore this idea of sex with men in uniforms."

***

"I don't want a big fussy do at all," she said, much later. "I'll want to make it something that is easy for Ted and Jean to feel a part of. The idea of a party in your garden at Langstone sounds great."

"Okay. If you don't want anything fancy, is there any need to wait? I mean, can we do it this summer?"

"If you're certain that it's what you want, yes we can. I'll talk to Ted and Jean and ask them to help me organise things. I know they're important to you, but to me they're like parents and I want them to know that they always will be."

"Let's go and talk to them now. They can know they are the first to hear the news."

"I think I should see them on my own first."

'mel, they love me and they know we're together. You seem to feel that you're doing something wrong?"

"I don't think it's wrong, but I'm sure that my getting married will bring back memories of when we were preparing for my wedding to Barry."

"I know you're just trying to protect them, but you can't honestly think that they need anything to remind them of him. I don't imagine a day goes by when they don't think of him. I also think they are waiting for us to get on with

147

our own lives. They'll be delighted, trust me."

"Come on then. Let's go home and break the news."

"Okay, but on the way, let's talk about something else. That way we can tell them we want to get married and they can help us plan how to do it. That will be better than us having it all worked out beforehand. "

***

"Congratulations," Ted said when they broke the news. "Let's have a drink and you can give us all the details."

"We haven't worked any details out yet. I asked her and she said yes. Then she said I have to go and tell Ted and Jean, I'll need their help, so here we are."

Jean smiled and leaned over to kiss Mel. "You're a good girl."

"We'd like to make it the first weekend in July. Do you think that leaves us time to prepare everything?"

"Three months' time – oh yes that's plenty of notice. The important thing first would be to book the service and wherever you want the reception."

"We want something simple in the registry office with just you and my folks. Then, I thought a garden party at my place might be good. We can invite everyone along to that."

"I'd like to do the food myself, but would you be able to help me?" Mel said.

"I'd love to, but keep an open mind about that. It would be a terrific amount of work, you know. We must go and have a look around the garden together. It's a long time since I visited, but I'm sure we can make it lovely. I imagine you'll be living there, after, will you?"

"Yes we will. It will be hard to move out but..."

"Of course you must move out, don't be silly. I've never been there, I'd love to come and look round before hand."

"Well good, we could use your advice on a couple of things. We've got to do something to make the garden

148

secure for Hope for one thing."

"Of course. It's open to the sea, isn't it?"

"Yes. Dad loves to sit on the porch and look out across the water. He never wanted anything to obstruct the view but he's happy with anything we want to do. They've moved into their flat, at last, and are totally content. They don't mind what we do to the house. It's mine now."

"What are you thinking of?" Ted asked.

'to be honest, we're baffled." Mel replied, "We don't want to restrict access to the sea, but on the other hand I need to know that Hope will be kept safely in the garden."

"Why don't you both come over tomorrow," Clive proposed. "We can plan the party, and while we're doing that we might think of a way of keeping the monster safe in the future. Let's have a picnic, you know, make a day of it."

CHAPTER THIRTY
Spring 1992

Gary walked down the ancient cobbled street in Chichester and felt pride again when he saw that The Gallery, which Julia had opened just over a year ago, was full of people browsing around the treasures she'd managed to display so well. The wind chimes tinkled as he opened he door and she looked up and smiled at him. She raised her hand in greeting. "Give me ten minutes?"

Nodding, he walked through to the galley kitchen and put the kettle on.

She joined him briefly saying, "I can't be away long. I've a party of Americans on their way here. They plan to shop for gifts to take home. They'll spend a lot but they expect personal service."

"I should bloody well think they deserve personal service, the prices you charge. Don't worry, I only popped in for a cuppa. I'm on my way out to Midhurst to price up a job."

"Did you get a call from Clive this morning?"

"Oh bugger! Yes, I was supposed to call him back and I'd forgotten. Did you talk to him? What did he want?"

"He's inviting us to his wedding."

"No shit! They've decided to get on with it then?"

"Yes. On the first Saturday in July Mel will be a married woman at last. Give the girl a gold medal – she's finally getting what she's been after for years. I just hope he makes it up the aisle."

"Christ Jules, you can still take my breath away sometimes. I get lulled into thinking you're not so bad and then you come out with something like that. You can be such a bitch."

"Oh shush, I've only said it to you. I won't let anyone else know what I really think. But I can't lie to you. I don't trust her and I think he's a mug. She's bad news and one day you'll admit it. There. I've said it once and it'll never be mentioned again."

"Oh right. So you haven't already phoned Deb to tear the poor girl's reputation to shreds then?"

"Deb is my best friend. We think as one, trust me. Now go and measure up your little plumbing job while I sell these tall, handsome Americans some very expensive British tat."

CHAPTER THIRTY-ONE
Spring 1992

Linda glanced out of the window just in time to see Steve pull up in his smart new car. She stepped into the hallway and managed to open the front door just as he reached it.

"Steve, come on in. How are you?"

"Hello boss." He smiled at Linda. "I thought it was time I came to see you in your new domain. Are you happy? Have you settled in okay?"

"That's what I wanted to talk to you about. Come up to the staff room and we can sit and catch up with each other. Thank you so much for helping me get Dad in here. He's really very happy. It was exactly the right thing at the right time for me and for Dad."

"I'm glad it's all working out for you. I just introduced you though, If you hadn't been the right person the board wouldn't have given you the job, they run this place, not me. They let me have an office here because I own the building, but I have no say at all in the running of things. My business is in the actual building, not the use of it. You got the job on your own merits."

"Okay, if you say so. You're looking very pale Steve. Is everything okay?"

"Fine. I'm just very busy at the moment. There's a huge old factory in Portsmouth that I have plans for. At the last minute the council wanted some changes made and I had to get it done overnight. I could have used a day off today but I needed to see someone here, and I couldn't miss the chance of a coffee with you."

"Come on then. Let's go and get a coffee, and you can tell me exactly what you plan to do with an old factory in Portsmouth."

"I want to knock it down, basically. I've been looking at the thinking behind the developments of shopping malls in America and I want to bring that kind of shopping, on a slightly smaller scale, to southern England. This place has access to the old docks and is fronted onto the main road. It's absolutely vast and I'm thinking of shops and walkways, picnic areas by the waterside and even a restaurant. A few little gift shops and stuff, you know, like Julia's place. Maybe a hotel. A space that families could come to for a couple of days."

"Wow, Steve, that sounds ambitious. Are you honestly thinking on such a grand scale?"

"No point in thinking small. I have hopes and dreams. And I have as much desire to improve myself as anyone else. I want to build something that will be bigger than anything my dad ever built."

She smiled at him. "That's a huge commitment. It must require a vast amount of time and money, and anything that needs all that probably has a workforce dependant on the decisions you make. I'm surprised that you've not talked about it before now. How long have you been thinking about this?"

"It's been over a year now since I first started things moving along, but Dad had already laid the outline out before he died. He'd been buying up little bits and pieces of land for years. He just wasn't quite clear what he'd do with it. But he never doubted it was the right thing to do."

"Who do you talk to when things worry you? I mean, you seem to have such grand plans. Do you not wish you had someone quietly by your side to share your success with?" she wondered.

"I try to work things out for myself. It always worked for Dad." He looked into her eyes. "But, why are you asking me these odd questions now?"

"I only just wondered if you were lonely. With Deb off and busy, and me living here, having moved, you must spend a lot of time alone."

"Don't be so daft. I talk to Deb every other day. I have a pint with Gary or Clive most weeks. I drive up and down the coast meeting friends like you for coffee all day every day. I barely have an hour to myself, so what on earth makes you think I'm lonely?"

"You talk to Deb every other day?" She was surprised.

"Yes. Why?"

"Oh, nothing. It's just that I hardly ever speak to her these days."

"Have you two had a row again?" he asked.

"Same one, ongoing. She's still sulking about me selling the house and moving Dad. We don't row but we aren't close any more. I think I've lost her."

"I don't want to hurt you, Lin, but you're driving her away. You've got to give her space to breathe; you've got to let her go."

"What do you mean "let her go"? She's gone."

"Stop phoning her all the time. You drive her mad leaving messages every day, and then she drives me mad by refusing to be straight with you. I love you both, but, between you, you're boring me to tears. Honestly, love, you need to get a life of your own or you will lose her.

"Now, tell me what you wanted to talk to me about and forget your bratty sister for at least today."

"I'm not really in the mood for confidences now. You've upset me, saying it's really my fault" She bit back a sob.

"You know what?" He stood up. "I can't be bothered going through it all again. I've told you both what I think, and now if you've got nothing else to talk about, I'm going to work."

"No, don't go just yet. I need to tell you that I'm leaving this job, or, at the very least, taking a leave of absence. I know you did put yourself out to find it for me and I appreciate it so much, really I do. It's just that Dad's safe and sound now, so I'm going on a walking break with Susie. What do you think?"

"I think it's time for you to do something just for you. And don't worry about the job. I told you that was all down to you, not me. I think it'll do you good. A bit of a break."

"Good. I'm going to do it. It'll be the best thing for all of us. I assume you'll keep an eye out in case Deb needs anything?"

"Well, yes. Of course I will, but where is this walking holiday going to be, how long will you be away?"

"A year, around the world, or at least a fair portion of it. Backpacking."

"Oh, be serious." He laughed, until he noticed the expression on her face. "My God, you are serious. It's not a wind up?"

"It's not a wind up."

"I thought you meant a fortnight in the Peak District or something. I can imagine Deb doing something ridiculous like this, but not you. I don't know what to say."

"I'm driving you both mad, apparently, so let's see how well we get on with distance between us. One question. Is there any chance that you and Deb might one day …?"

"Not a chance. Nothing like that could ever happen. I couldn't keep up with her anyway. She goes for a whiff of danger. I'm far too safe for her."

"Well, at least I'll know she's not lonely."

"What, Deb? I don't think so. Listen, I'm sorry for what I said. Think about it. Why not just have a couple of weeks away? Why a whole year and why backpacking? You've never done anything remotely like this before. I'll be worried to death the whole time you're away. I'm already regretting what I said." He was clearly upset.

"Well, don't. It had a ring of truth and common sense about it and it needed a very good friend to say it. Susie had suggested as much to me when she mentioned this trip, and I just told her she didn't know the people concerned or all of our circumstances, and therefore her opinion was not wanted. But you, well, you're family. We know all the important stuff about each other, don't we? Your opinion does count. It hurt a bit, but you were right."

"I'll sort some dates out with Susie and I'll keep you

up-to-date. And, to be honest, I quite like the thought of you being worried about me for a change. Now, tell me what you've been up to in your time off. Are you seeing anyone?"

"No. I'm not interested. I get such a buzz out of the business and don't have the time or inclination for anything else."

"Never?"

"Not since I was seventeen. I had a crush, but, nothing."

"Are you over it now or do you still wish that maybe …?"

"Business is everything for me now."

"Then let's stick to your business. What else don't I know about that? "

"I'm only just grasping the scale of it myself. It's a long story. Dad owned loads of places like this one. He turned some of them into flats and some he leased out to companies who use them for rest homes or offices and flats. So, all I do really is visit them and make sure the best use is being made of them. Some of the tenants are coming up to renewal time and I work with the solicitors on new contracts. Sometimes the right property comes on the market and I'll buy it and just sit on it until an opportunity comes along to rent it out. It's fascinating. I'm still discovering places I own that I didn't know about. I mean, everything was covered in the will, but we're still untangling some of the small print."

"So when people say that you own half of Portsmouth …"

"My business owns a fair slice of the south coast, to tell you the truth."

"And are you a millionaire? I know I've seen that reported in the papers."

"Don't believe everything you read in the papers."

"But you are very rich? I think I'd find it a bit daunting. It's a huge responsibility."

"I'm filthy, stinking rich," he laughed. "I've always

156

known it though, so I don't think of it in that way. I do think I'm owed it though, from Dad. He was a bastard through and through and he never should have married or had a kid. But, he was a brilliant businessman at the same time. Maybe you have to be one in order to be the other. I'll never be much more than a caretaker and I know that. I don't have his brilliance. But that's okay. I love what I've got. And I earned it, just not in the normal way."

"So you're okay then?"

"Top of the world, Lin. Don't worry about me. Perhaps it's a good thing that we can all worry about you for a change. In fact, I'm impressed."

CHAPTER THIRTY-TWO
Summer 1992

The garden of the house at Langstone looked wonderful as the wedding party arrived back after the simple ceremony.

Jean watched the laughing couple leading all their guests down the steps into the patio area and felt a sense of pride and happiness. She loved Mel and considered Clive almost a son. He'd been close to Barry but had become closer still to her and Ted in the three years since her boy had died.

Sometimes she ached for Barry, the pain had not diminished but had become manageable, occasionally something could catch her unaware and the pain would almost knock her to her knees, but then another time, a memory could bring a smile. And the smiles were becoming far more frequent. She shook herself and began to look at and enjoy the lovely things around her.

This was going to be a day of happiness through and through, and with so much to enjoy she knew there'd be no more moments of sorrow.

Her eyes found Mel, who was at that moment smiling sweetly at her. They gave each other a nod and the celebrations continued.

Mel was wearing an ivory dress that was trimmed with coffee-coloured lace that was stunning against her fair skin and blonde hair. The joy on her face was wonderful to see. Chrissie, as her chief bridesmaid, was also a picture in a coffee-coloured suit with an ivory blouse. Her happiness was moderated a little because she had the responsibility of making sure that the other bridesmaid, Hope, behaved herself. Hope was wearing a dress made from the same material as the suit Chrissie wore, and the three girls together were a wonderful sight.

"Come on, photograph time everyone," Jean sang out. She then proceeded to order them around to her exact specifications. "Clive and Mel together with Hope in front first, please. Bill and Mary, come and stand with your handsome son. Then, I want Bill, Ted and Clive. Now Mel, Mary and Hope." And on and on it went.

After Jean had exhausted every possible photo opportunity, they made their way to the seats that were laid out around a couple of huge tables. Every chair and table was draped with white cotton, tied into place by coffee-coloured ribbons. As a wedding present Ted had paid for the local hotel to come in and prepare a lunch in the garden, Jean and Mel, having decided that self-catering was far too much hard work. Jean, however, had decorated the garden as her gift.

"Jean, it all looks absolutely wonderful. Thank you so much. I knew you would give us something wonderful, but this is amazing. It looks like a film set," said Clive. "You've taken my breath away."

There were coffee-coloured bows and streamers on every tree and bush, and in between these were buckets of water filled with flowers. In the centre were the laden tables circled by chairs.

Jean smiled with pleasure at his words and began to direct everyone to their seats. "Clive, I want you and Mel here please, Gary next to Mel, then Hope and Chrissie, Ted and Julia over here, and then Bill and Mary here. Steve, I've put you here." And again it went on.

Ted said, "Enough Jean, calm down, love. Sit down, relax and enjoy the meal. Everything is perfect and you don't need to do any more. Not today."

She quickly said, "No, wait, Ted. You can't eat anything yet. I want to take another photograph. Of all the food."

"No more photos, please," they all groaned.

Jean shrugged happily and watched as they enjoyed the feast that she and Ted had spent hours planning.

As the music played quietly, all appetites were eventually satisfied and the sound of voices got louder and the clinking of bottle against glass grew more frequent.

Julia stood and stretched. "I envy you this place. What a luxury, to have a garden that's this private and leads directly onto the beach, Clive. It's heavenly. I could stay here forever. You'll get a small fortune if you decide to sell."

"It's not going to be sold, so that's never been relevant. We've couldn't get rid of it. It was built by one of my great, great, greats. No one else has ever owned it. Technically, it belongs to Mum right now," he said, looking across at Bill and Mary and raising his glass to them in thanks. "I've never seriously wanted to think of ending up anywhere else and we all agree it's a perfect place for Hope to spend a couple of years, so here we are. I've some old photos of it somewhere if you're interested. Of course, it's changed a bit over the years.

"There are a couple more changes happening this week, in fact. Jean and Ted gave us this fabulous lunch as a wedding present. But they're also giving us a wooden fence to circle the garden. It's great to be able to step onto the shingle or sit with your feet in the water, but we want Hope to be able to run about without us worrying, so the fence will be terrific. And just here, we're putting double gates so that we can open it right up for days like this, but then lock them up for Hope to play safely on her own out here."

"That'll cost a packet won't it?" she asked, always interested in the bottom line.

"Yes, but it'll keep Hope safe, so it's worth doing right," said Ted. "Now, who's for a glass of champagne?"

Jean smiled across the table at Steve. "How are the others nowadays, Deborah and her sister, I mean? Clive's always busy with his shifts, he says, and Julia is so caught up in business that though I see them both most days, I don't get much chance to keep up with you others as much anymore."

He leaned back lazily in his chair feeling the effects of

the drink already. "Deb's doing very well. She began her teacher training in Worcester and really loved it. She's doing some kind of work experience now. It involves running special classes for schools that are getting government support. It means moving around a lot, but it seems to really suit her. She's up near Newcastle at the moment."

"And does she still do much swimming?" Gary asked.

"Not so much. If she's lucky enough to be at a school that has its own pool, then yes. But her workload is extraordinary. I think she sleeps and works and not much else."

"Linda must miss her. Does she come home in the school holidays?"

"Not too often. I think the nature of their entire relationship has changed. For the better if you ask me," Julia spoke up.

"Ooh gossip. Lovely. Go on, dear, tell me more." Jean grinned and leaned forward. "Don't spare me, please. No one tells me anything. Come on, give."

"Well, okay. As you probably know Linda—"

At this point Ted stood and said, "If you lot are going to be gossiping, I shall take Bill and anyone else so inclined into the house and share a very nice bottle of Scotch I just happen to have brought with me for just such an emergency."

"I'm with you, Ted," Steve said.

"Okay, carry on, Julia. You were talking about Linda?" Jean said.

"Linda practically brought Deb and Steve up. Their mums were on the same maternity ward together. Deb and Steve were born on the same day, though his mum was quite a bit older, in her forties. Deb's mum felt sorry for her. She was quite ill and horribly depressed, I'm told. Anyway, his mum killed herself when he was nearly three or four."

"How terrible. Poor little boy." Jean said.

161

Mel shook her head but didn't speak.

Julia shot a look at her but carried on. "Deb's mum was worried about Steve, so she basically cared for him through the day and he was sent home at nights. When their mum went back to work, Linda, who's ten years older than them, just carried on looking after them both. Their mum died about five years later, but, by that time, they both thought of Linda as mum."

"Okay, so what's gone wrong with their relationship now?" Jean asked.

Julia drained her glass and filled it again, then continued. "Deb wanted to go away to teach. She was worried about going away because she thought that Linda didn't have a life of her own. She felt stifled because Lin just lived through her, you know, wanting to know everything, who she saw, and where she went. All she was ever interested in was Deb, what she was doing and where she went. She didn't go out except to work, she dressed like a middle-aged woman, and just worked and watched TV. When Deb first said she wanted to go away, Lin almost fell apart. She was frantic. I think that's what convinced Deb that she had to go. She told Linda that she needed to get a life of her own so that they could be more like sisters."

"The truth can hurt," Jean said.

"That's not what caused their big problem though. Linda's taken herself off on some kind of a mad walking holiday all around the world with some other nurse, and Deb's worried now that when she goes home, Lin's not there to look after her. That's the bit that I think is a good thing. I mean, Deb is my best friend, but she did kind of wipe her feet on Linda. Now though, she doesn't even know where she is."

"So Deb has lost her housemaid and she's regretting it. She'll get over it soon enough. We all have to grow up at some point," Jean said

Mel had been listening quietly. "That sounds very

162

brave, especially for someone who hasn't perhaps done very much for herself in the past. It's sad that her own sister can't be happy for her though, isn't it?"

"Oh, I think she is really. She's just uncomfortable with the thought of Linda being so far away. She's so used to having her fussing around her but now has to look after herself. But in her heart she's proud of Linda. When she gets back, they'll be fine," Julia said.

"You must keep me updated, Julia. I think we're out of time for today though. Come on, Mel. It's time for you and your new husband to escape. You go and sort the others out, and I'll start loading our car. Come on, Hope. It's time to go now," she called out to her granddaughter, who was having fun on the shingle with Gary's puppy Bo.

"Where we going?" Hope asked. She stood with her hands on her hips quite prepared to throw a tantrum if she felt so inclined.

"You're coming home with me and Gramps remember. Mummy and Clive are having a few days on their own and then you'll be coming back here to live. The party's over for today."

"And Bo?"

"Oh no," said Gary, coming out of the house and hearing her. "Not Bo. He has to come home with me."

"Why?"

"Because I'm scared of the dark and Bo looks after me," he said. Then he scooped her up and swung her up towards the sky. "Now, don't pout. You're the most beautiful princess in the world. If you're good tonight, I'll bring Bo to see you again in a few days."

"Promise?" She looked at him trustingly.

"I promise," he declared.

Jean watched the group happily making plans and saying goodbye. It had been a marvellous day. She'd been sad knowing that her home wouldn't be Hope's home any more, but those moments were made easier to bear by seeing how happy Mel and Hope were at the beginning of

163

a new life. A life that she knew would always include her and Ted. She was ready now to think about selling that huge house and looking for a smaller place to move into.

CHAPTER THIRTY-THREE
Autumn 1992

Gary and Julia barely made it to the train station in time, they were reluctantly due to pick up Deb. It was a last minute arrangement and neither of them could afford the time, but it seemed there was no one else to meet her and they felt they should. As they reached the platform, the train approached and they spotted Deb opening the door before the train had stopped. She never could wait for anything. She tossed her bags off the train knowing that Gary would catch them.

"It's so great to see you guys. How are things? What's happening?" She was all over them.

"All sorts. Come on, let's get your junk in the car and we'll find a bar. We can have a catch up and a drink," Julia said.

"That sounds like a plan." Deb sighed happily. "Give me all the gossip then. Are you two living together yet?"

"Yes, but not officially."

"What do you mean "not officially"?"

'my mum can't bear the thought of me living in sin, as she calls it, so I stay at home during the week and then come down to the flat for the weekend."

"Best of both words then. Mum still does your laundry and feeds you up, and then you get shagged senseless on a dirty weekend, every weekend. Result."

"It works for us. What about you? How's your love life?"

"Nah, nothing really." Deb shrugged her shoulders. "A girl can dream though. I'm happy working all hours to tell the truth. So, tell me about the wedding of the year."

"It was a shame you couldn't go. I would have had someone to talk to. It was all very sweet and familyish though. You know, Clive's parents and Ted and Jean. They seem to have become very fond of Gary, and, of

165

course, I spend a lot more time with Jean now she paints for me. It was pretty good though, to be honest. The food was fantastic and there were bottles and bottles of wine and champagne to drink. Jean had decorated the garden for the party and it was so clever. It was so lovely.

"In fact, I'm going to ask her to help me promote it as a business. Wedding and party planning."

"Wow. You're turning into quite a force in the business world. What do you think of all this Gary?"

"I'm too busy to worry. Our showroom will be finished in a month or so and we're planning a Christmas opening. That's going to take a huge amount of work. We'll only get one shot at it, so I need to make sure that I've done all I can to pitch the invitations and advertising properly." Gary looked very pleased with himself.

"And I suppose now you're a successful gallery owner and potential party planner, you're to busy to take time off as well?" Deb looked at Julia.

"Yes, that's about right."

"Everyone is becoming so grown up and sensible. Well, except for my sister, who seems to be getting less sensible as time goes on, bless her. Perhaps it runs in the family, cos I'm not going to be calming down any time yet." Deb declared. "Come on, let's get some more drinks."

"Sorry Deb, no can do. I've got a job to get to and Jules is planning an early start tomorrow."

"What! Oh Jules, come on. It's only one night! I'm so busy for the next few days, and there's some stuff I want to talk to you about. Please."

"Sorry, but no. I really would love to, but I can't. I've got to be really sharp tomorrow. Come on, let's go home and have some supper. I can recommend the Indian, but then it's bed for me." Julia could see Deb was disappointed.

"Not for me. I'll go and find Steve. He'll maybe have a bit more life in him. I've got so much to tell you. I've been seeing this shrink and he's helped me understand myself. I wanted to tell you all about it. I didn't travel all this way just to have a warm drink and an early night. Go on home, you miserable sods. I'll find someone else to talk to." Deb knocked back her drink and headed for the door.

"Come on, Deb," Julia pleaded. "Don't go off like this."

"Leave her alone, love. She'll find us in the morning. You know what she's like if she can't have everything her own way," Gary said.

At the last minute Deb turned around and said, 'don't worry about me. It really is okay. I love you both. Now, run along home and get some cocoa and a hot water bottle. I am going to get laid. Oh yeah!"

She walked out of the pub laughing at the look of either shock, or admiration on the faces of everyone within earshot.

CHAPTER THIRTY-FOUR
Autumn 1992

Mel took her drink out into her newly enclosed garden. It gave her a thrill like no other to think that she had a wonderful daughter, a lovely home and something she hadn't dared hope for, a husband that she was in love with. She very rarely thought about Barry. She had been very fond of him and she would have been a good wife to him. She couldn't think more about him because had he not died, she would never have gotten together with Clive. That was unthinkable. Life had turned out even better than she'd hoped. She came back to reality as the doorbell rang.

Chrissie had got into the habit of spending one morning a week with Mel and Hope at home and then one other day a week out somewhere with just Hope. Today was to be an at home day, Mel swung open the door to admit her friend. "Wow, look at you. I didn't know you were planning on changing your hair again. Turn around. Oh yes, it's very good. You didn't do that yourself, did you?"

Chrissie laughed, "I love it too. There's a great new place that's just opened up in Midhurst. They need more young stylists, so I picked up an application form for you while I was there."

"But I'm happy where I am," Mel objected

"I know you are, but it's taking the easy route, isn't it? Now you're getting your life worked out, I think you should get back in the saddle properly. And that does not mean putting perms into the blue rinse brigade. You need to get back into the high fashion end before you're too old."

"I'm only twenty-two, you cheeky cow. I'm not going to be too old for years."

"You'll lose your edge if you don't get back on track soon. You know, you'll get all middle-aged, develop a spare tyre and loose a couple of teeth. Then it's all over.

You need a bit of teenage competition to keep you sharp. Take a walk on the wild side while you still can, think about it anyway. Now then, you've been married almost two months, do you still like it?" The two friends laughed and teased as they headed into the garden.

Hope squealed. "Auntie Chrissie have you brought me a present?"

Chrissie dropped to her knees and looked the little girl in the eyes. "Of course I've brought you a present. You're my favourite girl. Look at this." She tipped up a bag she had been holding behind her back and out tumbled dolls and clothes of every size and colour. As the three giggled and fooled in the sunshine, they heard the doorbell ring again. Mel groaned and went to answer it. She frowned and stepped back when she saw who had come to visit her.

"Deb?"

"I'm sorry to just turn up like this and I don't want to interrupt if you have company. I'll come another time. I just wanted to talk to you alone." Deb tried to escape.

"No, no, don't be daft, come in. Chrissie will play with Hope while we talk if you like. Just come and say hello then we can sit on our own."

Mel introduced the two women and tried to put them at ease with each other. They had never met before, but it was immediately clear they had nothing in common. They came from different worlds and instinctively knew and distrusted each other. They circled each other like nervous cats until Mel decided she couldn't bear the tension any more.

"Chrissie, would you stay and keep an eye on Hope?" Mel asked. "Deb wants a quiet word with me. We'll go and sit inside, would you mind?"

"No problem, go ahead."

Mel led Deb into the kitchen and grabbed another glass. After giving her a drink, she turned two chairs toward the window. They sat side-by-side looking out over the garden to the sea beyond.

169

"It's a heavenly spot here, Mel. Thanks for letting me do this. It's something I should have done before now and it won't take long." She took a deep breath. "I want to apologise to you. I've not been a friend to you and I should have been. I'm so sorry." She looked as though she was almost in tears.

Mel was at a loss. "Okay, well thank you for that."

"Sorry, I didn't want to cry. I'm just so ashamed of myself."

"What on earth has brought all this on?" Mel asked.

"Oh God, everything really." Suddenly the words poured out of her in a stream. " It was hearing about you and Clive getting married, then I fell out with Linda, and she ended up going around the world to get away from me. I've been feeling so bad inside for so long. I can't go into all of it now, and it's not all relevant, but I've been seeing a counsellor, you know, to talk things through and try to clear my head."

She took a moment to pause but Mel was not sure what to say.

"It was like I hated everyone when I got out of hospital. You all seemed to be just getting on with your lives, as though me and Barry being there or not being there, didn't make any difference. I know that's crazy but it's how I felt. I came out of hospital and everything that I'd known before had gone and I couldn't seem to catch up. I resented you. I don't know why. It was so easy to just forget all about you.

"Then I heard that you and Clive planned to marry. I know that Hope had a lovely day and everyone was so happy for you all. Even Gary and Julia seemed happy for you both and were pleased to be invited. I didn't want to come. I didn't think you should be marrying him.

Mel bit her tongue. Now was not the time to tell this spoilt madam what she thought of her.

"I've been blaming you for Barry's death and my accident. I know that's ridiculous, but it's what I've been

170

feeling. Then everyone was telling me what a lovely girl Hope is and how much Ted and Jean love you, and how much you love them. I wasn't expecting to hear that."

Mel coughed and spoke at last. "What were you expecting?"

"I thought you would be a hard girl, a bitch that had trapped one of my friends and ruined his life. Someone who'd got it all worked out."

"Bloody hell," said Mel, "that was pretty tough on someone you'd never bothered to meet. So, now you've suddenly changed your opinion?"

"Not suddenly. I didn't absorb anything for a long time after the accident. The others had all got to know you by then, and I just felt almost as though you were taking my place, or taking Barry's place. I don't know what I was thinking really but I blamed you for it anyway. It was at Hope's christening and Ted's speech that made me start to realise that I may have been completely wrong about you."

"That was two years ago," Mel was totally confused.

"I know. And then it became easier for me not to think about you at all. But, now you and Clive have married and are genuinely happy, I felt I needed to clear my conscience. I'm sure you could have used a friend in the past few years and I'm sorry I wasn't there for you. As one of Barry's gang, I should have been. I think he'd be very unhappy with me if he could see how unkind I've been. Now that things are good for you, I wanted to come and apologise. It's too late to make a difference, but I needed to do it."

As she paused to catch her breath Mel spoke again hastily. She didn't want to hear anymore of this mad girls soul baring. It was all too late and what would be the point in prolonging things.

"Well, thanks for coming here to say all that to me. It must have taken a lot of courage and I appreciate that. Let's just put it behind us. Hope and I are very happy and our lives are very good. It's all okay now, I promise."

171

"I can see that. She's such a lovely little girl. I know we'll never be good friends now, but I want you to know that I'm aware that it's my fault and I regret the way things worked out."

"Okay, fair enough," Mel said. "Would you like to come and sit with us in the garden for a while and tell us what your intrepid sister is up to."

"Thanks, but no. I can't stay. I need to get back, early start in the morning. Heaven knows where Amazon Annie is at the moment, but, according to the postcards I get, she is having a lifetime of experiences in a very short space of time. She seems to be behaving shamelessly."

"Well, good for her," Mel said.

"It's taken me a while, but I agree. Bloody good for her. I must go now. Thanks for listening to me."

And as suddenly as she arrived, she was gone.

172

CHAPTER THIRTY-FIVE
Winter 1992

Gary and Colin walked around the newly finished showroom doing a final check before Gary's mum moved in the next day with half a dozen volunteers to do the "fluffy stuff" as they called it.

On Saturday, they were hosting an open-day that would involve coffee and biscuits being dished out by the truckload through the day to anyone and everyone. Then, in the evening, wine and cheese for the press, the Chamber of Commerce and any interested bodies from the council. Invitations had also been sent out to several of the hotels in the area with a hint that discounts would be available to local businesses provided they got in quickly.

"I'll admit you've done a fantastic job here. Putting a showroom on this site was a brilliant idea. I'm proud of you lad, I really am. I hope you're pleased with the results."

"What about the new name, Daniels Design?" Gary asked.

"I thought you were mad, but I built this business for you, so I had to let you make your mark, and you were right there an" all. I thought Bill was going to have a heart attack when he saw you'd done the DD on the vans just like the RR for Rolls Royce. They still laugh about it now down at the pub."

"That's the point though. Now everybody knows who we are and what we do."

"And what does your bit of posh make of it all? Does she think you're up to the mark yet?"

"I'm not just doing all this to impress Julia, you know. Of course, I want her to be proud, but this business was in my blood and heart long before she was. I'm doing this for all of us."

"Oh come on, I know that. I'm just pulling your leg.

Lighten up a bit. All the hard work's been done now. Relax and have a laugh. Enjoy a bit of time with your girl. You know I think the world of her. She's a treasure and you suit each other just fine. I'm only winding you up."

"You really do like her, don't you?" Gary smiled.

"Ah, she's grown on me a treat. And she comes from good stock. I remember when Tomar builders were here in Portsmouth. I didn't know old Tommy Marchant personally. He came from a much tougher family than I did. I do remember some of the tales though. He had it bloody hard did Tommy. Life as a poor kid in Portsmouth's no joke nowadays, but fifty odd years ago, it must have been unbelievable.

"But now, Tommy's son, that's your girls dad, well there a rich, respectable family nowadays. Amazing. Tommy Marchant's family have done very well. I think he'd be proud."

"You wouldn't mind her being a part of our family then?"

"Are you thinking along those lines? It's more the thing to just move in together these days, I thought, but it's not right really, I suppose. Not for a girl like that."

"I know that, Dad. Julia's the one for me. I want to marry her and I want to talk to her dad tonight. I wanted to know how you would feel about it, that's all."

Colin beamed at his son. "I'd feel just fine about it, if it's what you both want. If it's my blessing you want, you've got it."

Later that evening Gary was giving Julia a tour around the newly finished showroom.

"It's great, Gary, better than I had first expected. Tell me again what happens next."

"Tomorrow the cleaners are coming in to do a final polish up and I'll be here putting banners up. Saturday morning Mum's coming in to put flowers around the place, and we're putting coffee pots in all the kitchen displays. Doors open at ten o'clock, and we'll be giving

174

coffee and biscuits to everyone who turns up. Then, in the evening, we'll have a bit of a do for those with invitations only."

"I'm so proud of you, Gary. This has been a dream for so long and here it is done and ready for a grand opening. What are you aiming for next, I wonder?"

"Funny you should ask that. I was only saying to Dad earlier that there is something missing. Just one little change would make this more complete."

"Oh?" She looked confused. "Well, if it's just a little change, can't we do it now, Gary? I don't mind, you know, if it's that important."

"Well, okay then, if you're certain. Follow me." He led her to a small seating area and once she was seated he took a small box from his pocket and nervously smiled. "I love you, Jules. Will you marry me? Please?" He stopped suddenly, as nerves took control of his tongue.

She laughed in delight. "I can't believe it. You're actually proposing to me. Properly."

"I know we've said for ages that we would get married, but I wanted to do it properly once the time was right, and now it is. If you say yes, then I want to talk to your dad tomorrow."

"Wonderful. Okay then. Yes, of course, I'll marry you." She held her hand out for him to slide the ring onto her finger.

"Gary? Say something."

"I had a speech planned. I wanted to tell you how lovely you are and how special. How good and strong you make me feel. How proud I am to be seen with you and how much I love you. I said it all wrong."

"You said it all right." She kissed him. "Now, shut up." She kissed him again and again.

***

At last, the grand opening ceremony was over and Daniels

175

Design now had a showroom to be proud of. Gary, watched by Colin and Tommy Marchant locked the doors behind the last few stragglers on Saturday night. They'd all realised during the course of the evening that journalists would stay until there was nothing left to drink. Once all the booze was gone, they simply disappeared with it.

"It was a better turnout than I expected. I'd never have guessed so many people would turn out for a free drink in a plumber's yard," Tommy said.

Gary grinned. The day had been everything he hoped for and more. Having his leg pulled about his grand ideas was a price he was more than happy to pay.

"Was it all worth it, d'ya think?" Tommy asked.

"No doubts. We've handed out price lists to dozens of folks. I've got an appointment next week to price up bathrooms for a hotel refurb in Southsea, and we've picked up several bookings for regular plumbing jobs. Add that to the piece that should be in next week's paper and I think we'll be taking on another lad soon. This is just the start, you'll see."

"What have you planned for tonight then? Are you taking my daughter out for a slap-up meal to celebrate?"

"Not quite." Gary felt nervous. "I'd like to come and talk to you first if you've the time."

"There's no need for you to stand on ceremony. If you've something to say, spit it out," Tommy said.

Colin tried to slide away, sensing his son's nervousness, and knowing what was on his mind.

"I'd like to marry your daughter and I really want your blessing," Gary blurted out.

"And what if I don't give my blessing? What then?"

"I'll still marry her. I love her and I'll take care of her always. She loves me and she loves you, so I don't think you should ask her to choose. Do you?"

"To tell the truth, you've been the making of her, I think. Relax. I'll be more than happy to let you take that responsibility on. Let's all go out for a slap-up meal tomorrow to celebrate. On me."

CHAPTER THIRTY SIX
Winter 1992

"Are we millionaires yet then, love?" Ted asked. He'd been watching Jean unnoticed for fifteen minutes. She was looking better than she had for a long time and was much easier to be with. He loved her dearly and had been very worried about her and how she would cope when Hope moved out, needlessly it seemed.

"Not quite, but we're keeping our heads above water. Julia buying my paintings on a regular basis has made a heck of a difference to our budget, you know. In fact, I'm thinking about booking that holiday we've talked about?"

"I can't fancy another caravan holiday in Tenby, love," he groaned. "It was great fun last year when the sun shone, but when it rained, it was bloody awful."

She laughed and poked him in the ribs. "I was thinking of somewhere a bit more reliable weather-wise, as you very well know. How would you feel about finally booking a trip out to visit Peter and Sally? We've talked often enough about it."

"I know we have, love, but it's going to cost an arm and a leg. Do you think we've the money for Australia?"

"We don't now, no, but if I have another couple of months like the last few, we will have by this time next year. We could plan now to go over for next Christmas. We'd want to go for a longish time to look around, maybe all of December, so we'll need a fair time to make plans. They've been so kind to us coming over to visit us so often and they phone every single week. It would be wonderful to go over there and see where they live and see if it's somewhere we could get used to."

"I wouldn't like to have a Christmas without seeing our Hope though," Ted said.

"Well, no, neither would I. I'm thinking of all of us going, all five of us. If we decided now, it gives us a year

178

to make sure we've got the money to really enjoy ourselves. I can afford the tickets already, almost. Think about it, and then if you like the idea, we'll talk to Clive and Mel. I couldn't go if they didn't. I've mentioned it once or twice to Mel, but she didn't really take me up on it seriously, but now I feel more confident that we can do it, I'll mention it again."

"You're a wonderful woman, a treasure and a Trojan. Thank God I had the good sense to snap you up when I had the chance."

"You were never going to get away once I set eyes on you, so don't kid yourself." She laughed at him, relieved to see that he was perfectly happy even though Hope and Mel had moved out. She'd worried that it might be difficult for him. He always said she fussed too much, bless him.

CHAPTER THIRTY-SEVEN
Spring 1993

The weather was far too cool to use the balcony, but Linda and Deb were determined to enjoy the evening by sitting outside, with a bottle of wine, for as long as possible.

"I can't believe our timing," said Deb. "I've waited and waited for you to get back, and now just when you get here, out of nowhere, I get the chance to go away."

"I know, but it's okay, we've got this week to catch up, and then you can start your American adventure and it'll be my turn to get exotic postcards."

"Are you happy to be home?" Deb asked.

"Yes, very. It was a fabulous experience and I'm so pleased I did it. I feel so much more confident in myself. I had an absolute ball in some places and a bloody nightmare in others. I know I'll never do anything like it again, but it was absolutely the right thing for me to do at the time. Now I'm home I want to sort out a job and build a new life for myself."

"What sort of job will you look for? Something back in nursing?"

"Yes, it's what I know and what I'm good at. I've got a list of agencies to call but I won't start until you've gone. This week's for us," Linda replied.

"When I get back, I wonder if we should think about arranging a party for all of the gang and their respective add-ons. I think we've all moved on and changed so much already. Give it another year, which is how long I'll be gone, and we might all be able to get on well with each other. Do you know what I mean?"

"Yeah I do. Maybe we will, but you know a lot can change in a year. One day at a time is how I make plans. Enjoy the here and now. Speaking of enjoying things, how do you feel about missing Julia and Gary tying the knot, that would be a chance to meet everyone and see how you all feel about each other. How do they feel about you not being able to come back for that? I know you said you're bored with all the wedding talk, but she's still your best friend isn't she?"

"Of course she is. She's just a bit more focused than me at the moment, but we're still good.

As for missing the wedding, that's not a problem. They really are both totally focused on their businesses and building up a reputation there. The wedding's going to be out of this world. There's no doubt about that. But there's also no doubt that it'll be an advertising circus and a grand way of schmoozing the other businesses and council members in Portsmouth."

"Sounds tedious."

"Well it's certainly not going to be a relaxed friends and family bash. I don't blame them though. They're using what they've got to the max. I'm actually glad that I don't have to go, to be honest, and they don't mind at all."

"Um huh. I'm sure it will be spectacular. Steve's promised that he will send me a written report on who wore what. I suppose they invited him and Clive for old time's sake," Lin replied.

Deb laughed at her older but way more innocent sister. "Not quite Lin. They've invited Steve because he owns lord knows how much of the south coast. He's a local businessman, bottom line. And they invited Clive because someone has to be chief constable one day, and it just might be him."

"Yes, of course." Linda looked off into the distance. "It's quite odd but I forget sometimes how calculating some of your friends are."

"Well I suppose it looks like that."

"It all sounds much more like business decisions than friendship."

"I think it is in the real world though, don't you? When you want something in life, you think about who you know that could help you get it. You, and they, know that if you

181

succeed, you'll repay the favour in due course. Anyway, enough of them. This is our time, right?" Deb said.

"Okay, point taken. Let's move on to really important things. Would you prefer red wine or white?"

"What are we eating?"

"Um, cheese on toast," Linda said.

"Oh, red then, definitely."

Linda spent the rest of the evening at peace. She would enjoy this time with her sister, and then she would continue with her own life. Her time away had helped her learn what she did and definitely didn't want from life. She hoped that somewhere along the way she would find a partner and have a baby. That seemed to her to be the next step for her. A baby. Who knows what might be in her future. It was going to be something good though. She was suddenly confident of that.

CHAPTER THIRTY-EIGHT
Summer 1993

The gleaming car drew up outside the village church and Mel stepped nervously out.

Looking around her, she was unsurprised to discover that Julia and Gary had all the luck going again. They had indeed found a picture-perfect church in a picture-perfect village to get married in. Naturally enough, the weather proved also perfect, in the way only an English summer could be. The sky sparkled a brilliant blue with not a cloud in sight. Mel walked slowly along the path and she heard the unmistakeable sounds of a cricket match carried on the gentle breeze. It was all so ridiculously and perfectly English. Julia simply could do no wrong.

And here she stood, Mel from St. Agnes enjoying all this as one of the invited guests, almost as though she fitted in with this group of elegant, successful people. She crossed her fingers and repeated her mantra: I do belong. I do belong. I do belong.

For the first time in a very long time, she'd had several hours alone today. Clive had been busy all morning fulfilling his role as best man. Of course, she was used to being without him. His shifts with the Police meant that he was away more than he was at home, and she'd become accustomed to that and had learned to value the time they did get to spend together.

What was much more unusual was for her to be without Hope who, at three-and-a-half, was a confident, self-assured, little bossy boots, who followed her mum like a shadow. She was to be Julia's smallest bridesmaid and had spent the morning getting prepared with the other girls. She had reached the age where she simply would not be left out of anything. The original plan had been that Hope would get ready at home with Mel and they'd arrive at the church together.

Hope, however, had discovered that the other three, much older girls, were getting ready at Julia's house, and she insisted on joining them. Mel had been on edge all morning, expecting a phone call to say that Hope wanted her mummy and, in truth, she felt a little let down that the call never came. It was odd, arriving at the church alone. Perhaps that explained her nerves.

She made her way up the gravelled walkway that led to the lovely stone archway and wrought iron gate that protected the ancient church and grounds.

The soft, rolling hills led to the sea on her left and to even more downs on her right. The only sounds were the church bells and the murmur of other guests greeting each other.

She looked around to see whom she recognised. Steve was with a nice looking woman, who looked vaguely familiar, by the vast open doors being greeted by an usher.

She smiled and chatted to casual friends as she waited to be shown a seat. It was amazing how many people were here. Clearly, this was going to be, as advertised, the wedding of the year.

Mel couldn't spot any close friends, but in this mass of people that was hardly surprising.

Ted and Jean would be here somewhere though, and surely she'd relax soon, but, even so, she really didn't know how she'd last the day. Of course, she didn't really belong. Silly to have thought she could carry this off, really. It would be so nice to be at home wearing a tracksuit and playing with Lego or plasticine.

"You are far and away the hottest totty I've seen today. Are you on your own, pretty lady?" Clive said, as he crept up behind her, looking even more handsome than usual in his morning suit.

She smiled at him and her face lit up. "Hello, you fool. Is everything going according to plan?"

"I think so, or should I say, I hope so. Julia is acting like

184

the ultimate princess she would like to be. Every step has been planned with military precision, and we're all terrified that if something goes wrong, someone will lose their life.

"Gary's a useless wreck, but just about everyone's here now, and it's nearly show time. I'll show you to your seat before I go back to hold his hand, if you like."

"Lovely, thanks."

After ushering her to her seat, he strode to the front of the church and had a whispered conversation with Gary. A minute later the organ began playing the Wedding March.

Mel half-turned to see Julia enter the church. She looked like a *Vogue* fashion model. Her red hair was a riot of ringlets threaded with pearls, which lent an air of romance and drama to the simple-looking ivory dress that had been made to Julia's exact specifications.

Tommy Marchant walked proudly beside his daughter and looked Hollywood perfect, as did the adorable bridesmaids. The three teenagers walked abreast behind Julia and Tommy, and lastly, on her own, walked Hope. Her dress was a close copy of Julia's and she carried a basket of flowers. She clearly loved the drama of the event and graciously waved to everyone who looked her way. She looked like an angel and held the congregation in the palm of her hand.

When she spotted Mel, her voice was heard for the first time, as she stage-whispered, "Hello Mummy, I'm being a princess," as she passed regally by.

It was just the boost that Mel needed. Who cared about anybody else or their opinion, as long as Hope was here, happy and healthy? Nothing else mattered.

The ceremony was both moving and brief, and very soon the church was empty and peaceful once again. The guests made their way on foot to the landing dock across the village green. There, they found three lavishly decorated ferries, ready and waiting to take them to a surprise venue for the reception.

185

The bride and groom led the procession, followed by the proud, though slightly overcome, parents.

Giggling friends came next, relieved that all the formality appeared to be over and a party spirit was taking hold. The ushers and bridesmaids brought up the rear.

Clive and Hope held hands until she decided she was tired and no longer on princess duty, and therefore, could be carried. She boarded the last ferry thrown over Clive's shoulder in a fireman's lift.

The decorated ferries glided slowly across to Hayling Island, where the party disembarked, and, once again, in a procession followed Gary and Julia just a few yards along the beach to the golf links.

Jean had excelled herself this time. She'd worked alongside the managers of the club and they had been given a huge budget by Julia to create a fairytale setting for the bridal supper. The wooden clubhouse had been draped inside and out with swathes of pale blue and green chiffon. The tables were covered in cloths of coral and grey, whilst strings of pearls and silver chains hung from the beams and light fittings. The clubhouse had been turned into a pirate's treasure chest and the guests were the jewels. Odd-shaped mirrors were placed in unexpected places and hinted at treasures that were just out of sight.

Everyone was silent as they looked around at the gorgeous display. It was an underwater dream. At once, the silence was broken by excited voices exclaiming at the cleverness of Julia, hiring a designer for her reception. How brave, thought some, and how extravagant, thought others.

The fact that they were all chattering about her was all that Julia wanted. What they said really didn't matter. It was everything she hoped it would be so far. In this, as in every other area of her life, her desire to be the best had been achieved. It was a wedding to die for, but it was also the launch of her own wedding planning business, though no one else knew that yet.

After enjoying a delicious meal, Mel began to relax enough to enjoy a glass of champagne. Judging by the loosened collars and jackets on chair backs and loud laughter, many others were feeling as mellow.

Clive, whose duties as best man were almost completed, was leading the dancing with Hope in his arms.

Mel reached for a second glass of champagne when a voice said, "Would you mind if I sat with you for a while?"

Smiling, she looked up and said, "No, of course not. You're Linda, Deb's sister. Is that right?"

"That's right, and you're Mel, Hope's mum?"

"Is it the fate of some women do you imagine to always be someone's something?"

"I've certainly never been anything but Deb's sister and I never minded in the past. In fact, I loved it, but now I long to be "Linda" and have everyone know me without the qualifier."

"Um, I was Smelly Melly at school but now that I'm Hope's mum, or Clive's wife I'm much happier."

"It's amazing that I've heard about you for so long and yet we've never met. When I saw you sitting alone, I thought I should put that right. This champagne's a bit special, isn't it?"

"I know. It's wonderful stuff. I never drink normally, but, to be honest, I was feeling a bit out of my depth. I'm here because Clive is best man. I doubt I'd have been invited otherwise."

"Oh, me too. I came as Steve's partner," said Linda. "I'd much prefer to sit at home with my feet up and hear about all this second-hand tomorrow, but he couldn't come on his own. His invitation specified that. So I'm his plus one."

"More champagne, ladies?" asked a waiter.

"Yes, please," they choroused.

As the waiter moved on to the next group, Linda and Mel settled down to learning as much as they could about each other, both becoming a bit more relaxed with every sip.

"I can't think where I heard this, but I had the impression you had gone travelling. Was that wrong or have you been and returned?"

"Oh, I've been, for almost a year, in fact. I went with a pal from work. It was something I needed to do. It was a crazy thing to do really, but it turned out to be exactly what I needed. I was getting a bit old and stale far too soon, so I broke out. It was the best thing I ever did. Deb's away now though. She's doing an exchange programme at a school in Boston for a year. She's well into now and loves it. I think she'd like to travel more, with her work if she can, she's thriving on it."

"Blimey, a family of globetrotters!"

"Yes, I know it appears that way, but, in fact, neither of us had ever been anywhere or done anything until she recovered from her accident, it was as though Barry's death made us all take stock." She clapped her hand across her moth and turned scarlet. "I'm so sorry that was an incredibly stupid thing to say."

"No, don't worry. It's okay, I understand exactly what you meant, don't be embarrassed please. You must miss each other, you and your sister?"

"Yes, in a way it's a shame we couldn't have timed things to be away at the same time, but it's actually been very good for me. She just knows how to make friends and create a social life, it happens automatically for her but I've never been able to relax enough to let that happen for me, until now. I'd always enjoyed her friends and interests. In fact she once accused me of not living, just watching her live. I'm on a mission now to live my life to the full and develop my own circle of friends."

Linda sipped her drink then confided, "It's quite difficult though. Going away helped me so much with my confidence but I still find meeting people like this a trial. I'd feel much safer if I didn't bother, but I must."

"Safe? What do you feel you need to be safe from?"

"Oh, I don't know. Big groups scare me and smart people intimidate me, and I can never hold my own in a clever conversation. I suppose I worry that I'll appear stupid or boring."

"Most people are as genuine and friendly as you and me. Those are the ones I care about. Relax and be yourself and don't worry about trying to be something you're not. I know there are people here that prefer not to get close to me because they think they know what kind of person I am, and that I'm the wrong kind for them. I know they're wrong."

"But you seem to have everything going for you."

"I do. That's what I mean. My life is complete, I don't care what outsiders think."

"I think you've got the right idea. I hope we can keep in touch - I've enjoyed meeting you at last."

"Why don't you come out to visit us next weekend? If the weather's nice, we could go out on the water. We live right by the sea. With any luck, Hope will be acting a bit more like a child and not a princess. You can get to know her then."

"Oh, maybe I will, thanks."

At that moment, Clive came to their table and collapsed with a sigh into his chair. He grinned at Mel and Linda and said, "Those old aunties and kids have danced my feet off and now they're heading off so our generation can have a party, and I'm wiped out."

Linda stood up to go, but he begged her to stay. "No, no, don't leave us. If you go, someone else will grab me. Let them think I'm looking after you. Just for a little while longer."

"Let them think you're looking after Mel," she said.

Mel chipped in. "No. I must start making a move. Hope's had a very long day and if I don't get her home soon, I'm afraid she'll let herself down. Sorry, Clive, you're on your own. Linda, I meant what I said earlier.

189

Come and spend Saturday afternoon with us, if you'd like to?"

"I will, yes thanks. I'd love to."

Mel left the reception then, after making Clive promise to have a good time but not to drink too much. She knew he'd leave the minute he could and he probably wouldn't drink at all.

The taxi finally delivered her and a sleepy Hope back to the house at Langstone. As she walked in, a familiar feeling swept over her – peace and security. She had found them both here and she relished it. "Come on, princess, bath and bed time."

"Can I sleep in my princess dress, Mummy?"

"We'll see. Let's get a bath first and then a story."

As she tucked her sleepy little girl into bed, she kissed her forehead and breathed in the soapy, sweet baby smell and was overcome by a wave of fierce love. If anyone or anything ever threatened her child, she knew she would be capable of murder.

As she began her own evening ritual, she tried to ignore the nagging guilt she felt for not giving Clive his own child. He adored Hope, of course, but he so wanted a child of his own. He felt it would be a good thing for all of them, but she was terrified of the idea. She'd never quite got used to the idea that she'd got away with cheating over the identity of Hope's father and she couldn't help thinking that she'd spoil everything. Maybe by having another baby, it would be asking too much, pushing her luck. She could spoil everything.

She swallowed the little pill and put the pack back in its hiding place.

She felt shame when she witnessed Clive's disappointment each month, and the fear of him finding out was awful, but still she took those little white pills. Chrissie knew what she was doing and had tried to convince her just that week that she was making a mistake." I simply don't understand you", she'd said.

"He's such a good man and he loves you both dearly. Why won't you let him have his own child? You can't really think that God will punish you, do you?"

In her heart of hearts though, Mel felt that she'd been lucky to have as much as she had. He said he loved Hope as though she was his own and that would have to be enough for him.

She bustled about tidying up and pushed the cloud to the back of her mind.

CHAPTER THIRTY-NINE
Autumn 1993

Jean and Ted stood on the ferry that was carrying them from Southsea towards Hayling Island. The wind was brutal and they huddled together for warmth.

The variety of people using this method of travel between the islands changed with the seasons. Throughout the summer the boat would be full of holidaymakers, some from the hotels in Southsea going to Hayling for a change, whilst others from the campsites on Hayling came over heading for the shops of Portsmouth and Southsea.

In addition, there were students" bikes and backpacks filling every nook of space, and children who rode the ferry simply because it was a ferry.

At this time of year, the holidaymakers were all gone and the ferry became the preferred mode of transport for the locals. It was so simple to move between the islands with no need ever to sit on a bus or drive a car. The chief benefit though was The Ferry Inn, which was a far nicer place to sit and wait than any bus shelter.

Jean and Ted, having both been born and brought up on Portsmouth, thought they'd long got over the novelty of the whole experience. However, since Mel had married Clive and moved to Langstone with Hope, this particular journey was once again a magical adventure. One week they came to Hayling to spend a day with Hope exploring her island, and the next week she made the journey over to them. Jean was leaning on the safety rail looking for Hope before the ferry had left Portsmouth.

"You're excited, aren't you?" Ted asked her quietly. She turned to look at him noticing the tired lines around his eyes, but knowing that tired or not, he'd do anything to keep her safe and secure. They were a couple who'd learned over a lifetime together – firstly as school friends, and later, as each other's one and only lover – how to read each other's moods. Words weren't always needed but sometimes helped. Jean felt this was such a time.

"Yes, I am," she nodded. "I was a little sad when Mel and Hope moved away from us, but, of course, I knew it was the right thing for them both. I was terrified of the gap they would leave, but you know, it's worked out just fine. I love these days out we have with Hope now. And, of course, I can spoil her now she's not with us all day, every day. For a long time those two kept me sane, but if they'd lived with us for much longer, they'd probably have driven me mad. Now they've moved out, it's almost as though I've got permission to start to live a more normal life again. I suppose you're not feeling that way at all are you?"

He grinned at her and said, "I'd kiss you now but your granddaughter's waving to us."

And there she was, a tiny figure in bright red jeans and a floppy yellow hat, waving and shouting, "Look at me, Gramma, look at me!"

As quickly as possible, Jean was off the boat and running up the shingle. In one move, she had her arms around Hope and was swinging her around. "Hello, my darling girl. I love your hat. Have you got a hug for me?"

"Did you see me waving, Gramma?"

"Yes, and we heard you calling us. Hello, Mel, love. What a change in the weather, eh? At least it means we'll have the island to ourselves. I love it when the holidaymakers have gone."

"I just love it," said Mel, and then turning to Hope, she asked, "So what's it to be, walk first then eat, or eat first then walk? It's your turn to choose."

It proved to be a tough decision but, with a little prompt from Ted, they agreed to walk first and eat later. Walking on the shingle, they followed the water's edge, stopping at various times to point things out to each other.

There was nothing new to see, yet seeing it through Hope's eyes, kept it all it fresh and exciting. Looking back

193

across the bay, Portsmouth looked the same as ever. There were always a couple of people walking dogs and one or two hardy souls swimming or windsurfing.

Following the curve of the island, Portsmouth fell from view and the beach opened up for miles and miles. Every now and then, a container ship or passenger ferry could be seen on the horizon, heading into or out of the ancient port.

On their left, they passed the golf links where Julia had held her wedding reception. In warmer weather, they would often stop to watch the players and have a rest, but today it was more important to get out of wind.

Further on, the large houses of Hayling seafront came into view. These were wonderful, elegant, rambling homes, every one different. Only the seriously wealthy could have afforded a house here when this land had been developed and they made sure that every home was special.

These wealthy people had also made sure that no hotels, bars or restaurants ruined their little slice of paradise. The pubs that were on the seafront were small, friendly places that provided beer gardens with a sea view. A good lunch could be enjoyed but absolutely no cocktails or late night dancing. People that wanted that sort of thing could take a drive some forty minutes and find Brighton, where it was possible to find all kinds of entertainment. Hayling Island was in a time warp and intended to stay there.

Eventually, the foursome reached their first scheduled stop, the Coastguard Café. It was an old-fashioned tea and coffee shop. Very narrow and very dim inside, the wooden floor was crooked and creaky and the tables were all different shapes and sizes. The waitresses dressed in black dresses and white aprons and appeared to have been well and truly caught in the time warp.

Fish and chips to take away were sold from the front of the shop but here at the back pots of tea and homemade cakes were unadvertised but available. The café gave amazing views across the sea but offered shelter from the

194

weather. Summer or winter the wind blew hard on Hayling.

"Do you realise that we've been doing this once a week for eighteen months now?" Jean said. "What shall we do when term starts?"

"What's term mean, Gramma?" Hope's ears had pricked up.

"Gramma means what shall we do when you start school?" Mel explained.

"Not going to school for a long time. Picnic now, please."

As they continued their walk, they continued to suggest places to sit and eat their picnic, knowing that Hope always chose the same spot.

"Here we are," she announced at last. A breaker reached out to sea, which provided a shelter from the wind and also acted as a backrest. From this resting place, they could see the shoreline of another island over to their left.

For Hope, this was a place of magic and mystery ever since their first walk when she had said she wanted to paddle over to it. Ted had told her it was called Thorny Island and she would need a boat to get to it, but she wouldn't be allowed to land because the island was home to an army base.

Hope preferred to believe that unicorns, fairies and talking teddy bears lived there.

Each week Ted told her a fairy story which were all based on Thorny Island. As Ted embarked on this week's story, which included the little-known fact that Goldilocks and Cinderella were, in fact, best friends and went to the same school, on Thorny Island, of course, Jean and Mel quietly chatted.

"Gary and Julia are very pleased with the business the new showroom is bringing in, I hear," said Mel.

"Mm, been better than they'd hoped. Gary has taken on another chap to go on the emergency calls so that he can focus on the new installs. And Julia has come into her own

195

since finding a manager for The Gallery. She oversees that while running the showroom. She's come up with some brilliant ideas for publicity and seems tireless. There are a few government schemes aiming to get young people into work and Julia's doing what she can to help. It's all very impressive," Jean said.

"And Gary is evidently considering becoming involved in local politics. He's starting to make his voice heard. He feels very strongly that the council at a local level could do much more to help small businesses employ more young people than they are currently doing, and he's decided to get involved. He was trying to get Clive to talk to people he knows, to at least generate more interest," said Mel.

"I admire them both so much. They've turned out to be very different to the way I thought they might." Jean said. "I almost forgot to ask. How did your evening out with Linda go at the weekend?"

"Oh, it was more fun than I expected. We swapped life stories, most of which you know, but, of course, we didn't. I found her easy to talk to after a couple of drinks, and she and Chrissie really hit it off, which was lucky because Chrissie can't stand Deb.

When Linda got back home after her trip, she realised that she had to build a social circle of her own, so she started this, um, well, she calls it a dinner club. People have to sign up and fill in applications and then once a week they have a dinner evening, just as a way of getting people together. Chrissie said it sounded like a great way to meet single men, and Linda said it was turning out that way."

"Is she seeing anyone special?" Jean asked.

"Well, dozens by the sounds of it. Organising this thing has given her so much contact with people and she loves it. I don't know whether she'd like to meet someone special, but she says she certainly feels ready to have a baby. I think she's afraid of leaving it too late. I so hope she meets someone soon."

"But she's still such a young woman. Surely there's no need for her to panic yet."

"No, but she is thirty-five, so she wouldn't want to wait much longer before having babies," Mel said.

"No, of course. I'd forgotten that she's so much older than the rest of you. Thirty-five, hmm yes, she needs to get on with it."

"Yes, I know. Anyway that's enough about her, what are our plans for the weekend? Is there anything I need to be doing to help out?"

"No, Peter and Sally are on the way and we'll be meeting them at the airport tomorrow. We plan to stay at home quietly on Thursday. It's such a long flight from Australia and I'm certain they will want to just relax, so I thought a day to do nothing would suit them both. Then, on Friday, if you and Hope come across on the ferry as normal, we'll do a family tour of Portsmouth so that Peter can see some more of the changes taking place. Clive can come straight over when his shift ends and then when Hope's gone to bed, we'll have a few drinks and chat about everything. I think we've got everything organised for the holiday, but we can run over things together."

"What holiday, Gramma?" Hope piped up.

"Oh, you remember, I told you about our aeroplane holiday. We're talking about that."

"Okay." Hope tuned back into Ted's story. She wasn't interested but she wanted to make sure she wasn't being left out of anything.

Mel continued to speak. "I'm finding it all a bit much to take on board, to be honest. I loved the idea of moving to Australia, but Clive dearly wants us to have a baby, and I don't. I mean, say I did, I simply don't know how I could manage a new baby in a new country. I think it's all a bit beyond me." She stood up and turned away abruptly, but still Jean saw her brush a tear away.

Jean was appalled. "This is just a holiday, Mel. It's supposed to be a dream, a treat. If we all fall in love with

197

the place, we could think about moving in a year or so. If we don't all fall in love, then it won't happen. And if you're at all concerned, then we won't consider it for a moment. I thought you were as keen on the idea as I am. Your happiness is the most important thing to all of us."

"I am happy and I think the idea is fantastic. It's just that I don't want to be in a foreign country to have another baby and Clive doesn't seem to understand."

"If it's Australia that worries you, then don't go. If it's having a baby that worries you, then don't have one. Mel, you've got to do what's right for you. And only what's right for you. I've never seen you cry before in all that you've gone through. I think you need to take some time to think things through fully for yourself. Stop just going along with things and put your foot down," Jean said. "Take some time to think seriously about what you want."

CHAPTER FORTY
Winter 1993

Gary and Julia followed Tommy towards a wooden gate that was set in an otherwise unbroken brick wall in a shady, narrow street in Old Portsmouth. He'd promised them that taking a few hours away from work to spend some time with him would be time well spent, but they had to do it together. It was all very mysterious, but they were both beginning to feel deliciously like truants.

As they reached the padlocked gate, Tommy found a key in his pocket, unlocked the padlock and stepped through. He turned round and beamed at them. "Come on, come in," he urged them.

Julia knew at once that she had been here before years ago and had very hazy memories of the old house they were now looking at.

For Gary, however, it was love at first sight.

That ugly anonymous brick wall and locked wooden gate hid a treasure. It held safe and private the loveliest, little old cottage. Though shabby and overgrown it was also warm and mellow. It appeared to be a random hodge-podge of half wood and half stone. The wooden uprights, lintels, doors and window frames were weathered to a grey, white colour. The stonework was cream and grey. The entire building was dotted with verandas and balconies. It was as though bits had been added with no thought or plan yet it worked, it looked solid enough and was clearly very old.

The ground had been completely enclosed by the brick wall and the whole outside area had become a tangle of wild roses, nettles and fruit trees. Gary strolled around the little house and garden speechless.

"Shall we go inside and look around, or have you decided you love it already?" Tommy asked.

"I was daydreaming," said Gary. "What a great place

this is. I do love it and I'd love to look around inside. I can't believe this place is here. I've driven round this area all my life and I guessed there was a house here, but I'd never imagined anything like this. It's a dream."

Opening the huge front door with some difficulty, Gary stepped into a hallway with a wooden floor that contained two small doors and a narrow staircase. The two downstairs rooms were both tiny and each had double doors that let out onto a covered veranda.

Up the wooden staircase, the next floor held the main living accommodation. The entire floor was flooded with light and opened up to be one room. Every wall had a floor-to-ceiling window in it. One corner was given over to a kitchen area, but the rest was a wide-open space containing nothing but a very steep and very narrow staircase. The top floor held two rooms. This time though, they were both clearly bedrooms, each with a tiny basic bathroom.

"I've never known you be stuck for words before," Tommy said, as he slapped Gary on the shoulder. "It's basically just a few rooms tacked onto a staircase, this place. None of the rooms are big enough to do anything much with, so it's nothing to get excited about. Parking's a no hoper, but if you like it, it's yours."

Gary looked at him in shock.

Tommy nodded and repeated his words. "Yours if you want it."

"I don't know what to say. I mean, we can almost afford to buy somewhere for us. We're doing really well and we've been looking for the right place, but we're both so busy. It's been easier to stay in the flat until we get some time."

"I know all that. I also know your showroom has been open just under a year and an investment like that needs nurturing. You two won't have any time off for at least another year. And if you've got any money at all, you know as well as I do, it needs to be ploughed back in. You take money out of a business in its first five years, and it's the kiss of death.

"That little flat of yours is fine, I know, but it's not the right kind of place to take clients and councillors to. You're getting a name for yourself as the man to watch, and that's a good thing, but you've got to present the whole package. Pretty soon, you'll be invited to lunch and dinner and you'll need a place to socialise from. Your little flat just won't do.

"This would be perfect and it's yours. Well, it's mine now, but it was always going to be Julia's one day, and I think that day has come. You could move in here and both of you carry on with your work, no upheaval at all. It's a quirky place, but for a young, professional couple in your line of work I think it would work.

"If in due course you ever decide to start a family, there are a few things that could be done to make it more family-friendly, I guess. I've never wanted to do much more to it. It was my dad's home as a youngster and he was very unhappy here. Then, as an old man, he'd nowhere else to escape to really, so he turned his hand and brain to transforming it into something he could love."

"Tell us more about him please, Dad," Julia asked.

"It's all history now, love. It's not important."

"Oh, come on. You've said just enough to get us interested now. You've got to tell it all," said Gary.

"Well, just remember, the thing about family stories is they're usually only interesting to the people that were there at the time.

"My dad's dad was a wild one. He was a sailor and a gambler and much more, most of which is best left forgotten. Family tales say that he won, or even stole, this patch of land and the stone hut on it off a fellow he worked on a ship for. The other fellow had made some money and had no use for this worthless patch, which is probably why my granddad got away with it. Whisky and card games were at the root of it.

201

"Anyway, he, my granddad this is, moved into the stone hut that was the beginning of this place. He carried on his drinking and gambling and all the rest, and eventually got a girl into trouble. Because everyone knew about the fact that he was sleeping here, it was easy for her dad to find him. Having a knife held to his throat, was quite enough of an incentive for him to marry. He installed his new bride here and then got on the next boat heading out."

"Before the baby was born?" Julia asked.

"The day after they married he was gone, and he didn't come back for five years. Eventually, he moved back in, and though the details are mercifully unclear, I think he began to knock her around. I can't imagine how hard life had been for her, a young woman alone with a child. I don't know what she must have had to do to earn money to feed and clothe the two of them. I do know my dad said he'd no fear of death. He'd spent his childhood in hell, and nothing could ever be that bad again."

"They must have had some dreadful times."

They did, no question. And it made him what he was, good and bad. He was rude and intolerant, but he was honest and hard-working. He was also very determined and self-reliant. He thought fooling around with women was the most stupid, dangerous thing a man could do. He remained unmarried until his late forties. He did nothing but work and plan until then. I have no idea why he did finally marry. He never seemed to me to be a man who would allow himself to fall in love. Whatever the facts were, marry he did, and a year or so later they had me. He was very strict but not unkind to me. Distant is the best way to describe it. Distant. He'd built up a reputation as a builder, and I was trained from the day I could stand up to work alongside him. We worked well together, but it was only a work relationship."

"Did you live here as a boy?" Gary asked.

"No, my dad spent all of his spare time here, but alone. As I did more work for our customers, he gradually did

202

less. He worked here till he died, changing things. He built the balconies and the verandas and the wall around the garden. I don't think he ever loved it, but I do think he found some peace here in the end."

"When did all this happen, do you know? I mean, winning a place like this in a card game or a bet? It sounds like a story from the Wild West," said Julia.

"Well, now, let's work it out. I'm sixty-three now and I was born in 1930 when my dad was forty-seven, so he was born in 1883. His dad was living here when he was forced to get married, so it would have happened some time around 1882, I guess."

"It's unbelievable. What a fantastic story. I think it's fabulous, the house and its history. I'd love to live here. What about you, Jules, what do you think?"

"It's amazing. I do vaguely remember coming here once as a child but I'd forgotten all about it. Now though, I think it's absolutely perfect. There are more stairs than anything else, but I think there's a lot we can do. If we plan things we could make it super by getting the right pieces of furniture and rugs. I could put paintings up all the stair walls and display lots of art in the nooks."

She ran back up the stairs to the top floor, as Gary turned and shook Tommy's hand. "I don't know what to say. It's just..."

"Say nothing. I told you, it was always going to be hers one day. Look, I'm heading off now. You stay and make your plans, and we'll go over the details at the weekend. It'll need some work done. I've had various tenants in over the years, but it's not had any proper maintenance for I don't know how long, so look round carefully. I'll make sure the paperwork is in order so the place will be yours, but you'll be doing all the work on it. If you're sure that's what you want, let me know and we can get it all officially finalised next week.

"You come and shut the gate behind me now though. This garden would fill up faster than a free car park on the seafront if you ever forget to do that."

"Gary locked the gate behind Tommy and did a circuit of the garden once more. It really was small, no more than a border of about ten feet wide, but it entirely circled the house. There were all sorts of corners and nooks that had been created by the wooden additions on to what had been a square stone structure. As he stood planning things in his head, he heard Julia calling him.

"Gary come quickly, I've had a wonderful idea."

He walked inside and headed up the stairs, smiling and singing to himself. "Where are you?"

"Top floor, room on the left."

And there she was, standing in the weak sunlight, naked, and shivering and giggling. "I thought we could christen our new home. Come over here quick. I'm freezing," she said.

He laughed and swung her round in his arms. "It's November, you crazy woman. Of course you're freezing. I love you, Mrs Daniels, but do you realise we are only a stone's throw away from the cathedral? You're asking for trouble."

"It's trouble that I'm hoping to find. Now come here," she said.

As the sun faded away they grew warmer.

Much later, Gary sighed and then shivered. "It was a wonderful idea, ten out of ten, but I have to get some clothes on now. Let's try this again when the sun's shining."

"Actually, that wasn't my idea. That was a sudden flash of brilliance when I heard you coming up the stairs."

"Okay then. Let's hear the wonderful idea."

"I think we should have a Christmas house-warming party here during the day, not at night. Outside for a barbecue and picnic if it's dry, ground floor rooms and verandas if it's not. If we start to plan it now, we've loads of time. We could tell everyone it's an open day, any time between say eleven am and seven pm. Our families will

204

stay all day, I expect, and others can come and go as they please."

"Not nearly enough time. It's what, five weeks away? We'll never get anything done before then"

"But we could tidy it up enough to put on a bit of a show. We can do the real work later, but I think we could really do a great party here almost as it is. Make it the first and make sure everyone knows it's going to be an annual event. You know, we'd have to sell it up a bit, let them know they're the first invitees to something that will become more and more exclusive."

"I like the sound of it, but, honestly, we can't."

"We'll make it New Year then. That gives me a few more days and we can do it. Nothing structural, obviously, just a good clean and replace the broken windows. We should invite all your clients and all mine. Anyone we think we'd like to do business with could be invited. Everyone we know that we can count on to make up the numbers and put on a good show.

"Clive and Steve, of course. They both know important people. Clive's folks might come – a respectable, retired policeman is always nice. Linda could come. She's doing this dinner club and seems to be meeting every single businessman in the area. Chrissie and her latest girlfriend might make it. You know that will add a little interest and cause some gossip. It all helps to make a party memorable. And then, all the staff and some of the customers from the Gallery and the showroom."

"Whoa, that's a lot of people and an awful lot of work. Sorry, but I just don't think we can."

"It's a brilliant idea and I think we must do it. We'll definitely make it a New Year's do. It can be great publicity for us both. I'll plan it and do all the work. You must be able to see what an opportunity this is. Doing all that work might take my mind off having babies for a while."

"That was a bit below the belt," he complained. "Well,

205

if you're sure we can manage it, it is a great idea, and it will be fantastic advertising, but, you know, my time's fully booked. I've got to get this project for Steve in on time, or all the advertising in the world won't help."

"Don't worry, leave it to me. I'll get people to come and help. I'm good at that. Come on, let's go. I need to get busy."

CHAPTER FORTY-ONE
Winter 1994

The first day of the year looked as though it would be glorious. At ten-o-clock in the morning the weather was crisp and bright with a hint of sunshine to come. Linda and Mel were sharing a car heading to Southsea to attend Julia's house-warming party.

Mel laughed out loud. "Who, but Julia, would be perverse enough to decide to cook a barbecue on New Year's Day in England? But then, who but Julia could be lucky enough to have perfect weather for it? Everything she turns her hand to turns out to be a success. It's just like spring today. I bet she'll have a grand turnout and everything will run to perfection."

"Mm." Linda was staring ahead.

"Not in the mood for a party then? Or don't you feel like chatting?"

"What?" Linda jumped

"What's on your mind? Come on, fess up. We've haven't seen each other for weeks and you've nothing to say? What's wrong?" Mel insisted.

"I'm sorry. I know I should be asking you all about your trip to Australia, how the holiday was, and whether you going to move there and all your news. But, I think I'm pregnant and I can't actually think of anything else. I wanted to find out about you first, but I am just so overcome. I'm excited, scared and I don't know what else."

"Oh, Linda that's great news. Congratulations."

"It's what I've wanted for so long, but I didn't know it would be such a shock when it happened. I've only just missed my second period so it's early days yet. I've haven't told anyone yet because I want to be sure that Deb hears it from me first. We're due to talk tonight, so I'll tell her then, and perhaps that will make it real. I feel so guilty though; Julia has been trying for so long and it just won't happen for her."

"It will be a thrill for Deb though, I'm sure."

"I don't know how she'll feel about me being a single mum. I know she probably expected I'd get a husband first. To tell you the truth though, I've never really wanted a man. It was all about having a baby for me. I can live without all the other nonsense."

"Well I know that, come on, if you'd wanted a man, you'd have one. I've seen men eye you up and you are *so* not interested, it's funny. I've wondered for a long time if that wasn't the reason for the dinner club all along."

"Of course it was. I've had enough horny men over the last I don't know how many months to last me a lifetime. It was only ever a means to an end."

"So, running a sex club hasn't given you a taste for it then?"

"Ugh, no chance. And it's a dinner club, not a sex club. I needed to get on and get pregnant and I wanted nice friends as well. It's great fun. The members are all clean, smart professionals. That's all I needed to know. I can give my baby everything else."

"You're definitely going to be a single mum then? It's not easy, you know. I had Ted and Jean on hand, and it was still awfully hard and very lonely."

"Well, I've had an idea in my mind for a while, but it's a bit of a wild card, and now it's come to it, I've got cold feet. I don't know how Deb will respond and I'd really like to talk to you about it. Would you mind if we arrived a bit late to the party? I don't want Hope to worry if she can't find you."

"She won't. She's been there all day helping Jean titivate. Julia did some of the decoration but she wanted Jean to go over and finish off. She's absolutely shameless about roping people in, you know. Anyway, Hope went with her because Julia told her the party was to welcome her back and because they all missed her birthday party this year. She'll be strutting around giving orders left and right, and she'll have forgotten all about me. We can play truant for as long as you like. Why don't we stop at the hotel for a coffee and a catch up?"

They found a bar that was doing a roaring New Year's Day trade and realised that they'd never find a quiet spot, but they could at least be certain that no one would overhear them above the general din.

"Come on then, what's your plan?" Mel asked.

Drawing in a deep breath, Linda began to speak. "I'm going to ask Steve to marry me. Don't say anything yet, please, just listen. I know you and he don't get on terribly well, which makes me very sad, by the way. Nevertheless, I know and love him. Not in that way, of course. I don't really understand sex, it's just a lot of messing about. I only did it to get a baby and I don't see the need to do it again. I know that now, and I'm happy to have had the chance to find out that the reason I've been alone so long is because, in fact, I choose to be. I don't want to betray Steve's secrets in any way, but I know he plans to remain unmarried.

Now, if he married me, we'd be companions. We've known each other forever and get on very well. More than that, we do love each other dearly. We could have a happy family now that I'm pregnant. And the pressure would be off both of us. You know, all of that "When are you going to settle down?" nonsense that virtual strangers seem to think it's okay to ask."

Linda stopped and waited for Mel's reaction which was quick in coming.

"You couldn't really do that though, could you? I mean, it sounds like an easy solution now if you take all the facts on board, but one of you will find a person you love eventually, and then what happens? You'll have to divorce and your baby suddenly has its happy home ripped away. It's just too cold and clinical, and if you marry just to find a father for your baby now, you may regret it."

209

"Are you speaking from experience?" Linda asked.

"No, I am not. That's a horrible thing to say. I married Clive because he loved me and I loved him."

"I love Steve though, and he loves me. Just not in the way that married love is usually thought of. I just don't want to have the kind of marriage that most people consider normal. I want to have my own life and run it my way. I trust Steve more than anyone else I've ever met. I think it's a perfect idea and I thought you of all people would understand."

"What do you mean by that?"

"Oh, come on. You've haven't had the most conventional courtship and marriage scenario and it's worked out brilliantly for you. Why wouldn't it work for me?"

"It's a completely different situation. Clive isn't Hope's dad, but I married him because I love him and he loves us both."

"Steve and I love each other and he'll love my baby. It's actually very similar."

"You're refusing to listen to what I'm saying."

"Yes, I am. Because what you're saying is you just don't like Steve and anything I do that involves him would be wrong. That's illogical and I'm not going to agree with you. I hoped you'd be pleased for me and I truly thought you would be. Good God, you've had such a terrible time yourself, and people took you on trust and helped you out. I thought you'd look a bit more generously on people who actually might need your help or support. That's what friends do, you know."

"You're right, and I'm sorry if I put a damper on things. I know you love Steve and I'm sure he does love you, and that's all that matters. Forgive me? "

"Okay. But Mel, you've got to try to get over this thing you have with Steve. Give him a chance and try to get to know him a bit. Hope seems to like him and kids are good judges, you know. Come on, let's get to this party and hit

210

the booze."

"Well, I can, but you expectant mums aren't supposed to, you know."

CHAPTER FORTY-TWO
Winter 1994

Julia sparkled, her party had taken off with a bang, she'd had more help than she needed to get things ready and now, to top it all the Mayor had, as promised, dropped in. She invited him and his wife on a tour of the house and garden.

Gary, noticing that she was busy took the opportunity to grab a quick word with Clive.

"Steve looks a bit worse for wear. He's been knocking the booze back a bit too much, and so's Linda. Now he's getting a bit loud and he's just dropped a tray of drinks. Do you think you could help me out with him?"

"Sure, leave him to me. It's not like him though. I wonder what's happened to make him drink so much. I expected him to be networking like crazy today."

"Thanks. Julia will go ballistic if he upsets her party, and I feel I should keep my guests well refreshed. I've got no time for babysitting today."

"No problem. I'll see if I can get him to take a walk with me. That might sober him up a bit, and if not, at least it'll get him out of the way until the Mayor has had a drink and gone."

"You're a pal." Gary sighed with relief. "We'll get a drink together later when the rest of them have gone."

"I'll just go and tell Mel that I'll be gone for an hour or two."

***

Linda saw Clive come out of the house and waved him over frantically. Steve had leaned in towards Mel and appeared to be shouting something at her. She looked terrified and Linda was trying to pull him away from her.

"For God's sake, Steve, calm down and let her speak.

212

Don't be so rude."

"Well, she's talking a lot of crap, didn't you hear her?" Steve shook Linda's arm off him. "She says she thinks they'll move to Australia for a better life. There's nothing in England for them. Pretentious cow, up from the gutter and suddenly better than all of us. I've never heard anything so wet in all my life. It's about time she thought about what she was doing. You can't just disrupt things like that. She's nothing but—"

"I don't think you need to say any more," Clive interrupted him. "Come on, Steve, I'll give you a lift home."

"I'll come with you," Linda said..

"I'm not actually going home yet, thanks all the same," Steve glared at them.

Clive took charge. "We can go wherever you want, but we can't stay here, so come on. There are a lot of important people here today. Not just important to Gary and Jules, but important to you too. Don't let them see what a total prat you are in real life, shut up and come with me.

"Mel, will you stay here and help Julia, please? Don't worry, everything's fine. I'll be back in a while, and then we'll head for home."

Mel nodded, though no-one was looking at her, as they were both trying to get a very reluctant Steve into the car.

***

"Thanks for helping me. I couldn't shift him on my own," Linda said to Clive, thankful that at last she was heading home. Steve, now snoring loudly on the back seat was giving no more trouble.

Clive just shrugged. "It's okay. I just can't figure out what set him off. He's been drinking way too much lately, but he usually gets a bit bloody pathetic, to be honest. I've never known him be quite so nasty. I wonder what's going

213

on?"

"I'm afraid it's my fault. I just told him that I'm pregnant, and I think I probably should have waited until we were alone. I hadn't realised how much he'd had to drink, or how shocked he'd be. I handled things very badly, I'm afraid."

"Oh. I didn't know you two were ... ah, sorry, forgot my manners … Congratulations."

She sighed. "Thanks Clive. Don't worry, I know we're not a typical couple. Mel made that pretty clear earlier.

"Here's fine to drop us off thanks, If you can help me get him to the front door, I'll manage from there on. You can get back to the party, and Mel."

CHAPTER FORTY-THREE
Winter 1994

Mel was watching the pathway from one of the little covered verandas willing Clive to walk back into view. Her mind was racing. What had Steve said in the car about her? He'd been building up for a while. What on earth was wrong with him, and was Linda okay. And why the bloody hell did Julia expect them all to attend a party the day after an eighteen-hour flight? Over and over she played out the events of the day. Christ, where was Clive? He should be back by now.

The gate opened and at last he walked toward her. She moved over to him and he smiled as he put his arm around her.

At that moment, the Mayor decided to propose a toast. "Ladies and Gentlemen, raise your glasses please, and join me in thanking our hosts, Gary and Julia, on setting the benchmark for parties in the future. I envy them for the good luck they enjoy and applaud the good taste they have shown in choosing this fabulous, wonderful house. I look forward to next year's party and meeting you all once again."

As everyone raised their glasses for a goodbye toast, a sense of relief was felt. It had not been the friendly, relaxed gathering the friends and family had hoped for. Perhaps things would warm up once the busy little man left.

Gary and Julia smiled in delight at each other. The party had been exactly what they had hoped for.

Later that night, at home, Mel and Clive chatted about the events at the party.

"Steve was just being a pain all day," Clive sighed. "Sniping and sneering when he'd said he wanted to propose a toast. We all stood around thinking he was going

215

to say thanks for a great party, or something along those lines, but it was ghastly. He was being nasty about Julia and her ambition. He might have been trying to be funny, but I don't think he was. It sounded spiteful."

"I missed that bit. Linda and I stopped for a coffee and a chat on the way."

"I noticed you were late, and I gather she had something pretty momentous to tell you?"

"You've guessed?"

"She told me when I took them home. She and Steve are having a baby. I didn't know they were together and I couldn't think of anything to say. Bit of a shocker, huh?"

"Oh, you can be so dense Clive. He's your friend, she's mine, and neither of us had worked it out. Surely that tells you something. You hate me gossiping about your friends, but I could fill in the gaps for you now ...'mel offered.

"No, don't. I don't care that much about any of them. He found more to say about us possibly moving to Australia, than about being a dad, shows what a twat he is. I don't care about him I care about us. Which brings me back to moving to Australia We've all been there now and have seen what it can offer. Have you reached a conclusion? You were talking about it to Linda. Does that mean you've decided?"

She knew she should open up and discuss her fears with him, this whole Australia thing was moving on because she was letting it. But that might open a whole raft of issues, and it was just easier to go along with things.

CHAPTER FORTY-FOUR
Summer 1994

Linda scanned across the crowd of disembarking people, longing to see her sister again and hoping that they'd be able to get along with each other this time. In effect, they'd spent the bulk of the past two years in separate countries, so they should have both forgotten their differences, or grown up enough to deal with them. Of course, she'd got some news to tell her sister that could cause the rift to widen more than ever.

At last she saw Deb and all her nerves disappeared away as she rushed to greet her, thrilled that finally her sister was home, and amazed at how different she looked.

"Oh my God Deb, you look so different! You've gone blonde. It suits you, it's gorgeous. And you're so slim and smart. I've missed you so much."

"I missed you too, sis."

"Your hair looks fantastic like that," Linda said.

"So does yours." Deb replied loyally if not honestly.

"Are you tired, hungry?"

They cried and hugged each other, holding on as though they would never let go.

"I'm sorry I was such a cow before I went. I'll never forgive myself."

"Shush, forget it. It's all fine. I'm just happy to see you looking so well. I want to hear everything and I want to see every photograph. Come on, I can't wait any longer."

After what seemed like hours of listening, looking and laughing, the sisters realised that they were hungry, thirsty and in need of a bath and bed.

Later that evening, after bathing and resting they went out to eat. Heading toward the seafront, they agreed to eat at Maria's, a bar that proudly demonstrated its Italian leanings with an extensive and exciting pasta menu, lakes of delicious red wine and a stunning selection of Italian

217

opera music. There was, however, no Maria. The bar was owned by two brothers from Gosport who had never even been to Italy. Deb had loved eating there since they'd first discovered it. The food was good and cheap, the wine was not bad and cheap, but the best part was the fake Italian accents.

"So, we have a new member of the family joining us very soon and that's a story I need to hear more about." Deb said at last.

"You'll be an Auntie in late July. It's not much of a story, but I've got time to tell it now if you're ready to listen to it."

"Shoot."

"All my life I had you, dad and Steve to take care of and I loved it. But things changed. You grew up and you'll never be at home as you were before, Dad's being taken care of and Steve's a grown man now. That's all perfectly normal, it's me that was out of step. It was my dependence on you that was wrong and you helped me to realise that.

"What I needed was to become a mother. I didn't want to wait to get married though and I didn't exactly have a string of boyfriends. I was aware of time passing so I started a dinner club in order to meet attractive, clean, professional people. Mainly men. Then I began to have sex with them, one a week. A different one each week until at last I became pregnant. Then I stopped."

There was a stunned silence. Deb drained her glass in one gulp and waved for the waiter to fill it again. The waiter obliged and remained standing nearby, as fascinated as Deb to hear the end of the story.

"Are you serious?" Deb said with a voice half amazed and half in awe. I can't believe you sometimes. A thirty-five-year-old virgin suddenly feels maternal and starts shagging everything with a pulse."

"Well, I wouldn't put it exactly like that. But, yes, you've got the essence of it."

"Why did you have to have a different one every week?

Couldn't you find anyone good at it?" Deb struggled to contain her laughter. She failed and as she laughed, Linda joined in. When the laughter ceased, they wiped their eyes and held hands.

"Oh don't," Linda said. "It wasn't about the sex at all. I don't care if I never have to do it again. I just didn't want to know who the father was."

"Oh my God."

Linda smiled, smugly. She found she quite liked the feeling of being the unconventional one. The next bombshell was going to be a bit tougher though. Deb looked at her with something like admiration in her eyes. "Good for you Lin." She raised her glass in a gesture of respect.

Linda reluctantly related the story of her proposal to Steve, knowing Deb would hate it and all admiration would be lost. As Linda tried to explain her thinking behind the idea she could read the look in Deb's eyes. All respect had been replaced with something much closer to dislike.

"Well, I knew there was something else going on. You may be a new Linda in many ways, but I can tell when you're ashamed of something."

"I'm not ashamed. I was nervous because I knew you would be uncomfortable with idea of me and Steve as a couple at first but you'll see, this is the perfect ending for me."

"What about Steve, how can it be right for him?"

"I'm pretty sure he's capable of deciding that for himself. "

"Lin, please take a while to think about this before it's too late. Are you certain that this is the right thing to do?"

"It's a done deal. Steve and I both knew that a few people didn't or wouldn't entirely approve and we thought that the sooner we did it, the sooner everyone would get over it and start telling someone else how to live. So, well, we..."

219

"You've got married." Deb was stunned. "You wanted to do it, so you went behind my back. You and Steve got married on the sly because you know it's wrong and everyone who knows you will think it's wrong. Oh my God, Lin, what have you done?"

"We're married and that's it. You're the first person we've told. There's a party planned for this weekend to welcome you home and we'll make sure everyone knows before then. It will just be a one-minute-wonder and we shall ride the storm and it needn't be a subject of gossip for long."

"Gossip should be the least of your concerns. I can't think of anything worse than a party after that news. I'm worried about you, you've done something completely crazy. I don't know who you are any more. I think you've made a huge mistake, and the last thing we should be doing is announcing something like this at a party."

"I'm healthy, thirty-five and pregnant. I've just married a man I've loved forever. This is a good thing Deb. We love each other and we're looking forward to being parents. Can't you see this as the blessing that it is?"

"No, and I can tell you why. Steve has been my best friend all our lives. We have literally never done anything before talking to the other. Never. But he's not mentioned getting married. Now, that tells me either you're making all this up, or that he's as uncomfortable about the whole thing as I am. Obviously it's too late for me to say or do anything apart from wait to pick up the pieces. You know what I think, and he'll know soon enough. He's still my friend and I'll tell him my opinion. It's your life and as long as you're happy, then fine. But you should think about how shitty it is for me to know that neither of you cared enough to share this with me."

"Deb please don't be like that. We know that everyone is going to judge us and we just wanted to be together and do it quietly. Before the storm. I'm sorry you hate it so much but honestly, I'm happy and so's he. Now, let's change the subject for a while."

Deb couldn't speak so Linda filled the silence. "We've decided to have the party at Clive and Mel's place. We can't ask everyone to travel here and then squash into the flat. We've got the builders in at Steve's place getting it baby-ready, so having the party at Langstone means it's easy to get to from Portsmouth and it's no problem for us. And they've got so much space. I just love that house, with the garden running down into the sea the way it does. It's a great place for a party and Mel and I have become good friends."

"Does she know you're married?" Deb forced herself to speak.

"No. You're the first, I swear."

"Not such good friends then." Satisfaction brought a smile to her lips at last.

"I've invited everyone I can think of and most of them are coming." Linda continued describing her plans. "I've catered for more people though, in case you want to invite anyone you met in college or someone I may have forgotten."

Deb shook her head. "No, whoever you've invited will be enough. You'll have to tell me all you can about who's with whom. I don't want to put my foot in it. I've clearly been missing out big style on the gossip, so if there is anything else scandalous, do tell. No more about you though. I've had all the shocks I can cope with for now."

"Okay then, firstly Gary and Julia are nearly rich and locally famous. Everything they touch turns to gold. Her gallery is really well known now, and, of course, his showroom is open and doing very well. She's doing a lot of work now with Jean.

"Jean did the wedding decorating firstly for Clive, when he married Mel, and then for Julia and Gary when they tied the knot. Which incidentally is where my friendship with Mel began. Loads of people started to ask Julia to help them out with planning functions after that event, and between the two of them, Julia and Jean that is, they've turned that into quite a money-spinner. A bespoke party planning service."

"Yeah, Julia told me some of that the last time she wrote to me. Apparently, she's had to get a couple more staff to help them out. Do you see all of them often?" Deb asked.

"Yes, I do, oddly enough. I see more of your friends since you went away that I did when you were here. I went to the Christmas party at Gary's new house in Old Portsmouth. It's a dream of a place, really fairytale-like."

"Yes, I know. Julia's letter told me all about the house and the Christmas party. They sound very happy."

The sisters eventually headed for home and spent the rest of the evening quietly talking about all the people they knew and avoiding the one thing they couldn't yet agree upon.

Deb relaxed as the hours passed due to a combination of jet lag and alcohol. "So, what happened to make you so broody all of a sudden?"

"I was getting that way when I realised you were going. It took me a while to see that I'd been clinging on to you for my own ends, not yours. I wanted to be a mum, and getting to know Hope convinced me I had to just do it. She's clever and cute and she just made me feel that there was something huge that I was missing out on. It was an overwhelming feeling and I knew I had to get on and do something about it. Before time ran out. As soon as I was knew I was pregnant, everything fell into place. I'm happy, feeling strong and I know that everything's going to work out wonderfully."

"So much has happened in just a year. Keep talking. I can't stop thinking about you and Steve as Mr and Mrs." She dissolved into slightly hysterical laughter. "Distract me, quickly, before I throw up."

CHAPTER FORTY-FIVE
Summer 1995

The weather, after a damp start turned out perfect for the reunion party. Jean had found a bench under a tree and was happy watching the various groups of people and eavesdropping a little, but pretty much keeping on the outside of things.

Deb held her preferred spot, centre stage. She was a witty and unselfconscious talker who held her audience in the palm of her hand as she recounted tales of adventure in America.

"Quite a time she had by the sound of things. She should think about a career on the stage. She can make the dullest thing sound like fun, " Mel spoke as she approached Jean from behind.

"I didn't see you there, what are you doing hiding away?" Jean was always delighted to be with Mel.

"I'm just getting some shade and enjoying things from the sidelines like you."

"Well, come and sit next to me then. We can gossip about them all as we watch."

"Okay, you keep the seat. I'll pop and get us both a drink and come back." Mel walked to the self-serve bar and picked up a cold bottle of white wine and a couple of glasses. As she headed back towards her seat, the group on the lawn shifted slightly.

Gary, Clive and Steve were on barbecue duty and they were now tossing each other's chef's hats about and swapping ridiculous aprons. Their raucous laughter was a testament to how much booze they'd drunk. The smell of scorched sausage was another clue. Mel came back and sank gratefully into the seat.

"Gosh, it's hot. Perfect for a party, of course, but..."

"I know. It's tough on the back and ankles when you're pregnant," Jean said, very quietly.

223

"You guessed?"

"Of course I did. When were you going to tell me?"

"I was going to tell you all tonight. I didn't want to steal anyone's thunder today either. It's Deb's homecoming party really, and it's already been hijacked by Linda and Steve. Anyway there's only room for one expectant mum at a time. This is Linda's turn. I only had it confirmed yesterday. I wanted to tell you quietly and privately. I'll keep it to myself for a little longer."

"Well, we can talk all you want whenever you want, but I'm thrilled for you all. It's the most wonderful news."

"Yes it is. I was reluctant, as you know, but it meant so much to Clive that I decided to stop worrying and go with the flow. It will be good for Hope to have a little playmate, she needs to learn to share."

"And I'll have another grandchild to spoil."

"I was going to make a family announcement later, tell you all at the same time when we get home."

"You mean even Clive doesn't know yet?"

"No one knows except you. I couldn't trust him not to announce it to the world. He'll be so over the moon and I wanted a little time to think things through quietly, you know. Telling Hope properly, how it might affect us all with our plans to emigrate, and how do I feel about the changes a baby will mean. I'm enjoying having my own secret to myself for a few hours, I guess."

Jean smiled contentedly. "The thing is, life never goes according to plan. We've all got comfortable with making things happen the way we want. It throws a spanner in the works when something diverts us, but that's sometimes a good thing. Clive needs his own child, and as a couple you'll both feel one more connection. Hope will benefit from being a big sister. A change of direction is not always a bad thing. And I don't believe it will make any difference at all to our future happiness. Relax and enjoy it, that's my advice."

They were abruptly interrupted by a chorus of yells

224

from the chefs. "Grub's up, come "n get it!"

As people sorted themselves into groups around tables and mums tried to watch what their children were eating, the conversations moved into family matters. Holiday plans were being debated as various rates of exchange were balanced against average temperatures and the cost of flights and insurance.

"We're going on a big holiday soon, but it's a secret," announced Hope to Steve and Linda, who were seated either side of her facing Mel and Jean.

"Lovely, but if it's a secret you mustn't tell us," Linda told her. "That's what 'secret" means."

"Okay," Hope replied slowly, thinking about this. Jean and Mel exchanged smiles and carried the conversation on to the events that the police social club had coming up, which they planned to take full advantage of.

As the evening turned dark, Mel found Hope and attempted to get her into bed. This was difficult as she seemed to think that as everyone was at her house, they all had to read her a story before she could sleep.

Jean and Deb helped Clive and Mel tidy up the house, and Gary and Julia attacked the mess outside, while Steve took his turn in reading to Hope.

Linda put her feet up and sighed. She'd worried so much about what people's reaction would be to the news of her surprise marriage that she hadn't been able to enjoy the party at all. She was simply longing for her bed.

Deb had not warmed to the idea of Steve and Linda as a couple. In fact, she'd been sulking about it all week and today she was drinking far too much. As indeed was Steve. He'd seemed almost ashamed when their news was talked about, and she was left feeling furious and humiliated.

All the other guests had finally gone, and the small group of friends were sharing one last drink and enjoying the after party chat. Once all the debris had been cleared, Linda and Jean made a pot of coffee and went to join the gang outside after agreeing that they would try to wind things up as fast as possible.

Deb held centre stage once more, though this time she sounded aggressive. Clive, Gary, and Julia were listening to her and exchanging worried glances with each other.

"You're all so settled and dull," Deb sneered at them. "You're only my age but you all seem old and you're all so fucking boring. What's happened to you?"

"Life, reality. We're all growing up and working so hard at what we want to do. We're going to give it twenty years and then we can change direction if we want to, or retire to the sun. We'll be rich then and still young," said Gary.

"But that's what I mean. Talking about retiring at your age is sick. You should be doing something you love so much you never want to stop doing it. Until you've found that, don't stop looking," Deb retorted.

"Life's not like that," said Steve, reluctantly joining in.

"It is if you decide it will be. I think teaching is what I want to do, I'll learn everything I can and practise all I can, but I won't lose my own life. I've done a year in America and loved it. Next year I want to go to Australia or, I don't know, anywhere. I need new people and new experiences. There must be more to life than just this."

"What do you mean "just this", you ungrateful little madam? All this today was for you. We're all here to see you and welcome you back home. Don't be so bloody snotty. I've got the life I wanted and I'm working for the future we both want, and I don't need you to suggest that once again you know better than everyone else. You might have learned a lot at your fancy college, love, but you've not learned it all," Julia sounded hurt.

"Hear, hear, well said. Perhaps she needed to come home to us so we can knock some sense into her," Clive agreed.

Deb grinned and shrugged an apology. "I'm sorry. I know this party is for me and my newly-wed sister and I'm grateful. And if your businesses are giving jobs to people

226

and you're happy, then you should be proud of yourselves," she said to Julia.

"But it's not the same for you though." She turned on Steve. "You need to get a life. You can't spend your life slinking from one old people's home to another doing nothing. You're dodging life and taking the easy way out. Are you mad? Pack your bags and get away. Come with me. We could go to India, Thailand, anywhere. It's not too late, Steve."

"Don't start on me, mate. Not now. It's been a great day. Let's leave it, eh?" Steve said. "It's bed time."

"That's almost my point. You're not even passionate enough to row about it. The one thing I'm certain of is that it's not healthy to just stay here repeating the mistakes our parents made. Come on, I know you've gone and got married, but we all know it's a paperwork exercise, don't we? At least say you'll think about it."

"You're going too far Deb, so shut it, now. I'm very happy and even if I wasn't, I couldn't just walk away from everything here." Steve sounded more defensive than angry.

"Yeah, you could." She seemed determined to goad him. "I'm talking about in a year's time. And just for a year. You don't do any work now so don't try to kid us that you're needed here. There's a bunch of managers, or whatever they're called, running the business, and you just keep them happy.

"You crack on that you're this big important businessman, but it won't wash with me. You're a caretaker, that's all. Your dad put managers in and they're doing all the clever stuff. You're too young to be paddling through old lady piss. What's going on in your head Steve?" She turned to the others. "Tell him please. We need to help him get a life before it's too late. Come on, Clive, back me up. You're going for it. Packing up the whole family and heading for Oz. That's what I mean, Steve. Clive's married with a kid, yet he's still living an exciting life."

Clive, looking a bit embarrassed, said, "Er, well, we've not actually announced this, but, yes, we're all going to Australia quite soon. Certainly within the coming twelve months. How did you er …"

"Hope told me," Deb said. "She seems to think I've just come back from there and she wanted to know if I saw her new school. Sorry, but that's too big a secret for a little girl to keep."

"Oh no, it's not a secret. We just haven't started to talk about it to anyone outside the family. But there's no time like the present. Yes, I've got a job with the force out there and Peter and Sally have agreed that we'll live with them while we find a place of our own," Clive explained.

"That's so exciting for all of you. How could you have kept that to yourselves? It would have killed me," said Linda, leaping on the chance to change the subject.

"Well, you managed keeping your own wedding a secret, so I'll take that comment with a pinch of salt," Deb snapped at her .

"What about you, Jean? Are you heading off as well?" Julia asked.

"Well, yes, we're going too," said Jean, who'd heard the way the conversation was going. "I'm afraid you'll need to find another painter."

"Oh, bloody hell, Jean, how am I supposed to manage on my own. What about the party planning business? You can't just leave me in the lurch like this."

"We've six months to sort out a replacement, so it's hardly in the lurch. And maybe we could think about importing some Australian art and crafts for the gallery. I can start painting new scenes and impressions. I think it'll be great for the business.

"For now, though, I think it's time we called it a night. It's been a lovely day, but I'm ready for bed. Don't worry, I'll come over and talk to you tomorrow about business. I've tons of ideas." Jean headed into the house to say

228

goodbye to Mel.

Steve drained the bottle he was holding and threw it out into the sea. He swung around, almost losing his footing in the process, and looked directly at Clive. "You've got a great house you didn't have to pay for and a top job. Why would you want to uproot your family and give it all up?" he asked.

"We all want to try something else, that's all," said Clive. "If it doesn't work, we can come back. I feel now is the time to try it. You understand don't you, Deb? And you Linda? You've both been away and seen different things. Hasn't that added something to your lives?"

Deb nodded. "God yes. That's what I was just saying to Steve. Opening your mind to other people and experiences is a healthy thing to do. And I just wish he'd seen a bit more of the world before he and Lin got married."

"Why don't you get off my fucking case?" Steve retorted, "I'm doing what I want to do."

"Yeah, yeah, okay," Deb said, walking away.

"Yeah, it is okay. And I don't need any help or advice from a loser like you either." He turned to Clive.

"Loser. Who are you calling a bloody loser? Don't take it out on me cos she pissed you off."

"You're a loser. Call yourself a copper? You haven't got a clue. Didn't stop you getting suckered did it? At least I know what's going on around me."

Clive stood and leaned into him. "Watch what you're saying," he said very quietly.

"I just told you, I don't need any help from you." Steve was so close Clive felt his breath on his face. "The guy who took over where his best mate left off. What makes your life better than mine? Living in your dad's house with another man's woman. God knows what she's led you believe, but I tell you what mate, she saw you coming. And now you think you can just pack up and take Hope away from us. We're as much her family as you are, you dumb fucker."

229

Deb screamed as Clive dived onto Steve and the table supporting them smashed to the ground. Julia and Gary tried to pull them apart but backed away when they realised that though drunk, both men were genuinely furious and the blows they were exchanging were vicious.

Jean rushed from the kitchen after hearing the commotion, and, in a moment of sheer genius, turned the garden hose full force onto them both. They tried to fight on, but a combination of far too much drink added to the cold water made it impossible. They could barely stand and eventually gave up trying and slumped to the ground, exhausted, while Jean took control of the situation.

"You two," she said, nodding to Gary and Julia, "need to go home now. And you," she said to Deb, "need to think about your sister and get her home. I'll sort the rest of this mess out."

Clive and Steve were now shivering and looking ashamed.

Jean spoke to Steve. "Pick up everything that is broken and throw it away and then walk home. Next week I expect you to have replaced everything and sorted out your differences privately. I'm very disappointed in you both. Just go."

As Linda and Jean once again entered the house, they could hear Mel moving about in the bathroom above their heads.

"What a disaster. Steve always seems to drink too much lately. I'm so very sorry," said Linda.

"Nonsense. It wasn't just Steve. Most of them had too much to drink. That's the trouble with growing up. Every now and then people drink like they used to, forgetting that they're not as capable of managing it as they were. It was a great day with a bit of silliness at the end, that's all. If you mix men, beer and sunshine together in the right quantities, a fight can often end an evening. It didn't spoil anything for anyone though. Except themselves of course and with any luck they'll both have the hangover from hell tomorrow."

"It spoilt it for me though," said Linda. "I'm so upset with Steve and Deb. They both only ever seem to think only of themselves."

"Everyone had too much to drink, that's all," said Jean. "Don't make it more important than it was."

"Drunks don't lie, I've always heard."

"Of course they do. Drunks talk total nonsense most of the time. Now might be a good time for you to finally stop spoiling them both though," Jean told her.

"You could be right. Anyway, thanks for helping out tonight. It was a brilliant move with the garden hose. I must admit, for one spooky moment, I almost laughed."

"Yes, it certainly took the sting out of things, didn't it? It's a useful technique if you ever find yourself bringing up a son."

"Well, in a couple of weeks we'll know whether I need to buy a hosepipe or not, I guess."

"So soon?"

"I'm due late July, so it won't be long," Linda smiled nervously.

"Long enough to calm Steve down if you start now."

CHAPTER FORTY-SIX
Autumn 1995

Gary whispered gently, "When the time is right, it'll happen, love. Just wait and see."

Julia turned round to face him and smiled wanly. "I know, I know. Don't worry, I won't go off on the deep end, but I am going to go to a doctor. I've been patient, I've eaten properly, I stopped smoking, I hardly drink, and have sex so often that I'm bored and I WANT A BABY NOW!" The door slammed in his face and he heard her heels tapping across the marble floor, as she stalked angrily out of the showroom.

This had become, with varying degrees of passion and heartbreak, a predictable monthly occurrence, and Gary was absolutely sick of it. They both wanted a family and had stopped using contraception a few months before they married, but it wasn't happening the way they both thought it would. And this routine was ruining their lives. They would have to endure a week now of tears and tantrums, then two weeks of desperate, anxious, unsatisfactory sex, followed by a week of nail-biting anxiety.

Gary sat back down in the chair and reached for the emergency bottle that was kept in the desk and replaced monthly. He poured a generous shot and downed it. Then, as he poured his second, he became aware of a tapping on the showroom door.

"Oh shit, what now?" he muttered. "Coming," he shouted. As he made his way through the spot-lit showroom, he was surprised to see Steve leaning on the glass doors peering in at him. They'd quite never managed to restore their friendship properly. The disastrous end to the party at Clive's had added to the chaos that was almost created by him at Julia's party and made him an unreliable friend for someone with Gary's ambitions. He opened the door to him warily. "Steve."

"Sorry, Gary, I saw Jules drive off and I hoped to catch you alone. Time for a pint?"

"I've got all the time in the world if you're going to behave yourself. You start acting the prat and you're on your own. Let's go to the Nelson."

As they left the showroom and headed into the cool air Gary felt the effect of the two very large shots he knocked back. Moving into the bar of the old pub the warmth hit him hard and he sank gratefully into a chair. Settled by the old pot-bellied wood stove, a couple of large ones in short order each, and another in hand and all of a sudden things were beginning to look a hell of a lot better to Gary.

"I don't think we're spending enough time together. I'm working all day and she's tied up most evenings and weekends. She says she's desperate for a baby, but I think she's just too busy and doesn't know how to stop. I mean, yes, she wants a baby, but that's not the whole problem. This bursting-into-tears business is a bastard though. I mean, what should I be doing?"

"She always was a stroppy mare. Sorry mate, but its true. I mean, yeah, she's one of us on the surface, but she's a princess deep down, isn't she? She gets what she wants. That's how it's always been for her. She doesn't know any other way." Steve waved the barmaid for more drinks as he spoke.

"Well, she's learning now," Gary sighed

"I feel for you mate. Women, I swear there's not one worth the bother."

"It'll work out for us just fine, don't worry, I've never expected sympathy or understanding from you. What did you want to talk about anyway?"

"I've been thinking about that party at Clive's and I'm a bit bothered about it. I've seen Mel and Hope cos they came to see Linda when she lost the baby. I think I'm okay with them but I don't know how to approach him. I've always thought he was a bit of a dickhead and I know he thinks the same of me, but I feel like I should do something to bridge the gap."

"Leave it alone if you want my advice. I think you got away with saying something you shouldn't have cos most people were pissed. Most of them didn't catch exactly what you meant, but I did. I think you were lucky to have got away with a soaking and a black eye.

"Linda losing the baby and being so ill gave everyone else something else to think about. Really, if you dig it up, he'll think it through. If he'd realised exactly what you were suggesting, he'd have killed you. He loves Mel, as far as he's concerned, she's an angel. You suggesting otherwise is a recipe for disaster. Let it blow over. You'll bump into him sooner or later and when you do, act like nothing happened. They're all wrapped up in getting ready for the new baby now anyway. I don't suppose he's thought about you for weeks now. As soon as the baby is born, the whole family are off to Australia. I think he's got far bigger things than you to worry about. You should be worrying about Linda and not them." Gary drank his pint.

"You think they'll really go?" Steve sounded doubtful. "Linda reckons it's all Mel talks about now, but I didn't think it was that easy?"

"Being a copper is what got him the approval, and then the family business meant that Ted and Jean wouldn't have a problem going, made them all think that they could work it as a family. They've been thinking about it for a long time."

"They've got a lot of family over there, haven't they?" said Steve

"Not any more. Peter, of course, who we met at Barry's funeral. He and his wife have been back here to England several times since then. I don't think there are any more family members for either of them and they're closer now than they have ever been. Well, they've got Hope, of course, but no one else. Ted, Barry's dad, had a brother who went to Australia as a school kid when their parents split up. They basically kept one son each. The boys were allowed to write to each other but they didn't ever actually meet again. They'd both married and started families, and I guess they'd got used to not having each other in their lives. Anyway, Andrew, Ted's brother, died the year before Barry did. Peter was Andrew's son. He's been struggling to keep running his dad's business and still be a teacher, which is what he really wants to keep doing. Half of the business was left to Ted, so it makes sense for them to go. He's actually a pretty wealthy man now."

"How do you know so much about them?"

Gary smirked. "That's all down to witchcraft."

"Huh?"

"Linda, Jules, Mel and Chrissie used to meet every Thursday for a liquid lunch, shopping and scandal. Since various babies and husbands have arrived, they don't do it so much, but they all know what is going on in each other's lives. It's seriously spooky mate, and in case you hadn't realised, not one of us has a secret. Those four have some sort of unholy alliance that we will never understand. I listen to Jules and ask questions because if I don't, I get an unending monologue on Mel's pregnancies and why it's so easy for her and not so for Jules or Linda.

"It's like a badge of honour. They have their little upsets, just like any civilised coven, and one or another of them misses out for a while, but then they cast a spell or something, and the banished one is welcomed back. Anyway, when they're not communing with the spirits, they gossip."

He finished his fourth, or was it his fifth, whisky and signalled for another. "I tell you what Steve," he went on, "between Julia the shopkeeper,Linda the nurse, Mel the hairdresser and Chrissie the social worker, I know every secret worth knowing in Portsmouth."

"Terrifying," Steve winced.

Gary gave a mock shudder. "Anyway, is life as a married man suiting you? I guess things haven't been so

235

good for you two?"

"Grim. Lin is seriously depressed. I don't know what I'm going to do with her. She pops pills and drinks like a fish and there's absolutely no talking to her. And Deb is no bloody help at all. She's still showing off because we got together in the first place. Spoilt madam."

"Try for another baby, mate. That's the only thing you can do."

"No chance." Steve shook his head and ordered more drinks.

"Why not? I mean she's not, well, you know?"

'she's not anything. I just don't want to, that's all."

"You need to think about her, though, not you. Grit your teeth and think of England. Or whatever it is they say. Getting pregnant again seems the right thing to me."

"Yeah, but you know fuck all about it though. Witches coven or not, you don't know everything you think you do. Some things even witches don't talk about."

"I don't know what you're on about now and that's truth. "Nother drink?" Gary waved his arms, wildly catching the eye of the bored barmaid.

"Great, cheers. Let's get pissed and talk about football."

"I hate football. And I'm already pissed."

"So do I."

They giggled helplessly as the bored eighteen year old barmaid looked at them pityingly. There was nothing more sad than two blokes thinking they were still fit, getting pissed, and proving they weren't.

CHAPTER FORTY-SEVEN
Winter 1995

Jean stretched out her back and looked around at the rented flat they'd taken as a stopgap between selling the house and setting off for Australia. A container of their furniture was already on it's way and they were just left sorting through the last few boxes deciding what was saleable and what should be thrown or given away. They'd planned to have gone by now, but it was deemed sensible by them all to wait another six months, allowing Mel time to give birth and recover her strength before facing the final stage of the move.

"What shall we do with all these old decorations, Ted?"

"Uh?"

"ted. The Christmas decorations – shall I take them to the charity shop or put them in the bin? They're a bit shabby, but I imagine someone might find them useful. What do you think?"

"I think you're driving me up the bloody wall. Put them in a box, and we'll take them to the charity shop. Now, I know what's really on your mind. It's on my mind too, but they'll call if anything happens, don't worry."

"Shall I phone them?" she asked, but, right on cue the phone rang.

"Grandchild number two is imminent, Ted," Clive said.

"Okay, we're ready and waiting. See you at the hospital, Clive. Give her our love."

"Will do."

Ted hung up and smiled at his anxious wife. "Come on then, the action's started. Get your coat, and we'll be off. We'll reach the hospital a few minutes after them I expect, so I'll drop you off and go and try to park the car."

Jean paced the sickly sage green-coloured waiting room from window to door nervously, so preoccupied she didn't hear anyone come in. The walls were chipped, stained and

237

scribbled on. The floor was in an unspeakable condition, and as for the seats, torn, soiled and unwelcoming in the extreme. She spent her time thinking about how much nicer a hospital could look if just a little bit of care was spent on thinking things through. And if she could have the kind of budget people would happily spend on a decorating for a wedding, of course. She picked up a magazine and was certain it was the same one she'd picked up years ago when they waited for Hope to make her grand entrance. And here she was again.

"Gramma, my baby is being borned today," Hope explained as she rushed in for a hug.

"Yes, I know, darling. A new baby for you to look after. Are you excited?"

"Yes. No. Has Granda gone to get me an ice cream? I don't think the baby wants one."

"Granda doesn't know you're here yet, but if you want an ice cream, he'll get you one, although I think it's a bit cold for that. Chocolate will be better. Where's your Daddy?"

"He went with the nurse to help Mummy. She's a bit cross."

"Who's cross? Mummy, or the nurse?"

Hope laughed. "Not the nurse, silly. Mummy shouted to Daddy. Bloody is swearing though. You told me it's a bad word. You'd better tell Mummy off."

"I most certainly will. Come on, let's go and find Granda and get some chocolate, then we'll go and buy a surprise for Mummy if you like."

"But it's not her birthday."

"No, but she's having a baby for you, so I thought a present would be lovely for her. Just from you."

"Mm. Will I get a present too?"

A voice came from behind them. "What are you two up to now?" Ted asked.

"Granda!" Hope ran and flung herself into his arms. "We're going to buy a present for Mummy and me. I want

238

ice cream and shoes."

"Ice cream and shoes, huh? We'd better go and tell Daddy we're going shopping then, hadn't we?"

At that moment Clive came toward them.

"Everyone's quite happy. It's all looking good. She's doing well according to the nurses. I'm scared to death, mind you. But no one cares about me, do they?"

"Right now you're the last one anyone will think about. You want my advice, get used to it, son. You won't get a look in now for at least sixteen years," Ted said.

Clive nodded distractedly. "You all carry on, and I'll phone when something happens. Hope, be a good girl for Gramma and Granda please. I'll come and tuck you in later."

Jean smiled at him, "She's always a good girl with us. We'll go and get some lunch and then we'll be at home playing. You look after Mel and forget all about us. We'll be just fine."

Later as Jean washed up after lunch the phone rang.

"It's a boy. He's six and a half pounds with everything in good working order. Handsome little devil. He's got my eyes, I'm certain of it. Come round at about five and meet him," Clive said, half laughing, half crying. "Can I talk to Hope? Has she been good?"

Jean put Hope on the phone and then sat next to Ted.

"A boy, Ted. Can you believe we've got a grandson?"

They sat there quietly holding hands, both thinking back. Jean couldn't help remembering her own precious boy, just for a couple of moments. Why her boy? He was so young, with so much potential. Who decides who lives and who dies, and how do they reach such terrible decisions?

The door opened and Hope rushed in.

"Gramma, I've got a baby boy. I don't like boys very much and I don't want to play football."

Jean and Ted both welcomed the interruption and laughed as they counted their blessings.

239

"We'd better go and tidy ourselves up and then we'll visit him, I think. And I promise you won't have to play football this week."

"Daddy said I can choose his name, so I want to call him Bo."

Jean looked blank. "I don't think I've heard that name before for a little boy."

"Yes. It is a name. Bo is Uncle Gary's dog. I love Bo and he's a boy.

As they all walked into the room they could see Mel in bed, looking very tired but extremely happy. Clive, standing in the corner, turned from the window and they saw he was proudly holding his son.

"I'm just giving him his first sighting of Portsmouth. Come and say hello to the best looking baby ever to be born in this hospital. Jean, here, just look at the strength in his legs." He sat on the bed beside Mel and pulled Hope closer.

"Come and meet your baby brother," he said, sweeping her up in his other arm.

"He's very little!" Hope said, sounding surprised.

"He's only a newborn baby. He'll grow quickly if you help him. You'll be able to show him how to walk and talk. You'll help him button up his shirts and lace up his trainers."

"Is he going to live in my house?" she asked.

"Yes, of course. He'll live with us forever now."

"Will he go to my school with me?"

"Well, not yet. We have to help him grow up into a little boy first."

"Okay. Can he talk?"

"No, that's something else we'll have to teach him."

"Can he do anything?"

"Not very much yet. He needs to sleep a lot until he grows a bit."

"Oh okay." She turned away. "Gramma can we go now, I'm hungry?"

240

Jean glanced at Mel, who nodded, "Be a good girl and come and see me tomorrow. Perhaps we'll talk about names then."

"Okay, bye Mummy. Bye, bye Daddy. Bye Bo." She breezed out leaving Clive and Mel looking at each other.

"Bo?" Clive said.

"Gary's dog," Mel laughed.

"Genius."

CHAPTER FORTY-EIGHT
Spring 1995

Mel changed Bo and laid him down, praying that for once he'd go to sleep. She felt so tired and fed-up. She remembered feeling happy and energetic when Hope was a baby, but it wasn't like that this time. Bo was cranky and grizzly and Hope was horribly jealous every time Mel picked him up.

Mel stood up slowly and quietly, he sensed something and wailed. She sighed, picked him up and tried to soothe him, and, as usual, by some unfortunate fluke, this sent a signal to Hope.

"Mummy, cuddle me, Mummy," she demanded, consumed by jealousy.

"Come here then. I've got enough cuddles for you both."

"No, just me. I don't want Bo." Hope stared at her, waiting to see if she would put him down.

"Darling, he's a tiny baby and he's crying. Come and help Mummy cuddle him."

"Don't want Bo," Hope repeated.

Mel noticed with despair that her daughter had a wobbly lip and tears were welling up. Day after day she battled with Hope and she was overcome by a feeling of self-hatred. She found herself blaming her adored daughter for the fact that she couldn't cope. She'd struggled with Bo from the beginning. The overwhelming love she'd felt for Hope didn't come with Bo, and her feelings of guilt made her try to make it up to him. He didn't notice, but Hope did. Hope had come as a much-wanted baby, but there was no denying the fact that her pregnancy with Bo had been to appease Clive. Mel felt sure she now had to pay the price for her earlier manipulations.

She had allowed a situation to develop where her time was totally given over to simply keeping both children quiet. Actually enjoying her babies was a forgotten dream. She'd no time for housework, or Clive, or herself. It was a treadmill that showed no sign of stopping.

Bo quietened at last, so Mel laid him back down. She switched the baby monitor on and went to find Hope, who had stormed out.

Mel found her in the bathroom, redecorating the room with make-up and marker pens. The shirts that Clive wore so proudly to work were in the toilet and the door-handle was covered in toothpaste.

Mel saw red and, for the second time in a week, Hope was thoroughly spanked. She screamed so loudly that Bo woke with a start and he joined in the screaming chorus. With the sound of Bo's screams ringing in her head, Mel dragged Hope by her arm into the baby's room. She smacked her hard, once more, then closed the door and leaned against it feeling sick. Bo was screaming, Hope was shrieking in panic and Mel was sobbing.

She couldn't go on this way. Hope had been her world, her own little princess. How could she have hit her? She was turning into some kind of a monster.

"Mummy, where are you?" Hope sobbed.

"I'm here. I'll be back in a minute."

"You hurt me."

"Be a good girl and wait there just a minute, please."

"No. Now Mummy."

She opened the bathroom door and scooped Hope into her arms. "I'm sorry, sweetheart, Mummy's sorry. Come on, let's go for a walk, no housework today."

She held Hope and her heart broke as she realised her precious little girl was shaking, partly from sobs, but partly from fear. Fear of her.

"You smacked me too hard, Mummy," Hope said.

"I know, darling, I'm sorry." Mel had tears streaming down her face. She strapped the still screaming Bo safely into his buggy and headed to the bus station. Once on the Portsmouth bus, she looked at their reflection in the

243

windows opposite. They made a pathetic group. Mel and Hope were white faced and listless, while Bo was red-faced and whimpering.

The bus stopped and Mel dragged both children off and away from the glare of the matrons on the bus. All no doubt recognising her for the lousy wife and mother she'd turned out to be.

She marched resolutely down the road where Linda lived. As she got closer her pace quickened. She ran up the short path and leaned on the buzzer. All strength gone.

Linda opened the door.

"I can't cope any more. I've just smacked Hope really hard. Help me, please Linda. Jean's so busy at the shop, and Chrissie's not getting back from her course until tonight. I didn't know where else to go."

Linda ushered the tearful little group in wordlessly and took over for the day. At some point she must have called Clive and arranged for him to come to her house when his shift finished. She had insisted the three of them stayed with her until his working day was over, as she feared Mel's hysteria was not far from the surface and the situation could worsen very quickly.

When Clive arrived to pick them up, Mel began to unburden herself instantly. She had been trying so hard to run the home, keep her children safe and take care of Clive, that when she found it was all too much she knew that there must be something lacking in herself. Something that must be kept hidden at all costs.

"Bo is so difficult. He needs so much attention and then Hope gets jealous. I spend all day, every day, racing between the two until I get so tired that I'd feel happier without them both. That's when I have a couple of drinks." She was stung by the look of shock on Clive's face.

"You're never at home and you don't know what it's like, so don't look at me like that. You bullied me to have another baby, when you knew I wasn't ready and then you disappeared on bloody overtime every night and most

244

weekends. Help me get through it. That's what I need. I don't want more money and I don't want to be drinking every day."

He spoke up. "I'm not judging you, love. I'm gutted that you've been struggling so much and I hadn't realised. You're not on your own and you won't be struggling any more. We'll work it all out together from now on."

"I feel better talking about it, but it doesn't alter the fact that Bo is very difficult, and I don't know what to do with him." She was unconvinced by his words.

"Let's go home now love, and start to sort something out," He held Mels hand and then, turning to Linda, he hugged her. "Thanks for helping us out. You've been a real pal to us. How have you managed lately? We've been too busy to visit. I'm so sorry, we've neglected you shamefully."

She smiled tiredly. "You have rather, but I can see you've had your hands full. I'm getting there, thanks. As a matter of fact, Mel coming today helped me think of something other than myself. It's done me good. I'll phone you tomorrow to make sure you're all okay."

"Yes do. But we'll keep in touch more with you. Sorry Linda, we haven't thought of anything but ourselves. We'll get through this and we'll be better friends to you."

***

The next morning Mel and Clive went together to talk to Jean. She'd suggested they get together as soon as Clive phoned her.

"There's something wrong with Bo, I'm sure. He's so difficult." Mel was determined to make them understand. "I'm his mother, I should know."

"You may be right. Of course, you're his mum and you do know him best, after all, but you may possibly be wrong. You're comparing him to Hope, I imagine?" Jean asked.

"Of course I am, and she was a dream."

"Hmm, maybe, maybe not," Jean said. "Think back to that time. You only had Hope to think about and there were no other calls on your time. You were living with Ted and me, and between the three of us, Hope was cuddled and cosseted and never, ever had to share any of us.

"Bo doesn't have anything like as much cosseting, simply because we're not there to help. Hope comes first because she has been taught by us that she's the most important thing in the world and all we wanted was to keep her happy. Hope had three grown-ups dancing to her tune, full-time. Bo has half of two people. The reality is Bo just gets what's left over and that may be the problem."

"Oh that sounds so awful!" Mel protested. "Are we such terrible parents?"

"Perfectly normal I expect," Jean replied. "What would be awful is if we did nothing to change things. Bo is a tiny baby and he must come first. I feel partly responsible, I'm so caught up in being a businesswoman with Julia that I've lost sight of what's important. And, to think that I wasn't there when you needed me yesterday breaks my heart. That won't happen again. We must make some changes today. What can I do to help?"

"Could you cope with Hope coming here for a week to stay with you?" Clive asked.

"Of course, I'd love it. I'll begin letting her know how lucky she is to have a brother."

"Great. Make us all a pot of coffee, would you Jean? I'll go and make a couple of calls. I've had a thought. I'll be back in five minutes." He stooped to kiss Mel as he left the room. "Sorry love, I didn't realise how tough it was for you. You're not on your own anymore."

He went out and she could hear his muffled voice talking urgently. Jean was making the coffee and the room was silent. Mel leaned back and closed her eyes. Right on cue, Bo woke up and began whimpering, and Hope came

246

running in from the garden crying. "Mummy, I fell over."

Jean went to see to Bo, as Clive came back into the room and lifted Hope up above his head and twirled her around.

"Now then, ladies," he said, "you'd better decide what you want to take on your holidays next week."

"Next week?" Mel said. "A holiday next week. How?"

"It's all sorted out. My mum and dad will come to stay at our place with Bo. They'll be here on Friday night, so we'll all have the weekend together to get them used to his routine. Then on Sunday, we'll bring Hope over here to Jean and Ted's. Then you and I will head for the sun, alone, just the two of us."

"Oh yes," she sighed happily.

"Don't you want to know where we'll go?"

"Well yes, but it really doesn't matter. The great bit was when you said, just the two of us. It's never been just the two of us, do you realise that? We've never, ever, been on our own. Just the two of us."

"Next week we're putting that right. It's going to be exactly that. Just the two of us. And not just next week, from now on I want to make sure we take time for us. Next week is just the first step."

"Okay, so where are we going?"

"Only to Mum and Dad's flat in Eastbourne," he said. "A house swap seemed the best idea. Low cost and no disruption for Bo."

"Brilliant idea, Officer Gidson, you'll go far."

"Do you fancy going out for a drink tonight? Jean said she'd baby sit."

"Not really, no. I just want to sleep. I'm so tired. Sorry if I sound ungrateful but I'd reached the end of my tether. I'm exhausted."

"I understand. No problem. Come on, let's go home. You can have a bath and get into bed. I'm on duty as Dad tonight."

"You're so good to me."

247

"I will be from now on, will you be okay for the next few days? I can have next week off, no problem, but I'll have to do more shifts this week, that's the only thing."

"I'll be fine, really. A good sleep tonight and knowing that I've got next week off, I'll be able to cope with anything for the next couple of days. Honestly, don't worry."

**

The next morning Mel took Hope and Bo into Havant to have a little time with Chrissie.

"So, you're off on holiday next week. I'm pleased for you but I wish I'd realised how much you were struggling. Why did you shut me out Mel? I would have helped, surely you know I would do anything for you."

"I know, I think I was a bit mad for a time. I wasn't thinking straight. I should have told you and him I was struggling weeks ago, but somehow I felt so stupid, not coping. Sorry. He's been great and so has Jean. I think it was a shock to them both that I was so desperate that I ended up running to Linda, but if I'd have stayed on my own, I'd have killed one of them. I couldn't think how to get hold of you, or Jean, and there was no way Julia would have been able to help. It had to be Linda. She was the only one left."

"And how was it? I mean, you're not exactly close any more, are you?"

"Well, no, it's been so awkward, me having a second baby just as she lost her first. She wanted that baby so badly, you know. No, our friendship just didn't seem strong enough to get us through that. I can't stand Steve and she's all wrapped up in him. In fact, I've barely seen her since she lost the baby. I've been so tired and she's been so sad. Isn't that awful?"

"Well, yes, but you've had a hard time too. She was good to take care of you yesterday."

248

"She was great. She sat me down and took over completely."

"So, you're feeling happier now? I mean happy that you can cope?"

"Yes, I am. The worst is over now I'm certain of that, I won't try to everything myself again, don't worry. You won't be taking my kids into care yet. I'd been trying to keep everything exactly the same, but it couldn't go on that way. I should have asked for help a long time before I did. I should have been a better friend to Linda as well. I will be from now on."

"Despite you being in Australia. Or have you changed your mind about that? Is it still going ahead?"

"As far as others know, it's all going ahead. Between us two though, we're slowing the plans down. I'm not ready to face a life without you Chrissie, I felt so alone and scared recently and I tried to manage without you, practising for when we moved, but I found it so hard. I've told Clive and he's happy to stay if that's what we think is best. He'd agreed to go because he thought that was what I wanted. We are having a re think."

"Good. You look shattered, and quite frankly, hitting Hope like that isn't like you. I don't want you to snap again. It's a dangerous situation, you know."

"Okay, Mrs social worker. There's no need for the lecture."

"I just want you all to be safe. Every day I see how one moment of madness can change the lives of people forever, and I don't want that for you. I can help you here but you've got to start asking for help."

"It's all sorted, Chrissie, give me a break. I've told you, I've just to get through a couple more days and I'll be on holiday. After a whole week off, I'll be able to deal with anything. Honestly. It's cool. Now come on, let's take these kids of mine to the park and try to burn off some of their energy before it all turns into tears and tantrums again. Then, I'll be going home to pack for my holiday. I

249

won't snap now, you know me better than that, don't you?"

Next morning Mel smiled as she heard the gate creak open. Clive had come straight home after his shift again. And this time, she was determined to make sure he didn't regret coming home to her rather than have breakfast with his mates first.

"We're in here, love," she called out.

He strolled in looking tired, but happy to see them all up and waiting for him. "You must have been up for a while. Can I smell sausages and bacon?"

"You can. We decided you needed a proper home-cooked breakfast, didn't we, Hope?"

The little girl smiled and threw herself into Clive's outstretched arms. "Are you hungry Daddy? I made bacon for you, but then I ate it, so Mummy made some more."

"You ate my bacon? You little monster"

"Bo ate some too," Hope giggled.

"What, Bo ate some of my bacon? I'll have to have a word with him when I've sorted you out." Dropping onto all fours he began to growl and snarl as Hope ran squealing from the room. He stood and kissed Mel and then picked up Bo, who was looking sweetly sleepy. "Is he okay?" he asked Mel.

"Sure he is. Never better in fact. He's been awake screaming all night and has just been fed, so he'll go to sleep any-time now, and then he'll be ready to play us up all night again."

"Well, I'm home tonight, so I'll be on duty. This is great, love, breakfast all ready and waiting for me. Sit with me for a while and have a cup of tea. I'll put Bo to bed in a moment or two. He's okay just now."

They sat in silence for a while watching Bo who was trying so hard not to fall asleep. As Clive finished his breakfast, Hope rushed back into the room. "Daddy my bike is broken. Help me please."

As Clive moved towards the door, Mel said, "It's not

250

broken. She wants to try to ride it without the stabilisers on. I told her to wait and see what you said."

"Okay, I'll go and have quick look now, then I'm going to bed for a couple of hours."

"Okay, you sort Hope out, and I'll put Bo down."

Mel leaned back and sighed happily. For once, silence reigned. Bo had gone to sleep as soon as she'd laid him in his bed. Hope was squealing in delight as she practised riding her bike without stabilisers on in the back garden, and Clive was in the shower getting ready for bed. She had five precious minutes that were hers alone. No one needed her to do anything and everyone was safe. She slept.

She was vaguely aware of Clive creeping in beside her. She slept on for an hour or so wrapped in his arms, then woke as he began kissing the back of her neck. She stretched luxuriously and kissed him deeply. "What bliss. I'd better go and check on the monsters though," she whispered in his ear.

"We'll wake up like this every day next week, I promise," he said. "But without the monsters. I think they're fine, though. Bo will yell when he's ready and Hope is in the garden. The gate's locked and we'd hear if she needed us. Stay here, it's my turn. I need you now, and anyway, we ought to have a trial run. It would be a tragedy to have got away and realise we've forgotten how to entertain each other. Don't you agree?"

"Well, put like that, Officer Gidson, I do agree. What did you have in mind? Something like this, I wonder."

He groaned.

She smiled.

"Okay then, what about just a little bit of this then?"

He groaned again then gathered himself. "And now, for the lady…"

Their lovemaking was almost as good as it had been before Bo was born. And they both knew that everything was going to be okay as long as they had each other. They both slept, sweetly content.

Mel woke slowly and stretched luxuriously. For the first time for a very long time, she felt relaxed and happy. She'd come through the worst time and now it was all going to be okay. She just had to hold on for a bit longer. A piercing shriek from outside shattered the quiet and Clive turned over and muttered. She leaned to him and whispered, "It's okay, go to sleep. I'll see to the kids. I love you."

He smiled and let sleep take over.

Moments later her shrieks echoed through the house waking him abruptly. "My baby, my baby, somebody has taken my baby."

CHAPTER FORTY-NINE
2011

Chrissie looked around the bar and spotted Richard Dawkins in the midst of a group of people. He saw her at the same time and made his way over to her. She raised her glass to him. "Congratulations on the promotion."

"You helped me get it."

"And you're moving away my spies tell me?" She asked him.

"Best chance I'll get. New pastures and new colleagues. It's what I need. You?"

"No change. It suits me here. I can keep an eye on Mel and Hope, try to make things easier when I can."

"No happy ending yet?"

"Not quite yet. They're getting there but Hope has had it drummed into her for fifteen years that her Mum didn't love her and that takes some erasing. Then there was all that crap in the papers about who her father really was."

Mel had received widespread condemnation, mainly from those closest to her, once it became known that Steve, could have been Hope's father. It was suggested that had that fact been known to the police, then the investigation might have been conducted differently and Hope could possibly have been found years ago. The newspapers made much of this and for a time Mel appeared to be the most reviled mother in England.

"How did they cope with all of that?"

"Jean helped, the instant she set eyes on Hope she declared that she was the image of Barry as a teenager. She went on to prove it by digging out old photos and telling Hope about him. They've developed, or perhaps renewed a very strong bond."

"And Mel?"

"She's opened up to all of them, her family that is, about flirting with Steve and then meeting Barry later that

253

same night. She's also coming to terms with the knowledge that it was her visit to Linda, the day she slapped Hope, that set Linda off.

Since Hope has had her own little girl she's been getting closer to Mel. They all talk well together and sometimes they all cry together. It's uncomfortable but it's a stage they have to get through."

"Well at least they've all got another chance. It's up to them now."

"Yeah, it is. So, what's the latest on Linda from the police point of view?"

"Well, we all believe she was the one who actually took Hope. Whether or not she was coerced by Steve we'll never be entirely sure but they were in it together. Linda's convinced that Hope was Steve's daughter and that they saved her from a fate worse than death. Over time she managed to believe that Hope was her own daughter. That all fell apart when she realised Hope was pregnant and only Steve could have caused that.

He'd never had sex with Linda evidently and she coped with that by thinking he was asexual, realising he'd been messing with Hope made Linda realise what a terrible thing she'd done. She's lost all sense of reality and her story sometimes makes some sense and sometimes not. Is she crazy or is she wicked is a question for someone else. I've done my bit, with your help. So thanks."

"Good luck Rich."

"You too."

Coming soon from Nikki Dee

Sansome Springs

Nikki Dee is currently working on a novel set in Worcester, England.

The eighteenth century brought many changes to England, most notably perhaps the so called "canal mania". At last men and goods could travel the length and breadth of the country with ease.

The novel follows the path of one family through this dramatic and challenging period. *Sansome Springs* will be available in 2013.

About the Author

Nikki Dee believes she was born knowing how to read, and once started simply didn't stop. She reads for pleasure, education, inspiration, and occasionally to garner gossip from the gutter.

Nikki's fondest memory is of the day her father gave her her own library ticket and, along with it, the freedom to read what she wanted.

She began with the Famous Five and swore if she ever had a dog he would be called Timmy. Nikki moved onto Mallory Towers and developed an abiding love for midnight feasts, which, regrettably continues to this day.

Eventually she was drawn to the works of Jaqueline Susann and Grace Metalious though she prefers not to reveal all she learned at their knees. She then spiced things up with large portions of Agatha Christie and John Creasey.

By some miracle Charles Dickens crossed her path, he opened her eyes, and her mind. She went on to develop a deep appreciation for him, the Brontes and Thackeray.

In between reading and writing Nikki mis-spent her youth mired in Sales Management until one day common sense prevailed.

She gave it all up, opened a small book shop and devoted herself to writing (and reading).

Other books from WordPlay

Fallyn and the Dragons
by K J Rollinson

Three children are taken from their dreams to rescue the people of Nashta from the evil Prince Bato. To do so, Fallyn and his friends must learn to ride the island's dragons, and use them in a war that threatens their return to the real world.

Words on the Wild Side
by Georgia Varjas

Known on the performance poetry scene as a verbal volcano, the inventive and incisive Georgia Varjas has collected eighty of her vibrant poems in a single book that will make you think about modern life in a whole new way.

The Cardinals of Schengen
by Michael Barton

Jack Hudson, the UK Government's Foreign Secretary, is assassinated in his own home. In attempting to discover his brother's murderer, Peter Hudson finds himself in a race against time to save Europe from a secret society determined to see Europe become the Fourth Reich.

WordPlay ShowCase
by Various Authors

A collection of works by a series of writers, for some

of whom this represents their first time in print. The anthology covers a whole range of writing: factual, fiction, social commentary, and poetry.

My Gentle War (Memoirs of an Essex Girl) by Joy Lennick

This is the true story of a young girl whose family is wrenched apart by the heartache and tragedy of World War II. Community spirit and togetherness see her through the worst of times, and welcomes in the best of times.

COMING SOON FROM WORDPLAY

Fallyn in the Forbidden Land by K J Rollinson

A magical adventure that sees Allan, Eileen and Martin called away from the 'real world" to a medieval 'dream world". There Allan is known as Lord Fallyn, and he and his friends go to the rescue of King Rudri's dragons and battle against Prince Bato who seeks to depose his brother.

Looking Back, Walking Forward by Ian Alexander and Joy Lennick

This is a thought provoking, yet often funny story detailing the trials and tribulations of a man and a woman in search of happiness within their respective relationships, cleverly told from the points of view of the protagonists in alternate chapters.

Precinct 25
by Various Authors

25 stories, 25 murders, each taking 25 minutes to read. For those that like their New York killings potted, this is the perfect coffee table crime anthology.

Blowback
by Michael Barton

Peter Hudson returns in this tale of political intrigue that sees Britain's criminal masterminds linking with government ministers determined to make their fortune by cornering the illegal drugs trade.

Keep Write On
by Ian Govan

Published posthumously, *Keep Write On* is a collection of Ian's musings on life and, in particular, writing. There is wit, tinged with, perhaps, a little life cynicism here and there, that will make you giggle inside. All royalties from sales will be used by WordPlay toward "encouraging writers to write, and then getting them read".

Printed in Great Britain
by Amazon

76220584R00149